Nazi Treasure Hunt Book One:
Marsh War

Dale Cozort

To My Family and My Online and Real-World Writing Groups

Author's Note:

As with all my writing, **Marsh War** is made possible by my wife, who is also my long-suffering beta reader, and my daughter who respects my writing time, along with individuals in writers' groups willing to read pieces of the original rough drafts and suggest improvements.

Like most writers, I stand on the shoulders of previous authors, borrowing from and expanding on a body of science fiction stories and ideas that helped inspire me to write this book.

I would like to especially thank the following groups and people for their help:

Members of Point of Divergence, the alternate history writers' group, many of whom suffered through early versions of this novel, and especially David Johnson, Chris Nuttall and Kurt Sidaway for their critiques and suggestions. David Johnson also contributed cover ideas and content.

Members of the SM Stirling group on Groups.io, who commented extensively and very helpfully on the alternate history behind this novel and the novel itself.

Pat Shaw from the Writing Wombats who helped with the back-cover blurb.

If you enjoy the novel, feel free to check out my other novels and novellas on Amazon or your other choice of bookstores or drop by my website and my blog:

Website: www.DaleCozort.com

Blog: https:dalecozort.wordpress.com

Chapter One: Dietrich Lang Plots a Kidnapping

Mid-June 1949, Velikiye Luki, deep in the UN-occupied Western Soviet Union.

A man who called himself Dietrich Lang caught a glimpse of his past, a face that could ruin years of careful planning. He turned away, made his excuses and hastily got out of Velikiye Luki, Governor Sergei Meandrov's provisional capitol.

Dietrich Lang had been his name for over two years now. The real Dietrich Lang, Wehrmacht Colonel, was dead, his body in a mass grave outside Minsk. The Dietrich Lang name was useful. Unlike the man who currently used his name, Lang had never been a member of the Nazi party. He had a clean record, with no war crimes lurking in his past.

None of that was true of the man who now used Lang's identity, a man who was officially dead.

The man who called himself Dietrich Lang always landed on his feet. The man even Hitler considered ruthless ran a hand through thinning hair that, if he allowed it to, would streak with gray now. He didn't allow gray streaks or any sign of aging or weakness. His face was different now, with his nose and ears permanently, painfully altered and his hairline changed. Being recognized for who he really was would be fatal here, hiding in plain sight, with hidden allies who knew part of what he did, but not who he was.

Most of the people who could have recognized "Lang" were dead, many of them at his hands. Hannah Reitsch would know him though. Lang had no doubt about that. She wouldn't recognize his face. That had changed too much. She would recognize his voice though and maybe his posture and mannerisms. Hitler's favorite pilot. A woman with nerves of steel and reflexes that made her a world class test pilot. All that in a shapely blond package tailor-made for Nazi propaganda. After the war, she claimed she was just a young, patriotic German who loved to fly, exploited by the Nazis. Maybe those claims were true.

True or not, she was free and working with Governor Sergei Meandrov, a rogue Soviet General who worked with, then turned on the Germans and was now a provincial governor under the American dominated provisional regime that precariously ruled the western Soviet Union.

Hannah might not recognize Lang, but he had to assume she would. Governor Meandrov considered her a trophy and would insist on introducing her to his German friend, retired Colonel Dietrich Lang.

And then she'll recognize me.

Looking back, 'Lang' knew he rose too high in the Nazi hierarchy, though his titles never reflected his real power in the Reich. He pressed for power in a doomed Nazi Germany even after he realized the Nazi regime was doomed. He found a way out of that trap though, with his usual ruthlessness, sanitizing his trail by killing people who knew too much about him and especially about his role in creating the Final Solution. Why should killing Jews matter more than all the other Nazi murders, millions of deaths? He never understood the reasoning, but he understood the reality, so he erased his prominent role in that war crime.

The real Colonel Lang's close friends and family died along with the Colonel, never knowing why. The man who took his name often told himself that he should have killed his own wife and children too, told himself that they were a loose end that could unravel his new identity and his ambitious plans. Some remnant of the man he had once been kept him from taking that final step, though he cut himself off from them, allowed them to think he was dead, and cursed himself for his weakness. They could never know he was alive, even when he became the power behind the new Germany he knew would rise.

And now French intelligence thought 'Lang' worked for them. When it was in his interest, they were right. The dead-enders, the Nazis with hands too bloody to slink back into postwar German society, thought his organization worked for them, getting them papers and refuge more secure than anyone else could provide. Very few Nazis who came to his organization looking for new lives were ever found by the Allies or by increasingly sophisticated Jewish spy networks that hunted escaping Nazis. There was a reason for that success rate, though not one the Nazi refugees would like. Actually, he would be at the very top of their hit list if they knew why men who came to him for a new identity disappeared so completely.

The really big Nazis were dead now, at Allied hands, though Lang quietly delivered many of them into those hands.

Not all the Nazis he turned over to the Allies died at their hands. His allies in the French intelligence services found uses for many. German soldiers fought in the French Foreign Legion in French Indochina. Scientists went to secret French labs, though not all of them. Lang kept a few with militarily useful knowledge for himself, along with a few German physicists. Were the physicists worth the trouble? So far, no. atomic bombs? Still the stuff of science fiction, though French intelligence seemed to take the idea seriously and apparently thought that the Germans had been close to building one. As far as Lang knew, that wasn't true. Top German physicists claimed such bombs were impractical. German intelligence found fragmentary references to an American program called "The Manhattan Project" in the ruins of Moscow, but if the Americans succeeded, it was either after the war or too late in the war for the bombs to be useful. *By mid-June 1945, bigger bombs would have just bounced rubble higher in German cities and bounced the ashes higher in what was left of Japanese cities.*

How much did the French civilian government know about Lang's operation? Nothing that could be tied to them, nothing in writing.

He wondered how much ideology influenced his covert French allies. There were fascist elements in France before the war,

3

then more openly in the Vichy era. They had never been dominant, and were peculiarly French, trying to establish a French fascist state to compete with the Reich.

Fascism still lurked in France, six years after Vichy France rejoined the war on the Allied side and it was especially strong in certain parts of the French state. He suspected that his operations enriched those elements, funneling Nazi loot to French crypto fascists. Certainly not all the looted treasures he sent the French showed up in official accounts of recovered items, though prominent and identifiable pieces did.

He didn't regret splitting loot with his French backers. The split was a cost of doing business and he kept enough untraceable gold, dollars, pounds and francs to keep him in the lifestyle he wanted, fund his organization and give him a cushion if he had to disappear.

So many levels of deception. He could never pass as anything but a German, so he shed one German identity, too prominent to escape the Allies, for another. And the man who called himself Lang was, at least to the Allies, as dead as Hitler, Himmler and Goering.

Being both officially dead and allied to French intelligence had its perks. He lived in something approaching a castle, surrounded by riches, art legally bought by his perfectly legal businesses. Those businesses made money, though he was always slightly bemused by that. His trucks took the debris of war to central storage areas, where his men scrapped tank and artillery parts or salvaged spares to keep the aging tank and artillery parks of western Russia's warlords operating. Ironically, some parts ended up in Palestine, supplying both Jews and Arabs as they geared up for their inevitable war. He grinned at the thought. *Imagine me arming Jews.*

The salvage operations gave him influence among the warlords, supplying them and getting weapons away from bandits. More importantly, the operations gave him cover for his wealth and a plausible way that he could, if he chose, really get die-hard Nazis to South America in exchange for their loot.

He rarely kept that loot, except for gold or silver, though he did grab a few small, exquisite pieces for himself. Keeping anything was a risk and he sometime chastised himself for taking that risk.

Then there were the Americans. They were officially dead, but still risked bringing down his entire edifice. They would have to die eventually, but he regretted the necessity. *A man deserves his playthings.*

He grinned. That grin faded. Some Americans would never stop looking for their loved ones. Maybe he should dispose of his special playthings the same way he disposed of Nazis foolish enough to trust him. That was the logical solution, the risk free one. *But they're valuable too.* His allies in French intelligence might need a triumph sometime and be willing to pay for missing Americans. Could he still cash in? Maybe. That possibility kept the Americans alive so far, though they probably wished they were dead.

Lang focused on Hannah Reitsch. Should he kill her? Maybe. It shouldn't happen close to Lang's base of operations. Maybe in Lvov. A Ukrainian nationalist or bandit faction could do it, though such a high-profile target carried risks.

There was another option, though. Hannah Reitsch would know a lot about Governor Meandrov's security precautions. Meandrov was tough and competent, not the most important threat, but with growing potential. Lang might need to dispose of him someday. Then too, Hannah Reitsch could be an interesting plaything.

If she disappears, she may become even more famous, like Amelia Earhart. The thought amused Lang. He just had to make sure any search didn't lead inconvenient places. Maybe that search could even lead places he wanted the Americans to look.

One way or the other though, Hannah Reitsch couldn't be allowed to tell anyone who Dietrich Lang really was.

\#

"They won't fire on an American helicopter." That's what Colonel Rock, base commander at Fort Seminole, told Captain Joe

Murphy before sending him over the Pripet Marshes, scouting the route that Governor Sergei Meandrov would take when he flew south from his provincial capital at Velikiye Luki to Fort Seminole for a summit meeting with a US presidential envoy.

Captain Murphy didn't believe US helicopters were immune from attack, not completely. There was a time, two years ago, when the US army towered over all the powers of the world, but two years was a long time. *We built the world's best army, ran it down to a nub, built it again for the Donets War and let it go to crap again.*

In early summer 1949, the US army was going to crap. The decline stared Captain Joe Murphy in the face every day. Unmistakable. Congress figured World War II was over, so it was time to get the federal budget under control, but without reducing the Army's mission. *They thought they could save money in 1947 too and look what that got us.*

Captain Murphy fought in the 1947 Donets War, though he didn't have to. He could have gone back to civilian life. Staying in was a personal thing, mixing duty and a quixotic, deeply personal quest. *Looking for ghosts.*

That personal quest was why he was still in Eastern Europe, still prowling the western Soviet borderlands, now sparsely, insecurely garrisoned by too few US servicemen, along with a hodgepodge of "peacekeepers", officially under UN command. Almost every country in Europe contributed a few peacekeepers, paid for indirectly by US Lend Lease dollars, at least for another few months, or maybe longer if Congress renewed the program again.

Meanwhile, deep inside its pre-1939 borders, Stalin's Soviet Union brooded, bitter, bloody, with its cities in ruins, its people starving and with much of its western territory occupied by its former Allies.

Stalin and his crew hate us with an unholy passion now. Captain Murphy understood and sort of sympathized. The Soviets took most of the casualties in World War II and the Allies couldn't have beaten Germany without them, yet the war left the Soviet Union divided, with the Allies occupying the borderlands and even parts

6

of the Russian Soviet Socialist Republic, including the ruins of Moscow and Leningrad.

That result left a proud people who hadn't really lost the war with massive grievances for Stalin and his cronies to exploit. Exploiting those grievances kept attention away from the Stalin regime's many failings--the purges and the starvation, both before the war and during it, especially during the 1946-47 drought.

We had no choice. If the Allies hadn't followed the Germans into the old Soviet Union, Nazi diehards could have held out inside the Soviet Union for years. They did hold out there for years after the Allies chased them out of Germany and the rest of Central and Eastern Europe. The Red Army, ground down by years of war, disease and hunger and tied down by revolts in the Caucasus and Central Asia, showed no sign of pushing the Germans out, so the US, Britain and France, along with small contingents from almost every European country, went in.

And now we have a god-awful mess of former Soviet Union on our hands and no way to get rid of it.

Whatever else he was, Stalin was a survivor. From a low ebb in 1947, the Soviet Union seemed to be recovering scary fast. The Red Army was showing off a new generation of tanks, far more advanced than their late war T34/85s, and getting jets in service, ending a German and Allied monopoly on jet technology. And they were pushing to take back effective control of the Allied-occupied parts of the Soviet Union, not by open warfare, but by a sophisticated, bloody, deniable campaign of terror against former Soviet citizens who worked with the Allies.

If Congress doesn't watch it, if we keep signaling that we aren't interested, Stalin will invade. If he did, US and allied forces would be in a world of trouble, far too few men patrolling far too long a border and trying to control a huge war-torn stretch of the old Soviet Union that dwarfed any European country other than the Soviet Union.

What was lurking in the Pripet Marshes? Anti-German partisans prowled the forests and marshes during the war. They didn't directly attack Americans during the Donets War, but for the last two years they hid weapons and fought bitter little brushfire wars with anti-Stalin Russians, despite US efforts to round up the weapons and reconcile them to peacefully deciding the future of this land.

And those wars are about to escalate. At least US intelligence thought so, which was why Captain Murphy was flying over the Marshes to scout Governor Meandrov's route in a clearly marked US helicopter, an old Sikorski model. Clashes between partisans and anti-Communist Russian and Ukrainian governors surrounding the Pripet Marshes were escalating. The bulk of the Marshes were officially part of Pinsk Province, with an ex-partisan commander as governor. How "ex" was Governor Federov? Not very, according to US intelligence. The partisans didn't directly challenge the US, but didn't really disarm, though they brought in a few antique KV1 tanks to the UN depots which were supposed to hold the province's heavy weapons.

The Pripet Marshes were huge, almost half the size of Texas. Maybe the US army should have cleared them out after the Donets War, bringing them solidly under control, but it didn't. The US was tired of war and the army was wary of fighting in, quite literally, a quagmire, so the US accepted face-saving half-measures that gave the US nominal control.

And now it threatens to bite us on the ass whenever someone has to fly north to south.

Scouting Meandrov's route by helicopter wasn't Murphy's first choice. Yes, the helicopter could hover or land in a small field, but the air force had plenty of planes that flew slow and low more reliably.

It's a new toy in search of missions. The army also directly controlled helicopters, cutting out the air force.

Something bulky moved below him but was lost in the forest before he got a good look. The partisans could have a couple armored divisions down there or massed antiaircraft guns along Meandrov's flight path and Captain Murphy wouldn't see them.

Chapter Two: Hannah Reitsch Comes to Fort Seminole

Captain Murphy gradually relaxed. No one shot at him. Finally, he headed southwest toward Fort Seminole, the US army base northwest of Lvov.

Not far enough from Lvov. Lvov was an issue for another time, hopefully. *One unsolvable crisis at a time, please.* The US would almost certainly get pulled into a currently suspended Polish/Ukrainian struggle over the city and the disputed territory around it, but hopefully not soon.

Captain Murphy swung in for a landing, struck by how tiny Fort Seminole looked, a fragment of America dwarfed by the vast country it theoretically controlled. America was spreading here, though. A little Ukrainian farming village half a mile from the base had transformed into New Memphis, an American/Ukrainian town of several thousand people.

Captain Murphy landed on a field that still looked improvised two years after the base was established. He stood in drying mud. Mechanics came running. The helicopter sounds left his ears ringing and he shouted to hear his own voice. "Muddy hellhole in the spring. Freeze your ass off in the winter. Why are we fighting for this piece of crap land?"

He knew the answer. Mission creep. The Donets War finally destroyed the Nazi diehards but left the US and its allies controlling tens of millions of former Soviet citizens who didn't want Soviet rule, along with an unknown but large number who wanted the Allies out and wanted to kill Soviet citizens who cooperated with the Germans or the Allies. Pulling out would mean a bloodbath and could also make the Soviets a great power again. After Allies found

9

evidence of Stalin's bloody purges in the territory they occupied, turning the territory over to the Soviets was unthinkable.

Mission creep. It left too few US troops patrolling too much of what had been the Soviet Union with far too few resources. In the US, most people ignored the running sore here. They bought new cars, new houses and brought an unprecedented number of babies into the world.

I would be back there, going for a son or another daughter. Cindy wanted three kids, a son and two daughters. That would never happen, not unless...

Captain Murphy never spoke of his wife and daughter in the past tense. His mind told him that they were dead, killed in the 1947 diehard Nazi terror attacks on Allied occupation forces and their families in Berlin and other German cities. Those Nazis saw Germans realizing the war was over and accepting Allied occupation. In desperation, they launched bombings and raids throughout Germany, while rockets from Nazi-held areas of the Soviet Union rained down on any city within their much-expanded range.

And we showed Hitler and company why that was a very bad idea.

Fort Seminole, officially a joint US army/air force base, was on an upland south of the Marshes, though during the rainy seasons it felt like part of those marshes. It housed an airbase with a dozen P51 Mustangs and a few light reconnaissance airplanes, any of them better for the just completed mission than the old Sikorsky helicopter. The Army and the newly independent US Air Force were feuding again.

How do they work together well enough to win a war?

While Fort Seminole was a joint base, a fence separated the army and air force sectors, topped with barbed wire and guarded by armed men, though those men spent much of their time lounging near the fence, swapping stories. The air force had a decent all-weather runway. The army had a packed-mud field for the helicopters and light liaison planes the army was allowed under the interservice agreements. Two fields here were a waste of resources, but it reflected the interservice rivalry.

10

Fort Seminole theoretically housed an army battalion, backed up by two light armor companies and a few artillery companies. It had maybe ninety percent of its official manpower and he had no idea how many of the thirty to thirty-five light M24 tanks worked. Maybe two-thirds. Mud and a shortage of spare parts hit tanks especially hard.

Officially, the M24s were Fort Seminole's only tanks, but local armorers had patched together a dozen Franken-Shermans out of salvaged wrecks. They might or might not run and might or might not have ammunition for their guns, which ranged from standard 76-millimeter guns to heavier guns salvaged from German Panther and even Tiger tanks and by some magic of shade tree innovation crammed into Sherman turrets. At least they gave mechanics something to do while they waited for M24 parts, though getting a salvaged German King Tiger running was the latest off-hours project. The King Tiger's transmission was in pieces in front of it and Captain Murphy doubted that even the nearly insane ingenuity of the local mechanics could get the rusty, seized up engine going, though the mechanics worked harder on the giant German tank than they ever did keeping the US tanks running.

Fort Seminole's little contingent, less than three thousand men overall, wasn't meant to fight an army. It could keep down bandits, but mostly just showed the flag. If real fighting broke out, they would have to bring in divisions from Germany, where a dozen understrength US divisions patrolled, trying to weed out Nazis from German society before they gave a new German government formal independence, hopefully by 1953.

In reality, US ground forces were militarily irrelevant in the Western Soviet Union. Real military power rested in warlord hands, Russians or other former Soviet citizens who sided with the Allies to end German power here.

An unfamiliar female voice with a faint German accent said, "Helicopters are the future of flight. I'll have to try one of the new American ones some time."

Captain Murphy turned, startled. He kept his face impassive with difficulty when he recognized the woman. "Hannah Reitsch."

"You recognize me. Should I be flattered?"

"No," Captain Murphy said. "I would recognize Hitler or Goering or Himmler too, if we hadn't killed them."

Hannah pouted, while managing a hint of a smile. "I flew planes for my country. Unfortunately, my country descended into madness. Now we Germans live in a world that hates us."

Three US MPs stood behind her. One said, "She flew in ahead of Governor Meandrov to check the route."

"I heard that you were also checking," Hannah said. She looked as though she was about to hold out her hand to be shaken but didn't. "Captain Joseph Murphy, I presume. Whatever your views of my activities during the late war, we have a common goal. As one professional to another, may I offer you a drink as we pool information?"

#

New Memphis was either a Ukrainian town trying to act like an American one or an American one melting into a Ukrainian one. In any case, the two cultures blended there, with a Baptist church down the street from an Eastern Orthodox one, neither church far from the bars. The bars had US names prominent on their fronts, with Ukrainian translations below them.

Captain Murphy deliberately led Hannah to the one black-owned bar in New Memphis. ***Mr. Ford's***, named after its owner, was nearly deserted now, but in the evening it would bustle, with its stage filled with American and Ukrainian musicians, their music starting to blend, though the Americans, so far, couldn't match the athletic Ukrainian male dancers.

Mr. Ford was huge, at least a head taller than Captain Murphy's six feet and probably pushing three-hundred pounds. He looked genial, in a neat gray suit, but his face went rigid when he saw Hannah.

"He doesn't like Germans," Captain Murphy said. "And he can tell one at a glance."

"I don't imagine he likes people from your southern states either," Hannah said. "I'm surprised that you accepted my invitation."

I made arrangements before I accepted. Those arrangements included a brief verbal report to Colonel Rock, the base commander, and security arrangements. Captain Murphy carefully didn't look around the bar. One of his men would be here to monitor the conversation and follow Hannah when she left.

"We've both flown helicopters," Captain Murphy said. "That puts us in an elite group."

"Mine was experimental and I flew it indoors," Hannah said.

She could have added that she was the only person to fly several late-war German prototypes, many of them more dangerous to their pilots than to the Allies. Captain Murphy knew that from the intelligence reports.

They talked planes and helicopters for a while. She seemed open, unguarded and surprisingly young. She had to be in her late thirties, but she didn't look or act that old. Maybe she was just a kid who got used by the Nazis. *Or maybe she is good at manipulating men, including me.*

He guided the conversation to the shadowy time between the Allied occupation of Germany and the Donets War that finally destroyed the Nazis. "You went to the Soviet Union with Hitler, even after he lost Germany and they still featured you in their propaganda. Then suddenly you disappeared."

She nodded. "I wish I could tell you I suddenly saw Hitler for what he was, but actually I got caught up in petty squabbles between Goebbels and Goering. I'm not even sure which of them had me denounced for defeatism. I became a nonperson. I still believed in Hitler. He was a mix of father and God to me, even then." She studied Mr. Ford. "I've never seen a black man except in pictures. Does he really keep Germans out?"

"He doesn't make them feel welcome." An uncomfortable number of Germans still wandered the Allied-occupied Western

Soviet Union. Some of them lived in the area before the war, especially in the Baltics. Others were young and adventurous, seeing little for them in Allied-occupied Germany and some would be unwelcome back home. That was especially true in the Sudetenland and Danzig where local Germans terrorized their non-German neighbors late in the war. So, they wandered Allied-held parts of the Soviet Union, some training local armies. A surprising number married local women or developed informal arrangements with them.

Even with all the propaganda, men and women still screw if they get a chance, and sometimes they fall in love.

Captain Murphy glanced around the bar and wondered how many of the patrons recognized his companion. Hannah wasn't in the Nazi top ranks. She wasn't wanted for war crimes. She was famous though, a photogenic blond female test pilot who, if you believed the Nazi propaganda, was every bit as good a test pilot as she was a pretty face.

Unlike most Nazi propaganda, the build-up was true. Hannah genuinely was a brilliant test pilot. She had several firsts as a test pilot, genuine firsts that proved she had a great deal of skill.

She kept appearing in Nazi propaganda after the Nazis lost Germany and fled to their conquests in the western Soviet Union, test-flying advanced swept-wing jets that the Nazis produced in small numbers. Then, in 1947, she disappeared.

Superficially, that wasn't unusual. A lot of second tier Nazis disappeared with, so far, no trace. Hannah was unusual, though. She wasn't one of the pragmatic Nazis who tried to escape when they realized the Third Reich was doomed. Everything in her history said she was a true believer who would have fought to the end, would have taken off from widened stretches of highway in some experimental German warplane to fight air battles until the overwhelming Allied air superiority finally ended her.

That didn't happen, though. The young aviator never reached the Donets Basin where Hitler made his last stand. Instead, before the final apocalyptic battle, she disappeared. Captain

Murphy felt his body grow intense. Allied intelligence must have vetted her, but they might have missed something.

"Do you know who ordered or organized the Berlin bombing?"

Hannah ran a hand through her blonde hair. "I was never close to decisions like that, but I have some idea who made them. Hitler wouldn't have thought it up, not in 1947, but had to approve it. Who organized it? Goering? Goebbels? Not smart enough. Himmler maybe, or Heydrich. If your intelligence doesn't already know, it probably never will."

That was all too likely. He felt a flicker of pain go across his face. Hannah stared at him. "You lost somebody in the attacks. A friend? Family?"

"A wife and daughter." The words came out impulsively, but he didn't regret them. *It's not a secret.* "Bodies were never found."

"So, you'll never be sure they are dead. I'm so sorry." Hannah put a hand on his, the gesture apparently impulsive.

More than missing bodies kept Captain Murphy from giving up, though he didn't tell Hannah about that. Two bodies found in an improvised German prison after the Donets War were of the women from the same apartment building as Captain Murphy's wife, according to their dental records. That meant that at least some of the hostages made it out as German prisoners and lived until near the end of the Donets War. It wasn't much to keep him searching, but it was enough.

Hannah quickly withdrew the hand, glanced around the bar, then leaned forward and said, "We were followed. Your people?"

"Maybe."

"Or Governor Meandrov's people." Hannah grimaced. "He is a good man, but not a trusting one." She met Captain Murphy's eyes, her gaze frank and open. "I think you are here because you hope your family is still alive. If I hear about any English-speaking prisoners I will tell you."

"Thank you." Captain Murphy gave her his direct phone number. "The phone system is bad but getting better."

He rose to go, but Hannah stayed where she was. "I want to see if our followers stick with you or me."

I'm supposed to be an intelligence officer, but I only see Sergeant Duncan. Duncan was there on his orders, to follow Hannah if she ditched Captain Murphy. Were the other followers products of Hannah's imagination? Enough years in Nazi Germany would make anyone paranoid. Or maybe she liked to create drama. Then again, intrigue swirled around Fort Seminole. Diehard Nazis still lurked, as did German communists, Polish nationalists, nationalists from a bewildering array of Soviet nationalities, including men from Soviet Central Asia and the Caucasus Mountains. He had never heard of Chechens before he came here, and after a few encounters with the tough, feud-prone men. wished he never had to hear about them again.

Captain Murphy wished he could tell Sergeant Duncan about the other followers but didn't want to blow Duncan's cover, so he headed back to Fort Seminole, leaving Hannah in Mr. Ford's. Mr. Ford glanced at him reprovingly.

I brought a German into his bar and left her there. He wondered what the big black man would think if he knew how close Hannah had been to Hitler. *Maybe he does know.*

Chapter Three: Governor Meandrov at Fort Seminole

Lend Lease and the Marshall plan. Those were the US trump cards in the Western Soviet Union. the Holy Grail for Russian and Ukrainian warlords, US taxpayer money to staunch the gaping wounds of war and line influential local pockets. That money kept local powers grudgingly cooperating with US, French and Czech peacekeepers, at least on the surface.

American money made the US mission here sort of possible. Officially, American forces were here to repatriate German troops and civilians, round up Nazis, clear the debris of war and help return battered provinces to peace.

Those tasks would be hard working with competent, honest governors, but were nearly impossible under the men who seized power from the Nazis near the end of the Donets War after years of collaborating with them. Ex-Partisans like Alexander Federov were worse, acting as UN governors but with their allegiance still with Stalin. Still, US aid kept the provisional governors from indulging their worst instincts. It kept a dozen old feuds from flashing into open warfare and mostly prevented attacks on vulnerable US forces.

Still, pouring US money into these places was like trying to fill a bucket with the bottom rusted out.

Fort Seminole was far from any city Captain Murphy had heard of before he came there, except for Lvov, not far from the prewar border between Poland and the Byelorussian and Ukrainian Soviet Socialist Republics. On a map, the borderlands were neatly laid-out in provisional administrative districts, with UN appointed governors, paramilitary police forces and growing, US financed highway and telephone networks tying the borderlands together.

On paper, diehard Nazis and local militias were disarmed or in the case of local militias, incorporated into UN approved units, with their heavy weapons under UN control.

In reality, the roads, though a start, didn't fill the logistical desert from years of war, neglect, partisan sabotage and Soviet, then Nazi, scorched earth tactics tearing into already sparse road and railroad networks. How much of what the US was building would survive in the spring and fall muddy seasons anyway? The muddy seasons were a huge new challenge for US engineers.

Captain Murphy sighed. Governor Meandrov flew when he left his bunker in Velikiye Luki, randomly choosing one of four ex-US cargo planes from his fleet. All four planes went wherever he did, accompanied by a dozen ex-German FW-190 fighter planes with prominent US flags painted on them. This time he sent Hannah ahead of him.

Governor Meandrov's fleet must have landed while Captain Murphy was with Hannah. The Governor's bodyguards crowded the base while US MPs watched them warily. As the base intelligence officer, Captain Murphy would have to meet the governor and be available once the summit started.

Lots of listening to diplomats talk. That wasn't quite his definition of hell but came close. He sighed and went into the base command office.

Provisional Governor Sergei Meandrov's hand never strayed far from the Luger he carried, Captain Murphy noticed. That was true even in Fort Seminole, guarded by US soldiers and with dozens of his own guards nearby.

Back home, Governor Meandrov had an army, not a big one by US standards but well-trained and well-armed by western Russia's standards, though the heavy weapons he inherited from the Germans--tanks, planes and artillery—had to be worn out by now, short of spare parts and mostly immobile, with a remnant kept running by ruthlessly cannibalizing the rest. According to US intelligence, he had a few Sherman tanks too, though God only knew how he managed that. Officially, his tanks and artillery were stored in warehouses supervised by Dutch and French peacekeepers who patrolled his province. In reality, heavy weapons that worked were probably hidden.

General Meandrov's army probably didn't matter much. If the American and Brits kept the Soviets out, the governor's tough, truck-mobile infantry was enough to keep rivals out of his little kingdom. If the Allies let the Soviets back in, Meandrov would undoubtedly flee into exile or get a bullet to the back of the head.

We'll never let Stalin back in. Captain Murphy wished he felt more certain of that. Large swathes of the American public loathed keeping troops at the front lines and in scattered bases here, in the distant reaches of Europe. *But if we withdraw before we root out the Nazis and build something stable here, we'll be back doing all of this again in ten years.* Better to pay the price now rather than a far higher price later.

Provisional Governor? General? King? Warlord? Sergei Meandrov once a general in General Vlasov's Russian Liberation Army, did run a kingdom. He was effectively Tsar, though his official title was provisional provincial governor and he had to tolerate occasional sweeps by French and Dutch United Nations peacekeepers. They never saw anything wrong in his province. Captain Murphy figured that was partly because they didn't look hard.

Looking hard might upset a tidy arrangement. Sergei Meandrov's competent provincial police force kept bandits out for the most part, whether they be ex-German soldiers, Russians, or Byelorussian nationalists who hadn't accepted his rule. Most Byelorussians accepted his regime for now. They were too busy rebuilding shattered lives in the ruins left by too many armies fighting through the area's towns and villages, in a countryside so depopulated by war that wolves grew bold, accustomed to feeding on corpses and graduating to the wounded but still living.

The Command Office was the only frame building among the Quonset huts of Fort Seminole. It was also the only place in the base free of mud. The tile floor glistened. A hard-eyed MP had examined Captain Murphy's boots before motioning him into the corridors.

Meandrov leaned back in his chair beside base commander Colonel William Rock's gray battleship of a desk. The governor was a tall man in his forties, with thick black hair going gray, a broad face and an oversized, red-veined blotch of a nose. He sipped from a tall glass, after an orderly offered similar drinks to Captain Murphy. A less observant man than Captain Murphy would have thought the provisional governor was relaxed and confident, but Murphy spotted the signs. Meandrov was scared.

"I've given people in my province real peace for the first time since 1941," Governor Meandrov said. "Actually, to find genuine peace, a freedom from fear, people here have to go back decades, really to before the first World War. Since then, they have suffered through the Russian Civil War, peasant revolts, the war on wealthy peasants and Stalin's purges, which continued until the German invasion, though he eased back some." Meandrov grimaced. "When the Germans invaded, Stalin wrapped himself in the cloak of Mother Russia and called the war he brought upon us "The Great Patriotic War.""

Stalin. Governor Meandrov was good at keeping his face impassive, but it changed slightly when he uttered that name. What flickered across his face? Fear? Hatred? A mixture of the two, plus a reaction that uttering that name was a risk, that Stalin might suddenly materialize here, invoked by his name.

"I met Stalin once, when I was a Colonel in the Red Army," Meandrov said. "He had the coldest eyes of anyone I've ever seen. I still remember the way those eyes bored into me, as though he could see the fear and hatred in my heart. Then those eyes moved on and I survived." He sighed and focused on Captain Murphy. "I open my heart to you, maybe more than I should, because you don't understand the threat Stalin still poses. Yes, the Soviet Union is a shambles, with cities in ruins, with starvation and pestilence stalking the land, with railroads and roads battered to pieces. But Stalin's tentacles still reach far outside the land he officially controls, and he will rebuild."

Meandrov sipped his drink. Captain Murphy wondered if Colonel Rock spotted the subtle tension in Meandrov's posture, the way his hand stayed close to his weapon.

"I served the Red Army loyally until Stalin squandered my men in a futile attempt to carve through the Germans besieging Moscow in November 1942. The attempt failed, but my commanders kept pushing the offensive long after failure was obvious, when any fool could see that the Germans were about to encircle us."

Captain Murphy knew the rest of Meandrov's official story. After months of harsh German captivity, Sergei Meandrov joined General Vlasov's Russian Liberation Army. The Germans established the RLA as a propaganda tool rather than a fighting force and for long months it remained a propaganda tool. Sergei claimed he tried to resign and go back to prison camp when he realized what the RLA was.

He didn't resign, though. He claimed that Baltic Germans inside the Wehrmacht encouraged him to stay in the RLA and use it as an opening wedge to turn the German invasion away from its insane Nazi vision of enslaving the Slavs and into a mission of destroying Stalin.

"You Americans don't understand the choices people in the borderlands face, the choices I faced," Meandrov said. "When I remained in the RLA, I figured that if Hitler didn't shoot me, Stalin would.. But here I am, keeping part of Russia free of the Bolsheviks."

How free was Meandrov's province? French and Dutch peacekeeper reports spoke of a relatively benign autocrat compared to some provisional governors. He flaunted his anti-communism, a major selling point to the Americans. His political police could be harsh, especially to Stalin loyalists trying to burrow into Meandrov's province.

Meandrov's army started out German equipped and dominated, two divisions recruited finally, reluctantly, by the Germans in late 1944, when Hitler realized he simply didn't have the manpower to fight off the Western Allies and control his sprawling conquests in the East. Hitler never trusted the RLA and kept them on a tight leash, but gradually became more dependent on Slavs he despised as the Western Allies pushed the Nazis out of Germany and into the old Soviet Union. That mistrust was justified, as the Nazis found out in the end. Meandrov still had German military trainers and technicians, but French and Dutch peacekeeper reports concluded that Germans had little influence on his regime, which was more a throwback to Imperial Russia than to fascism or communism.

Even this far from the UN demarcation line, partisans still prowled. In areas like the Pripet Marshes, pro-Bolshevik partisans like Alexander Federov made the transition to provision governors and their provinces became centers for Stalinist subversion.

Stalin's assassins were out there, Captain Murphy knew. Governor Sergei Meandrov kept his hand close to his pistol for that reason. He wasn't sure why, but Captain Murphy had a sudden unexplained feeling that Stalin wasn't the only reason for Meandrov's fear, that there was someone the provisional governor feared even more than Stalin. Who?

Meandrov turned piercing gray eyes to Captain Murphy. "I hear you've met my newest pilot. What do you think of her?"

"She has a past."

"Young and patriotic," Meandrov said. "The Nazis used her like so many others." He leaned back, sipping from his glass. "I, on the other hand, used them." He smiled grimly. "We were trapped between two madmen, millions of us in Russia, and Poland. I only survive because I know who is who around me." He turned his hard eyes directly on Captain Murphy. "Captain Joseph Murphy. Chicago Irish stock. A widower. Wife and daughter among the officers' wives killed or missing in the Berlin explosions of 1947." He frowned. "I'm belatedly sorry for your loss. So unnecessary. The Nazis were madmen." The frown disappeared. "I see the Irish in you at a glance. So many people underestimate the Irish. You are, in your way, almost as good at bareknuckle politics as Russians."

Captain Murphy kept his face impassive. He wondered if Meandrov knew about his unofficial mission here, the personal one. That mission was partly for revenge. Somebody supplied and organized the Nazi diehards who killed or kidnapped his wife and daughter, along with hundreds of other American officer families, in a series of giant explosions that tore huge holes in Berlin's skyline months after the Allies took Berlin. It was a far more sophisticated operation than anything else the Nazi diehards pulled off. The Nazis took hostages, wired the buildings to explode and made demands. Did some of them escape with part of their hostages before they set off the bombs?

That was the hope that still haunted Captain Murphy. It was a selfish hope in some ways and a fear in others. Most of the hostages died in the explosion. If his wife or daughter escaped, it would have been as Nazi prisoners. Probably, no one escaped. There had been demands, attempts to exchange captives for high-ranking captured Nazis, but then came the explosions. A sophisticated attack seemingly came from nowhere with no real closure. US troops invading the Nazi pockets in the Soviet Union found no trace of anyone from the stricken buildings. They found no documents about who planned the attack and no one who knew who planned it.

How many US officers hoped or feared that their wives and children were captives rather than dead? How many of them volunteered for the brutal Donets War of 1947 because they hoped to rescue loved ones? Captain Murphy certainly did.

Emily would be ten now. Captain Murphy tried to picture his daughter as a ten-year-old. Emily would be tall like her dad and mom. She was already tall at seven. Her long blond hair would still fly when she ran, and her blue eyes would still have a smile in them.

"Awful thing," Meandrov said. "The Nazis brought a whirlwind down on themselves though. You were in the Donets War too, weren't you?"

Captain Murphy nodded.

"You weren't just in the war though," Meandrov said. "You were in the last fighting, when they cornered Hitler and his scramble-brained crew in the Donets Basin, and he blew the hell out of the place."

"That I was," Captain Murphy said. "Old Adolph had quite a funeral pyre when the slave-workers revolted."

The words sounded flippant, but they hid a final disappointment. The Nazis had thousands of Allied prisoners of war and some civilian hostages when the Allies closed in on them. The Allies fought that battle trying to save as many prisoners and hostages as possible and did save most of them. His wife and daughter weren't among the hostages found, alive or dead.

Captain Murphy kept his face impassive, with an effort.

"Am I bringing back bad memories?" Meandrov asked.

Captain Murphy shrugged, not telling Meandrov that he was in that fighting chasing memories and a fading hope. He was still here, his life on hold, for the same reasons.

The Allies fought the battles that wiped out the Third Reich for good in a hellscape of ruined cities and deep iron and coal mines in the Donets Basin in the eastern Ukraine. Thousands of die-hard Nazis died in explosions, fires or mine collapses that incinerated them or crushed them to unrecognizable human paste.

On the other hand, thousands of top Nazis, especially more pragmatic ones like Himmler and Goering, broke away before that final battle and tried to escape to the Baltic Sea, to waiting submarines that would have taken them to South America. The big-name Nazis didn't make it, betrayed by Russian collaborators or German subordinates trying to buy forgiveness for their own crimes and a place in the postwar world.

The smartest Russian collaborators changed sides at just the right time, when the betrayed Germans couldn't crush them, but the allies still found them useful enough to offer an attractive deal. Meandrov timed his switch perfectly and proved useful enough to keep power.

Meandrov ruled a swath of Russia from his provincial capital at Velikiye Luki. His domain extended deep into what had been the Byelorussian Soviet Socialist Republic, something that reflected a mix of power on the ground and cluelessness on the part of the western Allies. Putting almost a fourth of Byelorussia under a Russian warlord added another level of conflict to an area already

24

consumed by the feuds unleashed by the Soviet purges, years of war and the final scramble of betrayals.

Betrayal. That was a cynical word for what happened between the Nazis and their Soviet collaborators. Was it betrayal for anti-Stalin Russians to look to the Germans after nearly two decades of Communist-led barbarism that sent millions of innocents to execution or slow starvation? Was it betrayal when the brothers and sisters of people subjected to that treatment tried to use the Nazis against the people who oppressed them?

Given what the Nazis were, seeking their help wasn't realistic, but it was not betrayal in the usual sense. It was a desperate choice of one evil over another.

To Stalin, Meandrov was a traitor, a man marked for death. Meandrov seemed relaxed, in control, but his hand still didn't stray far from his Luger.

Chapter Four: The Opening Bids

"Alexander Federov." Governor Meandrov said the name like a curse. "He lived the same nightmare I did, even more so. Stalin purged his brother, who died in a Siberian work camp. Yet Federov is still Stalin's toady."

Alexander Federov, Governor Federov, was a partisan, fighting the Germans throughout World War II and striking devastating blows at them during the Donets War. He controlled the Pripet Marshes and a buffer around them when the Donets War ended. Rather than taking that territory from him, the US, getting the boys home as fast as they could, recognized him as provisional governor, along with former collaborators like Governor Meandrov, though in Federov's case, they trimmed his official control down to just the Marshes and even assigned part of the Marsh fringes to surrounding provinces.

They kicked the can down the road, and it snowballed. Captain Murphy saw that in 1947, when US negotiators put together the patchwork of provisional governors. Unfortunately, the US-drawn provinces were hastily drawn, with borders that looked good on a map but didn't always correspond to power on the ground.

"He's Stalin's toady," Governor Meandrov repeated, "And Stalin rewards him. His forces get stronger, while I barely keep mine operating."

As far as US intelligence knew, that was an exaggeration. Federov was dragging his feet on demobilizing his partisans and turning in heavy weapons, but that wasn't unusual among the warlords turned provincial governors. Meandrov's Sherman tanks were a particularly blatant violation of UN policy, though he probably found some loophole rather than simply ignoring restrictions. A lot of provincial governors had tanks or artillery pieces as war memorials, complete with plaques commemorating their capture from the Germans. Those war memorials tended to be in suspiciously good shape.

"Your intelligence won't spot what Stalin gives Federov," Governor Meandrov said. "You can't spot training, or ammunition, or elite forces or spare parts and mechanics to get knocked out Soviet or German tanks running." He sighed. "Federov is getting all that and more. He's also buying far more trucks than he needs."

"Unless the Red Army pours across the border, there is a limit to what Governor Federov can do," Colonel Rock said. "This is above my pay-grade anyway, which is why a Presidential Envoy is coming to sort it out."

Governor Meandrov nodded, but then went on, outlining what he wanted, mainly US heavy weapons. He also wanted the US to force Federov's people out of the northern and southern fringes of the Marshes, areas partisans still occupied, though they were officially in Meandrov's province or Ukrainian-run Ruthenia.

Captain Murphy didn't call the Governor on his hypocrisy but was keenly aware of it. Meandrov pushed the boundaries of allowable military power too. His men were well-trained, by German instructors. They were well-supplied with small arms and ammunition, courtesy of evacuated German factories Meandrov's people captured during the Donets War. They had armor kits to create dozens of improvised armored cars and a couple hundred "forestry tractors," based on Czech-built chassis that the Germans had used as tanks and later as tank destroyers. Meandrov probably had kits to turn them into tank destroyers too.

They're all arming for when we get tired of this crap and go home, but they all want us to crack down on their rivals. Could he blame Governor Meandrov for trying to use the US? No. The governor faced a nightmare with Stalin lurking on the other side of the thinly held demarcation line, getting stronger.

Mission creep. The US could help Meandrov and his allies get strong enough to take on Stalin, which would take years if it was even possible, or they could stay here. Leaving would mean millions of people killed or exiled. Nobody wanted that on their watch, but no one knew how to stop it in the long-term, forcing the US into improvisations that kept it from happening this month and then the month after that.

Meanwhile, Governor Meandrov waited, hands never far from a pistol.

Chapter Five: Envoy McCormick Comes to Fort Seminole

Captain Murphy saw immediately that Amber McCormick could wrap her father, Special Presidential Envoy Eldon McCormick around her fingers. Maybe she usually enjoyed the power that gave her. She couldn't be enjoying it this time. Getting to New Memphis meant a series of white-knuckle flights and primitive roads, ending up in Lvov, after which travel really got rough.

The US planned a highway from Lvov to Minsk, capital of the former Byelorussian Soviet Socialist Republic, now governed by Byelorussian nationalists under a UN appointed provisional governor. If you looked at a map, the Lvov/Minxk highway should give travelers convenient access to Fort Seminole. In reality, the US made great progress on the highway last summer, making it from Lvov past Fort Seminole all the way to the fringes of the Pripet Marshes. Then the fall muddy season hit, followed by winter, then the spring muddy season. The highway was a mass of potholes, though the spring and fall muds weren't as severe this far west.

Amber looked to be in her early twenties, probably a natural blond based on her complexion. Captain Murphy smiled at her, while thinking, *she'll wrinkle fast in the sun*. But Amber McCormick would never have to be in the sun long. Amber and her father were from old wealth, and it showed in understated self-confidence. People listened to and deferred to them.

Bringing Amber here was a huge distraction, asking for trouble, Captain Murphy thought.

Colonel Rock, the base commander, had leased the only decent restaurant in town for the meeting. They would need it for the leaders and their bodyguards, plus officers from Fort Seminole.

Special Presidential Envoy to the Provisional Federation of Eastern Europe. It didn't sound like a big deal. General Omar Bradley, Allied Supreme Commander for the European Theater, controlled military affairs. Envoy McCormick was President Truman's voice on the huge allied-controlled swath of Soviet borderlands, though, which meant he decided which of the squabbling provisional governors got how much desperately needed American "Rebuild Europe" aid..

The federation was a fiction, papering over centuries old feuds until the diplomats resolved them. Would there be an independent Ukraine? If not, how would territories it claimed be divided between a revived Poland and "free" parts of Russia? The Poles wanted every inch of their September 1939 territory and were trying to carve off pieces of pre-1939 Germany.

Envoy McCormick, Captain Murphy noticed with distaste, was newsworthy enough to attract stringers from the New York Times, a couple other newspapers, plus the big radio news networks—NBC and CBS. *One more complication.*

Peacekeeping. All allied European countries were doing it in the hotspots of Central and Eastern Europe, tamping down conflicts if they could, making themselves useful to the Americans so the flow of Lend Lease would continue.

Eventually, US taxpayers would rebel, and the flow would stop. Everyone in Europe knew that, though the consequences would be catastrophic to many governments even now, two years after major fighting in Europe stopped. Europe danced to the Lend Lease tune now, addicted.

That addiction should give the US more power in settling border disputes than it did. Europe had a thousand years of border disputes, with the most disputed areas too often in regions rich in coal, iron or industry.

So Eastern Europe seethed, diehard Nazis and Communists fed the discontent and the US tried to get Europe on a stable footing before Congress threw up its collective hands and relapsed into isolationism.

Any fool would know Amber was a way to get to her father, and Governor Meandrov was not a fool. He turned on an understated charm that surprised Captain Murphy. *The man changes faces well.* The Governor included Amber in the pre-dinner small talk, without being obvious.

Amber didn't seem to so much revel in the reflected power as assume it as her due. Captain Murphy wondered if the attention made up for the discomforts of this trip. He also wondered if she had any idea how dangerous it was in the wild borderlands.

She probably wasn't concerned about her personal safety. The Special Envoy had ten bodyguards, but Amber wouldn't see the need for them. In her world, real power wasn't about guns. Real power exerted itself long before violence was necessary. At least that was what Captain Murphy figured. It would be quietly exerted behind the scenes, in subtle ways that got things done, an unstoppable wave, not a spasm of bullets.

But then people like me make that power real. This was a different world from Captain Murphy's, and he was both uncomfortable and fascinated by it.

Despite her probable influence on her father, Amber was a sideshow. Special Envoy Eldon McCormick was the main event. Captain Murphy studied the envoy. He looked every inch the diplomat, his suit clean despite the hard travel, tall, square-shouldered, with an easy charm that had to hide a hard edge. The Envoy wouldn't have reached his position under a man like President Truman without an edge and wouldn't have lasted long presiding over this cauldron of hatreds if he wasn't tough and decisive.

"If we solve the problem of Lvov it will unlock a lot of doors," Special Envoy McCormick said. "But that city has a lot of history."

That was an understatement. Captain McCormick remembered visiting Lvov a month ago, sitting with his friends and taking in one last evening of civilization before they came back to Fort Seminole.

Civilization? That was a sad joke. They braved cold water to shower at their hotel and slept between distant gunshots too sporadic to sleep through.

Lvov was a city in limbo, at the center of an inevitable ruinous coming war, its people waiting.

Thousands of Poles waited to return to the ethnically divided city but after the Nazis left, Ukrainians moved into ruined, formerly Polish parts of the city and rebuilt among the ruins, clearing unexploded bombs and artillery shells. They figured it was their territory now, while the former owners bitterly opposed that idea. So yeah, war was coming again and when it came it would be bitter, pitting former neighbors against each other again.

"If you get the Poles and Ukrainians to agree on Lvov, you'll be quite the magician," Governor Meandrov said. "This whole part of the world needs a strong hand to sort out the mess that the empires made of it. Mixing peoples may be good for whoever rules the empire, but it makes for a horrible ending." He grinned. "If you put me in charge of the federation, I would sort it out. Stalin would sort it out too, but you've seen the mass graves from when he sorts things out."

Envoy McCormick sighed. "It would be a lot easier to keep Stalin out without the constant bickering. Every year, getting Congress to finance peacekeepers here gets harder. Someday they'll stop and everything we've worked for will go up in wrecked lives and burned-out neighborhoods. Then Stalin will come back, and everyone will wish they had settled their differences."

"That is the outcome we are trying to avoid," Governor Meandrov said. "But uniting against it won't be easy."

Envoy McCormick turned to his daughter. "I shouldn't have brought you. It's getting worse. This area is a witch's brew of hatreds. We're sitting on a powder keg and watching the flames burn along the fuse."

The powder keg part was right, Captain Murphy knew. So many hatreds here. So many dead. So many injustices crying out for revenge.

Captain Murphy understood the urge for revenge at a deep, personal level. Someone smart, patient and ruthless organized the diehard Nazi attacks on Americans and other occupiers two years ago, and cost Captain Murphy his family. Maybe that mastermind died in the Donets War. Captain Murphy hoped not.

I want them to die with my hands around their throat. But even now, two years after the attack, after the Donets War, after years of investigating in every free moment, he had no idea whose throat he wanted his hands around.

Chapter Six: Hannah Uses the Lady's Room

Master Sergeant Tony Duncan didn't flinch when Hannah Reitsch walked directly to his table. She sat across from him, smiling. "You're not bad at following people, but I've been followed by the Gestapo. Are you looking to buy me a drink or do you expect me to lead you to lost Nazi treasures?"

"Just having a drink," Sergeant Duncan said. He kept his annoyance at being spotted off his face, matching her smile. "But I don't mind sharing it with a pretty young lady."

"An American." Hannah leaned toward him. "Your hair is too long to be active army and your boots too scuffed. You can't hide the army training, the posture and the way you move, but many ex-Army men stayed here. So, you fit in as ex-army, maybe with a business that lets you roam the countryside, gathering intelligence."

"I collect scrap metal," Sergeant Duncan said. *How did she spot me?* Did she really know he was a spy? "I imagine men follow you for more obvious reasons."

Her smile widened. "So, you admit to following me. That means you owe me a drink."

He shrugged. "Do you always ask men who follow you to buy you drinks? That sounds dangerous."

"I'm a test pilot. I like danger." She toyed with a strand of hair. "But I only ask the handsome ones for a drink. They have to have scars too." She reached across the table, putting a hand on his wrist. "And you certainly have scars."

He moved his left hand off the table and changed the subject. "Hannah Reitsch. You aren't on wanted posters that I know of. What brings you to this hell-hole of mud and ancient wars?"

"Maybe the same thing that brings you. Why are you here?"

"This is good country except it's too cold in the winter, too muddy in the spring and fall and too many people hate each other." He smiled. "Despite all that, I like it. It's a huge country and the Pripet Marshes remind me of the swamps back home, only bigger."

"Your accent sounds southern."

"Our south is a big place, with almost as many hatreds as we see here," he said. "The big plantations pushed my ancestors out of the good land, into swamps and hills where they could barely make a living, then wanted our young men to fight for slavery. My ancestors told them 'Hell no' and some people still haven't forgiven us." He took a long slow sip of his beer, then stared at the mug. "You never get anywhere if you hate because someone hurt your great-grandfather and squabble over scraps of land too small to bury the people who die fighting over it. People have to get over that old crap."

"Is World War II over for you?" Hannah asked. "Am I still the enemy?"

"Two years is a little soon." He grinned. "Besides, my girlfriend would shoot my balls off if I got too forgiving."

"You look like a man content with a woman," Hannah said. "You aren't a good spy though. How many men followed me to this bar?"

"I haven't even admitted that I did."

"Four counting you," Hannah said. "I don't think the others were Americans."

"Maybe you're imagining the others," Sergeant Duncan said. "But Fort Seminole draws spies like a picnic attracts ants. You never told me why you're here."

"We moved aircraft factories east when Germany started to fall, one to Governor Meandrov's territory. He has German designers working to get the advanced prototypes into production. I want to fly them."

US intelligence would have checked the factory for anything unique and advanced, Sergeant Duncan knew, and would have debriefed the designers, but planes didn't have to be advanced by US standards to be useful here.

Hannah smiled at him again, but her eyes roamed the bar. "You are right that this is great country. And now it has me."

She seemed confident, brassy even, but something told him she was uneasy.

"This whole area is like the spring mud to you Americans," she said. "You came in to get rid of Hitler, but the mud sucks you in. I think you can't leave now."

Sergeant Duncan sighed. That might well be true. The US and its Allies drove the Nazis out of Germany and the rest of Eastern Europe, then paused on the 1939 Soviet border for long months, waiting for the Soviets to clear Hitler and his fanatic Nazi followers out of Soviet territory. A Soviet Union weakened by long years of war, rebellions in Central Asia, epidemics and the drought/famine of 1946-47 simply couldn't push the Nazis out, so after terror attacks by diehard Nazis, the Americans, British and French reluctantly remobilized and fought their way deep into the prewar Soviet Union in the Donets War.

The war wasn't the hard part, though it wasn't easy. Diehard Nazis made a last bloody stand among the great coal and iron mines of the Donets Basin in the Eastern Ukraine, using coal and iron from the mines to fuel industries they had moved east to get them out of range of Allied bombers.

We beat them again, dug them out of their bunkers and hide-outs among the mines. And now we may really be stuck here.

Sergeant Duncan's finger itched, the missing ring finger on his left hand, the scar Hannah mentioned. The finger didn't hurt anymore. At first the pain in the missing finger was worse than it could have been in a real, still attached finger, constant and weird, keeping him awake and somehow staying painful even when he was floating on painkillers that left wounds to his real body, the parts that were still attached, feeling distant and unimportant.

The finger was mostly just gone now, but sometimes, like now, it itched and that was a good sign trouble was coming.

Tony's wounds were healed now. He could march twenty miles on his mended right leg, with only the slightest limp, with his body routing around a chunk of calf muscle torn away by a German shell fragment.

He almost never thought about the leg, except when he was getting ready to undress before having sex, and the phantom finger, while weird, was a reliable signal of danger coming.

He glanced at his companion. Hannah was quieter now, her eyes never still.

"I think you sense it too," Hannah said. She was no longer smiling. "You've been to war, and I lived years among human snakes. We know when something bad is coming, even when we don't know how we know." She drained her glass, gave a small, lady-like burp and stood. "But right now, I have to go to the Lady's room."

Chapter Seven: The Search

"I thought you were good with the ladies." Captain Murphy grinned at Sergeant Duncan. "But she spotted you, flirted with you, then ditched you with the old Lady's room trick."

"And she told me I'm a crap spy," Sergeant Duncan said. "Was I being obvious? Does something about me say 'US spy'?"

"I don't see how she spotted you," Captain Murphy said. "Plenty of ex-US soldiers around New Memphis, supervising road construction crews or starting businesses. This is a land of opportunity, until the next war breaks out. So many things the locals need, and the Soviets or Germans killed enough of the smart locals that the rest are keeping their heads down until they know Stalin won't come back."

"That will take a while." Sergeant Duncan pulled one foot out of the mud, making a squelching sound. "She said this place is sucking us in like the mud does."

"She's not wrong," Captain Murphy said. "A lot of people see it, but nobody seems to know what to do about it, even our exalted Presidential Envoy."

"You don't sound like you think he's too exalted."

Captain Murphy wasn't sure what he thought about Presidential Envoy McCormick. Bringing his daughter here was a sign of weakness and a distraction, but McCormick seemed more knowledgeable about the Western Soviet Union than Captain Murphy had feared.

"He has a tough path ahead of him. Everybody wants us to fight their battles for them or pay them to fight their battles. Eventually, he will have to make tough decisions and make them stick."

"We should have cleaned Partisans out of the Marshes two years ago," Sergeant Duncan said. "We had the manpower then, troops trained and ready to go. Now we don't have the manpower."

There was enough truth to that to keep Captain Murphy from sleeping well. "Clearing the Pripet Marshes would have been a huge job," he said. "The Nazis never managed it and they were far more ruthless than our army is allowed to be." There was that, plus war wariness and unease at occupying territory that technically belonged to an ally, without that ally's permission. "But that's all in the past. We have to work from now."

He briefly flashed back to a morning in 1947, when, if he had known what was coming, he could have saved his family and a lot of others. "If I had a time machine, the Marshes wouldn't be my top priority."

"If I had a time machine, I would figure out where the Nazis hid their loot," Sergeant Duncan said. "And stash it somewhere I could find it."

That was an enduring mystery. The Nazis looted most of Europe of art treasures during their reign. A continuing trickle of those treasures were recovered, but a lot of them were still missing. "I bet they hid most of their loot in the mines at Donets and they're buried under a hundred feet of rubble, if they didn't burn in the coal seam fires."

Some young Americans in New Memphis were hunting that treasure, Captain Murphy knew. *There are worse things they could do with their lives.* At least treasure hunting was an adventure.

"At least I wasn't the only follower she spotted," Sergeant Duncan said. "She claimed she saw three others."

"Did you spot them?"

Sergeant Duncan shook his head. "She might have been screwing with me. The girl has a taste for drama."

"Maybe." Captain Murphy knew that spies from a dozen countries and factions lurked in New Memphis.

"Could be Governor Meandrov," Sergeant Duncan said. "I hear he's a paranoid coot."

"Definitely paranoid." Captain Murphy remembered the governor's hand, never far from his Luger. Hannah was a newly hired pilot. Meandrov wouldn't entirely trust her yet. "If he trusted the wrong pilot he might end up at Stalin's dacha. Stalin would love that."

"Could be Meandrov vetting her," Sergeant Duncan said. "But my finger itched." He pointed to the gap between his fingers. "When it itches, trouble is always coming."

That was undoubtedly the sergeant's subconscious picking up something, Captain Murphy thought. Sergeant Duncan was a good field agent, though apparently not good at following pretty blond ex-Nazis. He wondered how Hannah spotted the sergeant. Sergeant Duncan was good at playing ex-soldier. He had a regular route through the southern Pripet Marshes, collecting scrap and even had a Ukrainian translator/companion.

Captain Murphy put the question aside and worried about the upcoming summit. Were the Partisans really arming as much as Governor Meandrov said they were, or was the governor exaggerating to get US help for his own forces? US intelligence knew both the Partisans and anti-Stalin forces were covertly rearming, pushing the limits the US imposed to their authorized forces. The US wouldn't stay here forever, and they were getting ready for the post-US era.

Will we really leave? Every month the US stayed in the Western Soviet Union made leaving more difficult. Hannah Reitsch was right about the mud sucking the US in. Actually, it was obligations sucking them in. Stalin would kill people who worked with the Americans if he came back, and they were foolish enough to stay.

"Mission Creep." He said that aloud.

Sergeant Duncan glanced at him quizzically. "If that's officer-speak for getting sucked into this place whether we want to or not, you nailed it."

Colonel Rock came to the door. "At ease. Have you seen Hannah Reitsch?"

They both nodded. Sergeant Duncan said, "I saw her last. We talked at Mr. Ford's, then she went to the Lady's room and never came back."

"Governor Meandrov says she's missing," Colonel Rock said. "He wants us to drop everything and get her back."

Crap! Did the governor think she had been kidnapped or that she fled with security secrets?

"Maybe she just decided to spend the afternoon with a young soldier," Sergeant Duncan said. He paused. "I think I could have talked young Hannah into going to a hotel with me if I worked at it."

Captain Murphy thought about Hannah at the bar. Maybe she just felt comfortable around men. Being a female test pilot, she would be used to a male-dominated environment. Captain Murphy had gotten married young and didn't trust his instincts about female motives in a bar.

"She was supposed to talk to our air force people about a German jet prototype the governor found," Colonel Rock said. "It isn't flyable, and may not be anything special, but he's presenting it to us. Part of his charm offensive."

"And she was supposed to show us why it's special." Captain Murphy nodded. "If she went to a hotel with some guy, she is in a lot of trouble."

"The governor thinks she was kidnapped," Colonel Rock said. "He figures the Partisans want to sweat his security procedures out of her or disrupt the jet handover, or both. How long since you saw her?"

"Maybe an hour," Sergeant Duncan said.

"We've blocked the roads out of New Memphis," Colonel Rock said. "But an hour is plenty of time to get her out of town." He glared at them. "You were supposed to keep an eye on her. Get her back."

#

Sergeant Tony Duncan could almost pass as a Russian, but not quite. He still had a hint of a southern accent that marked him to Russians and keen-eared Ukrainians. Since he couldn't pass as a Russian, he advertised his American background when he went undercover.

He headed north along the new, but already crumbling, US-built highway in a battered army surplus jeep with English lettering on its side. LES ANDERSON, MILITARY SALVAGE. The jeep was half-full of scrap metal, parts from a burned out German STUG III that somebody probably died in. His Ukrainian interpreter and sometimes lover Ruslana Kostenko sat beside him in the jeep, her eyes wary, scanning the heavy forest around them. They were still officially in Ruthenia Province, in the fringes of the Marshes, but Ruthenian paramilitary forces got their butts kicked last fall when they tried to occupy this area.

Ruslana was normally at home in these forests. She knew the southern sections of the Marshes in a way only someone who grew up there could, knew every footpath, every cart trail, every village and every oxbow lake.

Her knowledge didn't extend across the entire swamp. The Pripet Marshes covered an area almost half the size of Texas, with thick, greedy mud creeping out to cover much of the western Soviet Union during the spring and fall muddy seasons.

Sergeant Tony Duncan knew a lot about the swamps for an American, both their geography and people. In his Les Anderson cover, he was an outsider, but a familiar and relatively trusted one. The ex-army man he played drove hard bargains for the scrap he bought but fit into the swamp culture in ways few Americans could.

But Hannah picked me out as a spy.

The swamps were Partisan country during World War II and the Donets War, and men who had been partisans still controlled it, though provisional governor Federov was officially appointed by General Omar Bradley, supreme commander, European Theater and approved by UN authorities.

Federov's still a commie. Was he also a kidnapper?

"I hear that you met this Hannah in a bar," Ruslana said. "Do you like her?"

Ruslana was pale, with long blond hair, in her early twenties. She reminded Sergeant Duncan of Hannah, confident, almost brassy. For some reason, they clicked in a way nobody had clicked with him in the states.

Sex was a short-term thing for him until he met Ruslana. He was tall, with broad shoulders and face and hair that attracted women, enough women and so easily that he never thought about long-term relationships. Should he be thinking of one now? He was on a mission. When it finished, the brass would send him somewhere else. Then eventually he would go home. Or would he? Would he fit in back in the US now?

His relationships before the war had been youthful bouts of physical attraction. After the war, the shellshock came to the fore often enough that women either fled from him or tried to save him. There was no saving him, because the problems were a mix of deep-seated fear and guilt at being the only survivor of an ambush that wiped out his platoon in the Donets War, when the US ordered its troops into the old Soviet Union to root out the last festering pockets of Nazis.

Ruslana seemed to understand his funks, the overpowering horror of his memories. She didn't talk about it but occasional bouts of silent brooding and sudden terrors deep in the night told him she had her own horrors. How could anyone in the Soviet borderlands avoid nightmares after decades caught between Stalin and Hitler, ruthless, mad tyrants without limits to their lusts for power.

Sergeant Duncan's men almost made it through the war. Another two weeks and the Donets War would have ended.

Did the Partisans kidnap Hannah Reitsch? Maybe they didn't have to. Maybe they paid her to join Meandrov, learn his security protocols and then leave. Why not? She had no reason to be loyal to Meandrov.

True, he sided with the Germans for a time, but in the chaotic fall of the German pockets, Russians and Ukrainian former collaborators bought their freedom and continued power by seizing big-name Nazis and turning them over to the Allies. Some of the more pragmatic Nazis played that game too, if they were small enough fish or valuable enough that they could get away with it. Himmler, Goering and many others ended up on trial at Nuremberg for war crimes because somebody thought turning them over to the Allies would bring them favor or paper over their own crimes.

Make yourself useful enough and all will be forgiven. That sounded cynical, but Master Sergeant Tony Duncan was cynical.

Despite hatreds from years of brutal war, even the Partisans employed Germans to train their paramilitaries, *The Germans are useful.* Local governors didn't throw away military talent, even if the men who possessed it had ravaged their country.

Not all the Nazis were gone. Many hid among Germans still wandering the western Soviet Union. Could some German faction have kidnapped her? She was well-known. Maybe diehard Nazis wanted her to front for them or wanted to kill her as a traitor.

"Too many old hatreds," Sergeant Duncan said. "If someone really kidnapped her, do you think they headed for the Marshes?"

"It's the logical place to go," Ruslana said. She turned, her light blue eyes suddenly intense. "The peace you Americans brought was always fragile. and it gets more fragile by the day." She sighed. "Maybe you don't see your army's power seeping away, but we do. We have to see it, living in the borderlands. We have to see power shifting, and we have to be on the victors' side, whether we love or hate them. So, if you show weakness, you lose allies."

Sergeant Duncan nodded. *Show weakness and this whole area will explode.* Aloud, he said, "The borderlands seem a world away to Americans. It *is* a world away; strange places they've never heard of and feuds they don't understand. Congress won't throw money at it forever. They would have pulled out long ago if they hadn't screwed up and left us weak for the Donets War."

He pushed the larger issues aside and focused on finding Hannah. His contacts told him there was traffic ahead of them, including a couple trucks that could be kidnap vehicles, but could also be normal traffic.

US planes flew over them several times, along with Governor Meandrov's FW-190s and French-built Dewoitine 520s with Ruthenian provincial paramilitary markings. Why were the Ruthenians flying early war French fighters? The fighters were probably surplus and cheap. The French had ties here too, left over from when French troops dragooned by the Nazis for anti-partisan work rebelled and Ukrainian nationalists helped them escape.

The new US highway let Sergeant Duncan move fast, despite potholes and occasional peasant carts. The carts were officially banned from the highway, but the locals sometimes ignored regulations in favor of a smooth ride, especially during the muddy season. The highway was eventually supposed to cut through the Marshes, firmly connecting Allied-occupied territory, but for now it only reached the fringes, with only Soviet-era roads reaching into the Marshes.

They left the highway and the forests closed around them.

"This is my kind of country," Sergeant Duncan said. "Except for the winter and the spring and autumn muds."

"That covers most of the year." Ruslana grinned at him. "Yet I think you love this land. You relax when you're in it."

Maybe too much. He slid naturally into his Les Anderson role, but he had a very specific mission. Was Hannah Reitsch somewhere ahead of them? He doubted it. The Partisans wouldn't mind interrogating her, but there were less risky ways to get information about Meandrov.

Did Meandrov's men hide Hannah? Maybe. Meandrov would profit by sowing distrust between the US and the Partisans, maybe even grab the Marshes with US support. But would Meandrov risk a scheme like that? Sergeant Duncan doubted it. Meandrov struck him as a chess player, a leader who thought in terms of years and decades, not risky schemes.

Which leaves us with no real suspects.

"There is another player in the borderlands," he said. "Somebody deep and smart and evil, manipulating Meandrov, the partisans and the others."

"Of course there is," Ruslana said. "Stalin." Her voice lowered when she said that name.

"Yes, Stalin, of course, but someone else too." He paused, then decided not to go on. What did he know that couldn't be explained by the known players? Stalin's agents were burrowing here, of course. So were intelligence agencies from every country of Europe. They wanted German scientists and their documents, German prototypes and Nazi loot. Some wanted chunks of ex-Soviet territory too. After two years of searching, most unique prototypes and big-name German scientists were in Allied hands, but much loot was still missing, and interesting prototypes still turned up.

Even with all that competition, his instincts still told him someone else was in the mix.

His missing finger itched, drawing him back to his surroundings. They were bumping along a dirt road, in the southern fringe of the Marshes. Something was missing. "When was last time you saw a peasant cart?"

Ruslana's eyes roved the forest. "You are slow, but you notice the important thing eventually." Her voice sounded strained, and her hands clamped around a rifle with its butt between the seat and the passenger-side door.

Trouble lurked in the trees and in faint sounds that lingered on the wind, too faint for Sergeant Duncan to identify, but not a normal part of the marsh. He checked his rifle.

The marshes erupted in gunfire before Sergeant Duncan figured out what the sound was. The gunfire was centered northeast of them, far too close and too heavy, both in volume and size of the weapons.

Sergeant Duncan was far too familiar with gunfire. This was dozens of light, fast-firing anti-aircraft guns. What were they shooting at? He didn't have time to care. He instinctively turned his jeep away from the firing.

"Tanks, a lot of them," Ruslana said.

Sergeant Duncan heard them too. There were aircraft too and at least one helicopter.

The helicopter was moving toward them, bringing unwelcome company. Spent, but still dangerous shells slashed through the trees, showering the jeep with severed twigs and leaves.

Sergeant Duncan felt the same helpless resignation he felt under artillery fire during the war. Shells and shell fragments came down where they wanted to and there was nothing he could do about it. Take shelter under the jeep? It wouldn't save them. Abandon the jeep and take shelter somewhere? He didn't see any place safer.

It grated on his instincts, but he stayed with the jeep, slewing through mud, ruts and potholes.

The helicopter sounds grew louder, then abruptly the helicopter appeared, maneuvering in ways no plane could, at treetop level, weaving between trees. More flak guns opened fire, closer to Sergeant Duncan and Ruslana. The helicopter changed course, but not before Sergeant Duncan spotted the US flag prominent on it. Was that Captain Murphy? He hoped not. The helicopter was in a hornet's nest of flak.

The flak seemed to come from nowhere, the guns invisible in the forest, but smoke plumes gave him some idea where the shots were coming from.

The Partisans are as good at camouflage as the rumors say.

Fixed wing planes swooped over, strafing. A bomb rocked the forest, too close, its shock wave splattering them with mud.

Were these partisans? If so, how many? Even with the marsh erupting with antiaircraft fire, Sergeant Duncan had no idea. A battalion? A division? A tank corps? The forest could hide an almost infinite force, though he wondered how they could move heavy weapons so far behind Allied lines.

Why were the men, whoever they were, shooting at a US helicopter? To disrupt the search for Hannah? To keep from being spotted? They would have been better off just letting the helicopter and planes keep flying. Were the shooters inexperienced and trigger-happy? Did Meandrov's planes provoke the attack? Or maybe someone wanted to bag a US helicopter and smuggle it to Soviet-held territory.

How far along was the Soviet helicopter program? The Soviets probably had something. They were good at copying US or German advances.

None of that mattered now, and Sergeant Duncan cursed himself for focusing on it while the flak still rained down. What else could he do, though? He had only a rifle and the jeep could only move so fast on this sad excuse for a road.

Flak kept opening up from new locations, making the ride a nightmare of falling shells and narrow escapes. The pilot was good, Sergeant Duncan realized, taking advantage of every trick a helicopter provided him, including a lot Sergeant Duncan hadn't realized were possible.

And suddenly the helicopter sounds faded, lost in the forest. The anti-aircraft fire stopped like somebody flipped a switch. That was impressive discipline, which scared Sergeant Duncan almost as much as the gunfire.

Ruslana was holding his hand with a grip so tight all his fingers, including the missing one, hurt. He gently pulled free, then looked her up and down, checking for wounds, before checking himself out the same way. Sometimes you didn't notice wounds, even severe ones, in the heat of battle. Fortunately, they both looked okay.

Sergeant Duncan let out a deep breath. "I'm getting too old for this crap."

Ruslana seemed surprisingly calm. Sergeant Duncan wondered again what she had been through in the long years when purges, famine and war stalked the Soviet borderlands. She never talked about those years but a few times that mask slipped. Not this time though.

They needed to get out fast. The heavy gunfire and especially the anti-aircraft artillery would trigger a response. The Americans, if their helicopter escaped, would be back with fighter-bombers. So would the Ruthenian air national guard, and Governor Sergei Meandrov's forces, both of whom claimed parts of the Marshes.

The forest noises gradually, cautiously returned to normal, with birds chirping and squirrels chattering. The underlying foreboding returned too, with more reason now.

"This is the kickoff of something ugly," Sergeant Duncan said. He needed desperately to figure out what.

Chapter Eight: Too Late to Stop a War?

It's struggling but I'll get it home. Captain Murphy hoped he was right. The helicopter's ride got more uneven, but the engine noise seemed reassuringly normal. He spotted the reason for the bumpy ride--a lot of holes, including one less than a foot behind him. "Crap! That was too close."

A lot of them were too close.

The helicopter seemed okay where it counted, and he was out of range of the flak. *What the hell did I run into?* Meandrov's warning about a Partisan buildup seemed more reasonable now. That was a lot of anti-aircraft guns for a Partisan force that supposedly had its heavy weapons under peacekeeper supervision.

What set off the attack? Nothing he did. He couldn't vouch for Governor Meandrov's planes or the Ruthenian Dewoitines. It wouldn't surprise him if either faction started a fight with him in the middle, but he saw no evidence of that. *Which doesn't prove anything.*

The helicopter held together the rest of the way back. Mechanics swarmed over it. One said, "I haven't seen that much damage since the war." He poked a finger through a hole. "Twenty-millimeter shell. Did you just start a war?"

Captain Murphy felt his hands shaking and pushed them into his pockets. At least he didn't get shaky until the action was over. "I didn't start anything and if Federov has any sense he won't start anything either." That was more hope than expectation.

He had to write up a report, and that report could start a war. He gave Colonel Rock a brief verbal report, just that his helicopter had been shot at, then went to his office to write the formal report. He started a couple times and discarded the drafts. His final attempt was carefully neutral, emphasizing that Governor

Meandrov's planes and Ruthenian planes were nearby, but also pointing out that he didn't see them do anything provocative. He emphasized how much fire he took, much of it from small automatic anti-aircraft cannons. That much anti-aircraft power would be enough for two or three divisions. That didn't mean those divisions were down there, but the forest would hide them if they were.

Was Governor Meandrov right about the partisan buildup? Maybe. Or maybe the partisans had collected anti-aircraft guns to ambush Governor Meandrov on his way back north and the search for Hannah stumbled into the ambush.

Too many possibilities. At least he didn't have to make decisions based on what little he knew. He glanced out his office window and was faintly surprised to see daylight. It was after seven in the evening, but summer nights were long here. He stretched, going over the report in his mind.

I'm procrastinating. That wasn't like him, and he mentally berated himself. He knew his report would go to the Presidential Envoy. *And that scares the crap out of me.*

He carried the report to Colonel Rock, knowing Rock would wonder what took him so long.

Envoy McCormick was in Colonel Rock's office, along with the Colonel. He nodded to Captain Murphy.

"Your helicopter got shot at over the Marshes, I hear. Tell me about it."

Captain Murphy glanced at Colonel Rock, who nodded for him to go ahead, then gave them the story, including the nuances he crafted into the report.

When he finished, Envoy McCormick nodded. "Whatever their reasons, they fired at a clearly marked US army aircraft, along with airplanes that technically belong to us. They'll need to tell us why."

Captain Murphy wondered what Meandrov thought about the firing. He had to know about it since his planes had strafed the area. "To be clear, as far as I know, the FW-190s strafed only after I was fired on."

The Envoy nodded. "I wish they hadn't strafed, but you might not have made it if they didn't, so I can't blame the pilots. Still, this is the kind of escalation I'm here to stop."

"Whoever is down there had a lot of firepower," Captain Murphy said.

"Which goes along with Governor Meandrov's fears." The Envoy shrugged. "We'll put additional forces on alert." He turned to the Colonel. "How much room do you have for reinforcements?"

Fort Seminole had quite a bit of room. It had housed a brigade and a few extra companies at the end of the Donets War, several times as many men as now.

Governor Meandrov joined them. "As I said, Stalin is building up in the Marshes. You ran into a piece of that buildup."

Captain Murphy told him the basics, adding that he had to discuss the incident with his superiors before he could get into details.

Meandrov nodded. "A good officer respects his chain of command."

Captain Murphy leaned back. How could Stalin get heavy equipment all the way from the front lines to the Marshes? Granted, the front line was long and US troops were stretched thin. Allies controlled long stretches of the front line--Czechs, French, Italians, and Romanians. Still, none of those countries wanted Stalin's Soviet Union as a closer neighbor. They couldn't prevent small arms from filtering through, but artillery, tanks and ammunition for the heavy guns would be difficult to smuggle in large numbers. Still, a lot of anti-aircraft artillery shot at him earlier today, and the gunners didn't seem short of ammunition.

Where did the Partisans get their ammunition?

That was just one more puzzle among many. Was it the same puzzle as Hannah's disappearance?

The crisis from the anti-aircraft fire put the search for Hannah on hold. Meandrov claimed that the partisans damaged one of his FW-190s, adding fuel to a fire that already seemed ready to flash out of control.

Meandrov seemed intimidated by Envoy McCormick now, Captain Murphy noticed. That hadn't been true at their earlier meeting and Captain Murphy wondered what had changed. The Envoy didn't seem particularly formidable and bringing his daughter into this snake pit didn't show great judgement.

Envoy McCormick used a base telephone to contact Governor Federov's office, summoning the partisans to meet him in the morning to explain their attack. The Envoy's tone was commanding, but Captain Murphy wondered how Governor Federov would respond.

He didn't hear the response, but Captain Murphy saw rage pass across Envoy McCormick's face, then disappear into cold formality. His voice was hard when he continued. "Governor Federov will be at Fort Seminole at ten tomorrow morning." He didn't threaten, didn't raise his voice, but Captain Murphy felt the power in the command.

What will he do if Federov doesn't show up? Envoy McCormick didn't mention that possibility after he hung up. He simply turned to Colonel Rock. "Be ready for a busy day tomorrow."

Busy could mean a lot of things. Captain Murphy wondered how Governor Federov and his partisans would respond to the summons. US forces in Fort Seminole were in no position to bring him here unwillingly.

Night was falling, finally, and Captain Murphy felt relieved when Colonel Rock dismissed him.

Amber McCormick sat outside Colonel Rock's office, leafing through a Time magazine. She looked up and smiled. "Time doesn't say a word about what is happening here. My father rushes around stopping wars before they get big enough for Time magazine, while America makes babies, buys cars and forgets about the troops keeping them safe." She gestured for him to sit beside her. "Tell me about this place, no secrets, just what I might read in Time Magazine."

Captain Murphy thought about his bunk, so inviting after this seemingly endless day, then sighed. "The base or the region?"

She smiled. "Start wherever you want, and I'll ask questions."

He started with Fort Seminole and worked his way outward. Her questions were seemingly naïve but cut to the heart of the issues the US faced here. *She picked up a lot from being around her father.*

"The area around Fort Seminole was Polish territory before the war," she said. "The Soviets took it when the Nazis invaded Poland. Why can't we give it back? It belongs to Poland, right?"

It isn't that easy. He wondered how much background he could give her before he put her to sleep. Probably not enough to answer her question. There was one simple answer, and it was the most important one. "Stalin says he will send his army here if we let the Poles into those territories. He may be bluffing, but nobody wants to find out. A year ago, he probably *was* bluffing. Now I'm not so sure."

He told her a little about Poland's minority problems between the wars, with mostly Polish cities nested deep in mostly Ukrainian or mostly Byelorussian or mostly Lithuanian countryside, and Poland ruthlessly imposing its rule. "Poland would have been better off supporting independent buffer states between them and the Soviets, but they didn't, and they paid a price when World War II came, and the minorities wouldn't fight for them."

He didn't tell her much about the US military in the area, just generally that far too few US troops were trying to control far too much territory. "It took the Germans two or three million men to control the part of the Soviet Union we control with a tenth as many. That doesn't count our allies, but still, it's way too few. Your dad is playing a weak hand, and that hand is getting weaker."

Captain Murphy immediately regretted his frankness, but Amber just smiled. "Something to keep in mind: My father never bluffs." She glanced down at her magazine. "You're a smart man, well informed, but to you power is guns and planes and tanks. I quite like guns and am very good with them, but real power doesn't come from guns. My father understands that. You'll see." She stuffed her Time magazine into an oversized purse and touched his arm. "You must be very tired. Maybe we'll talk more tomorrow."

Chapter Nine: Hannah Calls

Sergeant Tony Duncan and Ruslana raced southwest toward Fort Seminole and New Memphis in the battered jeep, seeing nothing of the men who fired at the helicopter. Sergeant Duncan relaxed slightly when moments of quiet stretched to become hours. Cart traffic, which had vanished before the anti-aircraft fire, resumed.

Sergeant Duncan wondered how the locals knew to disappear. Ruslana probably knew, but she probably wouldn't tell him. He was an accepted part of the marshes, but still an outsider.

The emptiness reminded him of the Marshes two years ago when his unit fought through them against sporadic German resistance. Then the locals hid, protecting meagre possessions from both Americans and Germans. There was plenty of room to hide in the Marshes. Soviet partisans put them to good use when the Germans occupied this area, with tens of thousands of partisans controlling the countryside.

The Marshes, like Lvov, were a suspended war, ready to start again any time. The Marshes were actually worse than Lvov. Multiple factions lurked and prepared for war—Stalin loyalists versus anti-Stalin Russians, Russians versus Byelorussian and Ukrainian nationalists. Even Poles had a stake here. They held western parts of Byelorussia and Ukraine between the wars and would love to grab what they lost and more if they could.

Scattered enclaves of Poles dotted the countryside and when Poland was strong it used them to claim the area. Poland was devastated by war and German occupation, but strength is relative, and the Polish recovery was years ahead of the Soviet borderlands, its army well supplied with older model US Shermans and its air

55

force equipped with late-model US piston-engine fighters, surplus now that the US air force was transitioning to jets.

The Polish army was formidable in a Central and Eastern European context, but the many disputes along their borders meant the UN couldn't use them as peacekeepers here. They did most of their work in the Balkans or Eastern Germany, with some units on thankless missions in Asia against diehard Japanese who still didn't believe the war was over. The Polish efforts brought in US aid, vital for rebuilding the battered, much-fought-over country.

Was Hannah in the Marshes? After his encounter with anti-aircraft fire and strafing, Sergeant Duncan couldn't bring himself to care much.

"This could be the start of a war," he said.

Ruslana studied him. "You understand that the war never really ended, don't you?"

He did, but months of traveling through the Marshes without violent incidents lulled him. He wanted the war to be over. He liked the Marsh people, whatever their language or political affiliation. They needed to live their lives without huddling in ruined villages with bombs and artillery shells falling around them. They needed to live without fear of being rounded up by Stalin's thugs too.

They stopped a few times on their way back to the fort, while Sergeant Duncan chatted with his contacts. He found no evidence that Hannah Reitsch had ever been nearby. On the other hand, the swamp held its secrets, as the anti-aircraft fire proved.

He dropped Ruslana off at her room in New Memphis and got back to the barracks a little after dark, wondering if this was his last night of peace.

#

Hannah Reitsch called Captain Murphy not long after sunrise, on the direct number he had given her. She sounded calm. "I figured you would be up."

"Where are you?"

56

"In Lvov."

"We may have started a war because we thought you were kidnapped." Captain Murphy felt a flash of anger. *If she shacked up with someone overnight I'll strangle her.* Actually, Governor Meandrov might strangle her first. *Unless he put her up to it.*

"I *was* kidnapped." Hannah's voice still sounded calm. "I escaped. Actually, one of them recognized me and let me go."

Captain Murphy tried to make sense of that. "Where are you in Lvov?"

She paused briefly. "I'm using a phone in a cafe called Tranquil Gardens. You can't miss it. Half the front looks scorched. Fighting must have gotten close."

That might not make the building stand out much in Lvov. The city saw bitter fighting in the war, when the Polish Home Army prematurely rebelled against the Germans.

"How did you get down there?"

"I don't know," Hannah said. "They grabbed me, blindfolded me and drove me somewhere near here in a truck. I didn't see much." Her voice became more intense. "I don't know who kidnapped me, except they were Germans. I don't know who to trust. Can you meet me here? Don't tell Governor Meandrov."

"You don't trust the Governor?"

"I trust the Governor." She paused. "But I don't know all his people well enough to trust them."

"Are you in danger now?" Captain Murphy asked. "Anyone following you?"

"I don't think so, and I'm pretty good at spotting people."

Captain Murphy remembered how she spotted Sergeant Duncan. *And he is good undercover.* "I'll be there to pick you up. Try to remember everything you can about the kidnapping. What did you hear? How many turns did you make and when? Write it down."

She agreed and hung up. Captain Murphy stood staring at the phone for a few seconds, wondering if he was being conned. Governor Meandrov could have had Hannah drive to Lvov, then reported her missing. Why? To drive a deeper wedge between the

Americans and Governor Federov's Partisans? Would Meandrov risk playing that game? Why not? If Hannah stuck with a vague enough story, it would be difficult to prove she was lying.

Then again, Governor Meandrov had enemies and Hannah might have information those enemies could use against him. Maybe somebody didn't like the prestige that having the famous aviatrix as a pilot gave Meandrov. The politics around here could be cutthroat, but also sometimes remarkably petty.

In any case, he rousted ten men he had worked with before, including Sergeant Duncan, and arranged for two jeeps to meet them at the gate. They headed down the US-built West Highway toward Lvov. Captain Murphy was going over what little Hannah told him, trying to make sense of it, then he realized that he didn't recognize his driver. A second later, he did. *Amber McCormick.* He swore. "What are you doing here?"

"Driving to Lvov."

"You can't be here."

She smiled. "Of course, I can."

"We're on a mission. How did you even know we were going?"

"I figure out a lot of things. For example, I know you're going to rescue Hannah, but not from anybody hostile. Did she spend the night with some soldier? You aren't heading to rescue her from kidnappers."

How did she figure all that out? Captain Murphy didn't care. He had a strong impulse to tell Amber to stop the jeep and leave her at the side of the road or make her turn around so he could leave her at Fort Seminole.

"Does your dad know you're here?"

"I'm an adult and don't take his orders. Does he know you're going to pick up Hannah Reitsch?"

Actually, he didn't, though Captain Murphy left a note for Colonel Rock.

"Don't worry," Amber said. "I could go to Lvov on my own. This way I get an escort. You aren't going anywhere dangerous, or you would bring more men. I get to visit Lvov and ride back with Hannah Reitsch. Everybody wins."

And if I take her back to base, she'll just get another jeep and follow us. Captain Murphy didn't formally okay her presence but decided to drop the matter. "If this gets dangerous, we'll put you in a hotel and you can make your own way back."

"Of course." Amber smiled. "It's a beautiful morning and we're going to the big city, getting Hannah Reitsch back, defusing a war and making dad's life easier. So, relax. Smile."

Captain Murphy kept his face expressionless. *God, I hope this goes smoothly.* Hannah didn't think her kidnappers had followed her if there really were kidnappers. He kept circling back to that. If she had been kidnapped, why would the kidnappers release her? On the other hand, if Governor Meandrov ordered her to hide, why let her call him? None of this made sense. Was it a trap? What would anyone gain from capturing or killing a few US soldiers? His intelligence connections might make Captain Murphy worth grabbing, but the kidnappers had people in New Memphis, so why not grab him there?

"This makes no sense." He didn't realize he said that aloud until Amber glanced at him.

"Care to explain?"

"No. Just having you here is already irregular enough." He turned to her. "You have no idea how dangerous the borderlands can be. This isn't New York or Washington, where money or who your father is makes you safe. Here or in Lvov, if you wander off, all it takes is two or three bandits and nobody will ever see you again."

"Ever read Ransom of Red Chief?" She asked. "Kidnapping me would work out far worse than that did for the kidnappers, and they paid to give the kid back."

He opened his mouth to respond, then closed it, not knowing where to start telling her how unrealistic that was. Bandits or factions out here would have her tied up, raped and dumped in a ditch with her throat slit so fast she wouldn't get a chance to tell them who she was or why attacking her was a bad idea.

"I know that sounded naïve," she said. She patted a revolver in a holster on her hip. "I know how to use this."

"You can't take that into Lvov," Captain Murphy said. "No civilian guns allowed, at least not on the street."

She shrugged. "My words are far more dangerous than that revolver, most of the time." She turned back to her driving, then added, "Dad taught me that. Words and money, that's where power comes from. Guns are for when the enemy has already lost long ago but hasn't figured it out yet. Even then, use them like a scalpel, not a bomb."

"You live in a different world, normally," Captain Murphy said. "You don't understand this one."

"Oh, but I do." She quickly summarized the things that puzzled him, then added, "Governor Meandrov could find far less risky ways of turning us against the Partisans, but if he chose a fake kidnapping he would ride it further." She steered the jeep around a gaping pothole. "You're lucky I came. When Hannah tells her story, part of it will be lies. You won't know which parts. I will."

Chapter Ten: Lvov

Hannah sat at a scarred table with scorch marks on one edge in the semi-repaired part of a noticeably scorched cafe in Lvov, sipping a drink and looking calm and sophisticated.

Captain Murphy felt the tensions around them, felt the inevitable ruinous coming war. This had probably been a Polish-owned restaurant before the Polish Home Army revolt five years ago, before the Germans massacred or chased out most of the local Polish population.

The survivors wanted to come home, but this was Ukrainian-claimed territory now, claimed by right of their work clearing away unexploded bomb and artillery shells left over from the revolt. The former owners bitterly opposed those claims. So yeah, war was coming again and when it came it would be bitter, pitting former neighbors against each other again. *Hopefully we'll be gone before that happens.* Captain Murphy couldn't be sure of that. Every year getting Congress to finance peacekeepers here got harder.

Czech peacekeepers in United Nations uniforms sat in a cluster near the bar, armed and wary, though Hannah and now Amber drew their attention.

"You led us into a witch's brew of hatreds," Captain Murphy told Hannah.

The witch's brew part was true. Lvov was a mostly Polish city deep inside a countryside populated by people who were definitely, adamantly not Poles, though they hadn't quite decided if they were Ukrainian or a separate Ruthenian nationality. Poland controlled the area between the World Wars after a brutal little war with Ukrainian nationalists and wanted it back. The Soviets annexed it in 1939 and added it to the Ukrainian Soviet Socialist

61

Republic, brutally suppressing both Poles and Ukrainian nationalists.

The Germans pushed the Soviets out on their way east. Now, in 1949, two years after the collapse of the last Nazi holdouts in the Eastern Ukraine, the Poles wanted Lvov back. So did the Soviet Union. The Ruthenian Provisional Government's claim was backed by effective possession of the city, though French and Czech peacekeepers, under the United Nations flag, nominally controlled the area.

Peacekeepers mostly kept Ukrainian and Polish factions apart, while the Soviets licked the wounds of war, epidemics and famine and stirred old hatreds. They waited for the Western Allies to get tired of spending men and money trying to administer the parts of the Soviet Union they held, or the Soviets got strong enough to push them out.

Witch's brew. The Czech and French peacekeepers who mostly kept the Poles and non-Poles from killing each other here would eventually leave, but for now they still brought in much needed Lend Lease dollars for their countries. The peacekeepers postponed war here, turning rivals from bullets to intrigue and stockpiling weapons.

Lvov was still a mess, five years after the Polish underground Home Army's revolt against Nazis here, but seemed to be recovering, a tentative, fearful recovery that could shatter at any moment.

Hannah greeted Amber McCormick with a smile that had something of a cat eying a rival in it. "And who do we have here?"

Captain Murphy wasn't quite sure how to explain that one, but Amber said, "Lie detection specialist, ma'am. I'm particularly good at reading women."

Hannah's smile broadened, though it didn't get more friendly. "What happened to me will sound unbelievable, but if you can really detect lies, you'll vouch for me. Here is a test, though. If I told you that I slept with a famous German rocket scientist, would I be lying?"

Amber stared at her. "I don't think so. It's hard to tell when you don't care if we believe you or not."

"I went to the ladies' room at Mr. Ford's in New Memphis. Somebody stuck a gun in my ribs, hustled me out the back door, put a hood over my head and made me get in a car. They tied my hands, drove me for a long time, then took me into a building, then into a basement. They questioned me in German about the Governor's security arrangements. They left me tied to a chair for a long time, then one came back and told me that he didn't want me to die because I did so much for Germany during the war. He drove me to Lvov, still with a hood over my head, cut the ropes around my wrists and told me to count to thirty before I took the hood off. When I took the hood off, I was a block from here. When the stores opened, I called Captain Murphy." She held up a hood. "This is the only thing I have from the kidnapping." She held up her hands. "You can still see the rope marks, but they prove nothing." She turned to Amber. "Do you think I'm lying?"

"I think you don't care what we believe," Amber said.

"Oh, I care very much," Hannah said. "These men intended to kill me. I accept the risk of dying every time I test a new plane but dying with no control over my fate and not even knowing who intends to kill me is not an experience I intend to repeat."

Her nonchalant attitude slipped near the end of that sentence. Captain Murphy noticed a slight tremor in her hands. It went away, and she seemed as calm and in control as ever. *Is she afraid and controlling it, or is she a very good actress?* Captain Murphy wasn't sure. He glanced at Amber, who just smiled at him.

"The kidnappers spoke German," Captain Murphy said. "Was it their native language?"

Hannah nodded. "I think they were from the Sudetenland. Not Bavaria or Prussia."

Sudetenland made sense. The Nazis fought a bitter little war within a war to hold onto Sudetenland, deliberately alienating local Germans from their Czech neighbors. When the German military was forced out, Sudetenland Germans fled with them. The Czechs wouldn't let the refuges return, leaving aggrieved Germans roaming the US-occupied western Soviet Union.

"Diehard Nazis?" Why would they kidnap Hannah Reitsch though?

"I didn't hear anything that told me they were Nazis," Hannah said. "But they're probably used to not talking like Nazis."

"What else could they be?" Sergeant Duncan asked.

"Communists, maybe," Hannah said. "The Communists were strong in Germany until the Nazis took over and are rebuilding their power."

Can I believe any of this? Captain Murphy wasn't sure. "Can you remember anything that could tell us where you were?"

"Maybe." She closed her eyes. "Get me a car and I'll try to retrace my route."

Whoever released her in Lvov drove straight on a paved road for several minutes. If Hannah was right about how long the kidnapper drove on that road, then the ride took them into an area without many paved roads. The kidnapper made two turns in the trip to Lvov to release her.

The soldiers worked backwards. The last turn was probably from one of two roads and the other, earlier turn could have been from any one of three roads.

"That gives us six possibilities," Captain Murphy said. He was in the lead jeep, with Hannah, Sergeant Duncan and four soldiers. He had ordered Amber McCormick to stay in Lvov, with one soldier as a bodyguard. Hopefully she would respect the order, though he had no real authority over her.

The jeeps split up to save time, staying in radio contact. This was sparsely inhabited countryside, hollowed out by the many armies fighting through it in the last decade. Even tough peasants, canny in the ways of hiding food, young men and daughters, could only survive so many armies fighting through their lands. Scrub trees and vast fields of thorny plants, chest high, with tiny blue flowers sprinkled among the thorns, dominated what had been peasant fields, with clusters of larger trees around the remains of peasant shacks. Rusty cultivator machines were barely visible, buried in the weeds.

Captain Murphy did a doubletake when he spotted a German Stug III self-propelled gun among the brush, its main gun pointed at them, but then he saw that the vehicle was burned out from a side-shot that had penetrated its armor. A fair-sized tree grew through a hole in the armor, lifting one corner of the multi-ton vehicle. He pointed the Stug out to Sergeant Duncan. "Good salvage. I'm surprised nobody has stripped it yet."

Some peasants were rebuilding, clearing fields and repairing shacks. *It's hard to completely wipe out peasants. They're tenacious.* He tried to imagine living through the wars this area went through in the last decade. The Soviets took it from Poland in 1939, then the Germans took it from the Soviets in 1941. It suffered a sputtering four-cornered war between Soviet partisans, Ukrainian nationalists, ethnic Poles and German occupiers for the next seven years, before the Allies forced the Germans out.. *No wonder the countryside is so empty.* Yet peasants survived and were rebuilding. *I just hope we can keep another war away from them.*

They spent the morning combing the roads, looking for anything matching Hannah's memories. They finally found a match almost by accident. Sergeant Duncan noticed a tire track on the muddy shoulder, apparently heading nowhere. They stopped and pulled aside a carefully camouflaged gate, revealing a gravel road with deep ruts from traffic during the recent rainy season.

"This has my missing finger itching," Sergeant Duncan said. "We may be blundering into something too big for us to handle."

Captain Murphy nodded. Whatever was down the hidden road could easily be too much for two jeeploads of soldiers.

"How many voices did you hear?" he asked.

Hannah closed her eyes. "Four men talked, all Germans." She paused. "One of them spoke English briefly. He told someone to shut up."

Four men. But how many others didn't say anything? He focused on the English. "Did you hear anyone speak English before the guy told them to shut up?"

She closed her eyes again. "If I did it was too faint for me to be sure it was English."

She had some idea how many people walked with her into the building, based on footsteps.

"More than four. Probably less than ten."

Captain Murphy called their location and what they had found back to the other jeep, then sent men down the road to scout. He turned to Hannah. "Gravel road, a pause and then onto paved road, right?"

She nodded, "This road fits but I can't be sure."

He pulled the jeep inside and closed the gate. Someone was hiding down the road. A bandit gang? Hard-core Nazis? Polish or Ukrainian nationalists training for their war? A secret partisan base?

Die-hard Nazis were most likely if this was where Hannah had been, but could he believe her story? This was a woman who spent a lot of time around Hitler and other top Nazis. Even if she started out as the naïve German patriot she claimed to be, would she have stayed that person after being around Nazis for years? He doubted it.

The scouts returned, telling him that the road led to a large apparently deserted World War 2 era German warehouse.

"We probably have the building in our archives," Sergeant Duncan said.

That was probably true. The building was visible from the air. The US would have searched it during the Donets War. Then locals would have stripped it of anything useful. Then somebody moved in. The number of tracks meant this wasn't a one-shot hideout for the kidnapping.

Did someone want us to find this place? Why? A trap? Leading the US to an enemy hideout? There were easier ways to kill a few US troops or point this place out to them.

I'm letting my mind run me in circles. He shied away from the English order Hannah overheard. The possibility of American prisoners would cloud his judgement, though a lot of Americans went missing during the war. Chances of prisoners being anyone he knew were vanishingly small. Still, the possibility lurked, raising irrational hopes. He mentally cursed himself for letting those hopes seep in.

Chapter Eleven: The Hideout

Captain Murphy hesitated. He needed more men but getting them would take time. He had contacts in the Ruthenian provincial government, but could he trust them? They might even be behind the kidnapping. They weren't the most likely suspects but might want to stir up trouble between Governor Meandrov and the partisans. Ukrainians might consider ethnic Russians fighting each other a cheap victory. Given their history under the Tsars and Soviets, he couldn't blame them.

What about French and Czech peacekeepers? Both had substantial numbers of Communists in their ranks. If the kidnapping was a partisan operation, the peacekeepers might tip the partisans off.

He radioed Colonel Rock at Fort Seminole. The Colonel promised him air support if he needed it and promised to send reinforcements as soon as possible, which meant in an hour or two. *Can I wait that long?* Whoever used the building knew Hannah was gone and that she might lead someone back here.

"We'll scout the building," Captain Murphy said. "Very carefully. We're probably outnumbered."

The other jeep should get here soon. He radioed them to deploy to give covering fire but not enter the building.

After all the worrying, the building was a disappointment at first. It had evidently been a German truck repair depot. The first and apparently only floor contained a few rusted truck carcasses, stripped of everything usable. All the tools were gone. Field mice peered boldly at the intruders from the corners.

There was no sign of an elevator or basement.

"Are you sure this is it?" he asked.

"No." Hannah surveyed the building. "There was a basement." She paced forward, eyes closed. "It sounds right."

They stayed ready for battle, rifles poised. Sergeant Duncan stepped outside, then poked his head back in. "Trucks have been here recently." He pointed to a truck-sized door. "They drove in there."

Muddy tracks led to the door, but there was no mud inside. Captain Murphy turned to the floor. "No dust. No animal tracks near the building." There were field mice inside, but he saw no sign of larger animals. Back home, raccoons and squirrels nested in abandoned buildings. Something would nest here if the building was really abandoned.

Somebody was using this building regularly and cleaning the floor to avoid leaving tracks inside. He saw no sign of humans though.

"There is a basement and an elevator," Hannah said. "Unless there is another building like this one close by."

Another building was possible, but the truck traffic pointed here.

"A hidden basement," Sergeant Duncan said. "We could get our butts shot off if we find it."

That sounded all too possible to Captain Murphy, but they had to search the place. If there was a hidden door, where was it?

Hannah retraced her path. "They probably drove the truck in through the overhead door." She closed her eyes. "I felt two bumps, so they drove all the way in." She stood where she would have been when she got out of the truck, then paced forward. That led her to the north wall, to a dust-covered window. "No door here, but the windows are dusty, and the floors aren't." She retraced her steps, then paced at an angle. That took her to a blank stretch of wall. "That's the right number of steps."

They discovered that the building extended several feet at the point she indicated, with the extension hidden behind a cluster of saplings. Once they knew where to look, they found a truck-sized concealed door and pried it open, with Captain Murphy half-expecting—he wasn't sure what. Heavily armed Nazis? Nazi treasures? A rocket factory? Adolph Hitler? Captain Murphy's wife and daughter? Bandits?

Instead, they found a bare room just long enough for a truck to park, and an elevator shaft. The elevator was one floor down, apparently stuck there. Other than a slow dripping sound, the room and the elevator shaft were silent.

"This is where they took me, but they're gone," Hannah said. " I can always tell when a house is empty."

"Does that include secret Nazi hideouts?" Sergeant Duncan asked. His voice sounded loud in the empty room, and he cringed. "Sorry."

"If they didn't know we're coming, they do now," a soldier said.

Captain Murphy stared at the elevator shaft. It was like an unopened box. As long as they didn't go down there, a basement might have any of the things he thought of earlier. Something there was important enough to visit regularly and work hard to keep secret.

They needed more firepower, but anyone down there might have already fled. For all they knew, he might call in peacekeepers or Ruthenian paramilitary forces. Until he knew what was down there, reaching out to other forces was risky though. If he found something valuable, French or Czech peacekeepers might grab it, or Poles and Ukrainian Nationalists could both try to grab it, starting their war.

I'm borrowing trouble. He hesitated partly because until they explored the hidden basement, there was a faint, almost vanishingly small, chance his wife and daughter were down there, the English-speaking captives. *And when we go down there, that chance will go away.*

Chapter Twelve: What Lies Below

There's no one down there. Sergeant Duncan wasn't sure he really believed that. He also didn't know if he wanted it to be true. If there was nothing down there, if Hannah's kidnappers fled, nobody would shoot at him, always a good thing. It would be a disappointing end to this adventure, though. His missing finger throbbed. Not an itch. A throb. An itch signaled danger coming but not imminent. A throb, though, said disaster loomed.

That's superstitious crap. He told himself that but didn't believe it. He climbed down to the top of the elevator, landing silently on wooden slats. The elevator mechanism was in good shape, with signs of recent maintenance.

The wooden top had cracks between the slats, but below them was darkness. If someone was waiting in the elevator, they knew he was up here. *So, I might as well take my chances.* He pointed the flashlight at a crack, his sidearm poised. Nothing. He worked the light around covering the entire elevator, then found a hatch and lowered himself into the elevator.

He did a cursory search outside the elevator, finding nothing. "Looks deserted," he said into the radio. "Send a team down."

A couple soldiers joined him. One said, "It's empty. They're always empty. Get your hopes up for a fight or finding treasure and they're empty."

"And maybe boobytrapped," the other soldier said. They kept their voices low. The darkness seemed to consume their words, and their flashlight beams.

Still no sounds. Sergeant Duncan turned out his flashlight and motioned for the others to turn off theirs. He didn't bother closing his eyes. The darkness was absolute. He stood, listening. Nothing. He smelled something, though, actually two things. One was exhaust, and he couldn't identify the other, though it made him uneasy. *I've smelled that before and it was bad, very bad.*

He turned the light back on and began the search. The underground area extended under the building and into a tunnel leading away from it. He started with the area under the building, radioing up his findings.

A room matched Hannah's description of her captivity, including a narrow table with unlocked handcuffs and manacles attached to it. Another room held two dozen bunks, while another looked like a kitchen, strewn with empty US army ration containers, probably stolen. Yet another room was a miniature weapons factory, with a few crudely made half-finished Walther P38 sidearms left behind. Another area apparently made rifles, judging from the machinery, though nothing was left of that production. Cartridge reloading tools sat in one corner, along with spent cartridges, but no gunpowder or primers.

"They were making maybe a hundred pistols a week," Sergeant Duncan said. That was a drop in the ocean compared to the number of German, Soviet and Allied weapons washing around the region. Still, it would be good to shut down the operation.

A huge gear sat in one corner, too big for a truck or tank. A ship? A U-boat? That was possible, though why here, so far from the ocean? A few German U-boats were still not accounted for, though they must be running short of spare parts if their crews hadn't scuttled them. So maybe they were trying to repair a U-boat part here. That would make this a more important base than he figured. He wondered why the men here had abandoned it in the face of a US force they could have easily beaten. But once they started the fight, more US forces would pile on and whoever was in charge probably knew that.

Another room, at the far corner from the sleeping quarters, was a bomb-making workshop, with a trip wire attached to enough explosives to make his skin crawl. *Crap! We're going to die down here.* The explosives would have brought the ceiling crashing down. *Did they set a timer to back up the trip wire or scatter more traps down here?* He radioed up about the explosives, adding, "We'll need explosives experts. We also need to get everyone up top away from the building."

Was the tripwire the disaster his missing finger was throbbing about? Apparently not. It kept throbbing.

"Do you want to come up and wait for explosives experts?" Captain Murphy asked.

Hell yeah. Actually, Sergeant Duncan had mixed emotions. He wanted to see what was here, discover any dangers or treasures himself. Then there was the terror of being buried alive, or dead. "Somebody has to find out what's down here. We'll keep going for now."

That was partly fueled by not wanting to look scared in front of the men who accompanied him. *If I was alone I would leave skid marks getting out of here.*

They slowed the search, but Sergeant Duncan remembered the twisted German mine-planting ingenuity and wondered if they should withdraw and blow the place up. At the same time, the basement kept giving little clues on who used it, enough to keep him searching. He would have gone back up if ordered to and been relieved to be out, but when Captain Murphy gave him the option of coming back up or continuing the search, ironically he felt compelled to continue searching. *Bastard. He knows I won't stop unless he orders me to.* He wondered if the other soldiers felt the same mix of fear and overwhelming, compulsive curiosity. Probably.

They finished with the basement, seeing signs of hasty evacuation, but nothing to identify the kidnappers. Exhaust fumes should have mostly cleared in the tunnel, but they seemed thicker there. He pointed that out and tightened his grip on his rifle. "If they're going to fight why abandon the factory part?"

That didn't make sense unless something went wrong with the evacuation. He visualized men struggling with flat tires or overheating engines and expecting someone to stumble over a tripwire any second.

It felt slapstick, like slipping in mud while charging a machine gun nest, but situations like that happened in war and could turn deadly.

"If we come under fire, fall back," he said.

They kept going down the tunnel, but hugged the sides, with flashlights searching the darkness. The flashlights made them easy targets, so one soldier turned his off and hung back.

A heavy truck-sized door blocked the tunnel, with exhaust fumes seeping under it.

He updated Captain Murphy, then tried the door. It was locked, apparently from the other side, though he found and operated the opening mechanism on their side. A field mouse stood eyeing them curiously, wiping its whiskers, seemingly unconcerned but mildly curious.

"Locked or jammed." The lock resisted their efforts for long moments, then they finally pried the door up about a foot. Exhaust gas puffed out. The mouse took two steps away from the door, then fell, twitching.

"Gas! Get back, now!" Sergeant Duncan was sprinting down the tunnel before the words were out of his mouth. He didn't worry about tripwires, just sprinted to the stranded elevator, helped the other soldiers up and climbed up himself.

He paused at the top, started to grab a breath, but kept going until they were out of the building, then grabbed a large, hungry gulp of air.

Captain Murphy stepped out, his rifle ready. "Are they chasing you?"

"No. Gas." He wondered briefly if he had overreacted, if exhaust fumes killed the mouse, but exhaust wouldn't kill that quickly. He knew the Nazis killed Jews, Communists and anybody else they took a dislike to with gas, though they didn't use gas on the battlefield. There were rumors that Allied troops had blundered into nightmarish gasses that the Nazis produced, but if that was true, it was highly classified.

"We explored the basement, but there is still a lot of tunnel to explore." He savored the fresh air and sunlight, then noticed that his missing finger was still throbbing. "They must have left a truck running so the exhaust would hide whatever other gas they used." He noticed his hand trembling on his rifle. He tightened his grip, willing the trembling to stop. "I used up one of my nine lives down there." He turned to the captain, suddenly intense. "I think something bad is about to happen. Old soldier's intuition."

Captain Murphy nodded. "I've learned to take that seriously." He turned to the other soldiers. "Stay sharp. This may not be over." His eyes searched the field of thistles. "Which life was that? Number eight?"

"Somewhere around there." Sergeant Duncan closed his eyes. "I need to call it quits. Go back to the states, buy a car, knock out kids and live the American dream."

"Any sign they're still down there?"

"Probably not," He thought through their time in the tunnel. "No voices. No sounds except the engine they left running. They probably just left a trap for us."

More soldiers arrived from Fort Seminole, including explosive experts, who quickly took charge. Captain Murphy and Sergeant Duncan walked back to the road, where they left the jeep. Captain Murphy looked around. "Where is the other jeep?"

Before they figured that out, Colonel Rock came on the radio. "Is Amber McCormick with you?"

"No. She should be in Lvov."

One of the guys from the missing jeep shook his head. "She said you wanted her to stay back. She was in the second jeep the last time I saw it."

Captain Murphy looked around. The second jeep was gone. He stared at the radio and mouthed, "Crap!"

And that's what my finger was trying to tell me. That made no sense, but Sergeant Duncan believed it completely.

Chapter Thirteen: Dietrich Lang Gets a Surprise

Dietrich Lang knew something was badly wrong. He didn't know what it was, but he hadn't survived near the top of the Nazi hierarchy for over a decade by ignoring his instincts. In that bare-knuckle world, with rivals clawing for him and the western allies trying to kill him, he developed a sixth sense for trouble.

Kidnapping Hannah Reitsch went off without a hitch and the kidnappers supposedly now held her at one of his minor workshops near Lvov. Something was wrong though. He heard it in the voice of the guy he phoned there for a carefully worded conversation to see what, if anything, they had discovered from "the package."

His man in charge at the warehouse was lying. Lang could hear it in his voice. The guy was also terrified. Lang didn't confront him over the phone. He just brought the conversation to an end and collected a squad of enforcers. They headed for the workshop without a word, traveling the highway that the US had so conveniently built from the Marshes south to the Romanian border. That highway wasn't an autobahn, but it wasn't bad. especially given the toll the horrible muddy seasons and winters took on roads. It was almost as good as what the Germans built.

Lang smiled. The highway would last longer than the US occupation here did. The Americans had no strategic vision or taste for extended conflict. They mobilized in huge spasms, crushed their enemies and then went back to their homeland, surrounded by oceans that they now controlled beyond any dispute, firmly displacing the Royal Navy as the world's greatest sea power. If the enemy didn't stand up to be crushed, the Americans lost patience.

Was that still true now that the US emerged from World War II as by far the strongest country on Earth? Lang's plans counted on that continued US pattern, and nothing in US postwar actions so far went against that pattern. The US was trying to occupy not just one but two great powers, or significant parts of them, with an army a fraction of the size the Germans used to occupy the conquered part of the Soviet Union. That couldn't work in the long run, and Lang was betting his future and the future of Germany that when the cost grew too high, the Americans would hastily patch together some face-saving peace treaty, then abandon Europe to its bloody fate.

The ride was smooth, but Lang's gut clinched. Why was his man at the warehouse lying to him? Why was he afraid? Did his men kill Hannah when they tried to torture her? Did they somehow draw attention to the workshop? What was he driving into? He should have stayed out of this, whatever it was. He had people capable of handling whatever was going on at the warehouse. But that thinking left him trapped, a spider at the center of his web, unable to leave. He enjoyed being outside, enjoyed the sun and a sense of danger. He didn't know what he was driving into and that felt good.

The workshop had two entrances. He picked the less traveled one, the one that led to an escape tunnel built in the last stages of the German occupation at a high cost in dead slave laborers.

That let him show up with little warning, hopefully not allowing his men at the workshop to get a story together. His men swept through the check point at the tunnel entrance and through the tunnel, arriving at the main workshop without warning. The German in charge of the workshop, a former Luftwaffe sergeant, glanced up from assembling a rifle and went pale. He went to attention and saluted. "What do you need sir?"

The man was sweating despite the chill in the basement workshop. The men around him paused, eyeing Lang warily. Lang hesitated. There were more men working here than he brought with him, tough, experienced soldiers. A fight here could end his plans. So could any hint of weakness. *I was stupid to come here, but I have to push through.*

"Where is our prisoner?" His voice was mild.

"Not here," the sergeant said. "She escaped. She's on foot so she couldn't have gone far." The man kept talking, but Lang tuned him out. An escape was far worse than never having kidnapped the aviatrix.

"How long has she been gone?"

"Shortly after you called," the sergeant said.

Lang nodded to one of his men, who pulled his sidearm. "Don't lie. It makes it more difficult for me to clean up this mess."

The sergeant gulped. "I don't know how long. We noticed she was missing ten minutes before you called. I figured we could find her. No need to bother you."

"But you haven't found her." The trip here took about an hour, and Hannah was gone before he started. She would have started out on foot, but an attractive young lady like her would find some other way to get around, certainly in an hour or more. He nodded. "We have to assume that she is out of our reach and will bring the Americans here. Fill trucks, starting with the most vital equipment, then things we can live without."

The poison gas could be useful, but it was bulky and dangerous. It could stay. He had the sergeant take him to the room where Hannah had been held. No sign of her bonds being broken. They must have been unlocked. One of his men must have released her. He felt his anger flair. Stupid. Probably a guy with more hormones than sense. Who? He didn't have time to find out. *Which means that I have a use for the gas.*

"Scout everywhere to make sure you leave nothing that tells searchers who you are." He added, "All personal documents go into my car. You'll get them back when we've made our escape."

"We have a few of your special prisoners," the sergeant said.

The prisoners would be a burden, but if they were still alive he must have decided they were valuable. "Bring them."

He helped the men dismantle the workshop, bringing around trucks and loading them. Most of these were good, loyal Nazis, but at least one was a fool, a security risk he couldn't afford. He let no hint of what he was thinking reach his face, and even congratulated the men on their speed. When they finished, he motioned one of the men he brought with him over and whispered to him.

#

The gas wasn't one of the nasty types that German scientists invented just before World War II. It was an older one that had been around and very effective late in World War I. Lang didn't want to be anywhere near the tunnel when the men from the workshop died. It wasn't that he was squeamish, just that he had a healthy respect for what even the older war gases could do and how tricky it was to use them. He drove away from the tunnel in a carefully maintained, but non-descript jeep, with a single bodyguard and two of his special prisoners, both carefully hooded. The other men he brought with him would make sure the workshop men died in the tunnel then drive away in the trucks full of vital components from the workshop.

He drove quickly, his instincts telling him he might not have much time. He still didn't know how long Hannah had been gone or where she went, but he had a bad feeling about the escape. That feeling got worse when his bodyguard opened the gate and he saw a US military jeep parked on the shoulder not far from the gate. The jeep was empty, but the engine was still warm. Lang wanted to speed away, but whoever was in the jeep could be watching them. *They probably saw my face.*

Were they part of a larger group? Probably. If Hannah reached the Americans with her story, they wouldn't send just one jeep, or if they did, that jeep would be followed by a lot more. Lang felt a moment of near panic. *I may have just lost everything.* He could run, but if the soldiers from the American jeep were watching, his escape would be temporary. *I have to kill them before they tell anyone else I was here.* He pulled a knife and motioned to his bodyguard. "Find them and kill them." That was high risk when he had no idea how many Americans were here, but he could see no other way. The remainder of his men wouldn't arrive for long minutes, long enough for the Americans to get away or get reinforcements. He had to do this with his own hands and those of his lone bodyguard.

How many Americans were out there? He studied the mud where they had stepped out of the jeep. Only one set of footsteps, from the driver's side. The tracks led to the gate, then into the thicket on one side of it. There was something odd about the tracks. They were small and didn't leave anywhere near the mark his tracks did. Small and light. Only one person. That made no sense. Maybe the rest of the jeep's complement got off somewhere up the road, leaving only the driver to check out the gate while the others covered him. That would explain it. He nodded. The Americans would have covered the gate. Were they still there or were they moving toward the workshop? No way to tell. He motioned for the bodyguard to circle wide while he followed the trail. That gave him the dangerous part of the mission, but anything they did here was dangerous.

Lang felt a kind of thrill he hadn't felt in a long time, though. He wasn't skulking or planning now. He was staking everything on a throw of the dice. He would kill the Americans, or he would lose. It was that simple and it felt good.

Whoever made the tracks was short as well as light, able to slip through brush he had trouble squeezing through. He tried to gauge how comfortable they were in the thicket but couldn't. They didn't go places an experienced soldier would go to cover their trail, but whoever it was put tricks in the trail that he had to puzzle out, delaying and frustrating him. He didn't have time to play tracking games. More Americans would be on their way. *We have to end this.* He also had to be patient, he knew. The tracks he followed could easily lead him into an ambush.

The chase was taking far too long. He paused briefly, listening. Nothing. If there was a jeepload of Americans out here, they were good at skulking in these thickets. A bunch of backwoodsmen? The German army ran into the type during the war and learned to fear Americans who still lived a 19th century existence in out of the way corners of the US. There weren't as many in World War II as in the first World War, but they were still as formidable as the stories from World War I suggested. If he was stalking a jeepload of those types, he would be lucky to get out alive. At the same time, a wild, irrational part of him wanted to pit himself against men like that.

The more rational part of his mind told him he was being stupid. He didn't have to prove himself, especially not against illiterate backwoodsmen who could shoot the eyes out of a squirrel or whatever the hell Americans like that did instead of going to the opera.

A shout broke the silence, followed by a curse in German. Lang ran toward the sound, leaving caution behind. He plowed through the brush and found himself in a little clearing. A young woman stood over his bodyguard, trying to pull the guy's rifle out from under his prone body. She seemed unarmed except for a heavy stick, which she gripped when she turned to face him. "He tried to grab me. I hit him. I think he's hurt." That was in broken German, mixed with sobs.

What the hell? A woman out here? Why? Lang tried to recognize the accent. It might be Ukrainian, but the woman was sobbing so hard he couldn't tell. "Have you seen anyone else out here?" Lang asked in Ukrainian.

The woman shook her head, still sobbing. She turned to the bodyguard. "I'm sorry. Can you help him?"

Why was she out here? More importantly, where were the American soldiers?

Lang crouched beside his bodyguard and felt for a pulse. Some instinct warned him, and he ducked, taking the blow from the woman's stick on his shoulder instead of the back of his head. He rolled with the blow and grabbed the woman's legs, bringing her down. She kicked him hard in the ribs and turned to run. Lang drew his Walther P38. "I will shoot you if you take another step."

The woman stopped, though the way she held her body told him she was thinking about running.. She turned, continuing to sob. "I'm sorry. The Americans chased me, made me ride in their jeep. I thought you were with them."

That might make some sense of the situation. He wondered if he should knife the woman now or try to find out more about the Americans. "How many were there?"

She sobbed and said something he couldn't make out. Behind him, the bodyguard groaned. "What happened?"

"You got hit by a girl," Lang said. "Some bit of fluff the Americans were playing with." Maybe the Americans weren't here because of Hannah. Maybe they were on leave and messing with local women. That happened sometimes in most armies, and the US army was going soft with occupation duty. He wanted to believe that because if it was true he could creep away from this fiasco and lose only the workshop and the men dying in the tunnel.

"We'll need to kill her." He said that in French, hoping the bodyguard knew that language. The woman stiffened slightly. *Did she understand what I said?* He took a closer look at her and swore. She wasn't a peasant, though she was doing a very good job of acting like one. Her clothes were too expensive and her hair too neat, manicured. Who the hell was she and what was she doing here? That was a mystery he would have to explore later. He aimed his sidearm at her and said in French, "If you want to live, tell me so now."

Chapter Fourteen: Envoy McCormick Sets a Deadline

Captain Murphy expected a tongue-lashing when he got back to Fort Seminole, and that was a best-case scenario. He couldn't think of much of a defense. Bad judgement, yes. Losing control of a situation? He couldn't dispute that.

They found the second jeep behind a second hidden gate, further down the road, apparently where the tunnel led. He belatedly posted guards there.

Reinforcements, including explosives experts arrived, pushing him out of the loop on investigating the mystery building, even before Colonel Rock called him back to Fort Seminole. He drove back to the fort to face whatever punishment he faced for allowing the Envoy's daughter to finagle her way into a dangerous search and get captured.

Hannah Reitsch rode back with him to Fort Seminole, along with Sergeant Duncan. Hannah kept looking back toward the building, as did Sergeant Duncan.

"I'm expecting a boom," Sergeant Duncan said. "That place is an explosion waiting to happen."

"You saw everything I said was there, though," Hannah said.

Sergeant Duncan nodded. "Pretty much. Awfully good place to get blown up."

"You're headed for something worse than getting blown up," Hannah said. "You lost the most powerful man in Eastern Europe's daughter."

Captain Murphy wanted to tell her to shut up, but instead asked, "Remember anything else? Anything that tells us who was in charge?"

"If they were Nazis, they were quiet about it," Hannah said. "No Nazi slogans, even when I was blindfolded in the basement. They didn't appeal to me as a German pilot or as a Hitler loyalist, and they didn't accuse me of being a traitor for working for Governor Meandrov."

Captain Murphy thought about that. Most of what Sergeant Duncan saw in the basement pointed toward diehard Nazis, including the apparent U-boat part. The Germans here would be used to hiding their beliefs. Would that carry over when they were alone with someone they thought had Nazi ties?

Was Hannah telling the truth about what she heard down there? Probably. This was a valuable base for local Nazis, or whatever group used it and her escape forced a hasty evacuation, with the group leaving valuable equipment behind. If she was still a Nazi sympathizer, her actions made no sense.

Maybe she wanted us to find them. In the convoluted world of the Nazis, deadly feuds were common. Did they continue after the war? Maybe Hannah was using Americans to attack rival Nazis.

Captain Murphy tried to relax. He needed to figure out why Hannah was kidnapped but saw no way to do it. He knew Nazi factions lurked among the Germans in the borderlands, but US intelligence rarely infiltrated them or got useful information from the few they caught. That could be ominous, suggesting sophisticated counter-intelligence operations or it could mean the Nazis here were few, and disorganized. He suspected most of them were laying low, figuring the US would eventually get tired of the seemingly endless drain of occupation and go home.

Those were all problems for the future. Right now, he needed to survive his reception at Fort Seminole. He felt a surge of resentment. If anybody was at fault here, it was Envoy McCormick for bringing his headstrong daughter into this maelstrom of competing factions. *But I didn't handle her well either.* What he could he have done differently? Left Amber at Fort Seminole? She was right when she said she could just follow them. Left her in Lvov under guard? The guards had no authority over her.

"If she wanted to get herself kidnapped, there wasn't much I could do about it." He said that aloud but cringed when the words left his mouth. "But I was the commanding officer. It's my responsibility."

"This is another time I'm glad I'm not an officer," Sergeant Duncan said. "My finger was telling me the whole time that things were headed south."

"Your finger?" Hannah asked.

He explained about the missing finger itching or throbbing, adding, "The doctor says it's all in my head. My subconscious picks up things the rest of my mind doesn't. Whatever it is, it works. I know when the sledgehammer of God is about to slam down on me, even if I don't know where it's coming from."

When they got back to Fort Seminole, MPs ushered Captain Murphy into base headquarters. Another group of MPs took Hannah and Sergeant Duncan to the barracks.

Presidential Envoy McCormick showed no sign of anger. He sat calmly beside Colonel Rock; his face impassive, while Captain Murphy made his report.

Captain Murphy wondered if Governor Meandrov knew Hannah was back but didn't ask. He kept to the facts, focusing on the mystery building and saying the bare minimum about Amber to let them know why she was with them.

Colonel Rock let him finish the report without interruptions, then nodded. "We'll discuss how a civilian ended up where she did, but we have more important things on our plate." He nodded to Envoy McCormick. "The Envoy has a few things to say."

Captain Murphy braced himself, but Envoy McCormick asked, "You know about the Galatian oil fields?"

"Sure. Clusters of small oilfields east of Lvov that add up to quite a bit of oil. Not Texas-sized, but enough to matter. The Soviets sabotaged them so thoroughly that it took the Germans years to get them back in operation, then the Germans sabotaged the wells themselves when local Ukrainians went over to the Allies. They still aren't back up to their prewar production."

"Production is way up," Envoy McCormick said. "And while it isn't a lot of oil by US standards, it gives whoever owns it a nice boost. Our intelligence claims local Poles plan to seize some of the biggest fields, with support from elements of the Polish government. If they seize the fields, it will set off a row of dominoes. It means war between Poland and Ukrainian nationalists. Then Stalin will scent weakness and pull something. He already partially mobilized, trying to keep it secret. I figure he will start border skirmishes to tie down our troops, then have his tame partisans grab something." He sighed. "Probe with bayonet. It's an old Soviet strategy. If the Polish army gets involved, the Soviets say they'll cross the demarcation line and push the Poles out. We're bringing in quick reaction forces from occupation duty in Germany. It will look as though we're reacting to my daughter being kidnapped, but we've planned the move for weeks."

How would the kidnappers react to US forces piling in? They could kill Amber and dump her body. *We may never know what happened to her.* Captain Murphy wondered if Envoy McCormick understood the risk. *He can't let that change his decision.*

Captain Murphy wanted to ask what the kidnappers demanded but decided not to. Let the ambassador bring up the kidnapping if he chose to.

"Any news from the mystery building?" he asked.

Colonel Rock glanced at Envoy McCormick, who nodded. "Go ahead."

"We found bodies," Colonel Rock said. "Fifteen men died trapped in the tunnel. They were moving poison gas, and something sprang a leak. They died fast, but in a lot of pain. Somebody closed a door in front of them, probably to save themselves.." He grimaced. "Nasty way to go, even for dead-ender Nazis."

"Actually, we found some evidence these were German communists," Envoy McCormick said. "Nothing solid, but the communist cells are careful and professional." He turned to Colonel Rock. "Let's bring the governors in. It's time to put the fear of me into them." He turned to Captain Murphy. "Stay. You'll want to hear this."

Governor Meandrov came in, escorted by two MPs. The partisan governor, Alexander Federov followed. He was a huge man, a head taller than the MPs who escorted him and bulky, a bear of a man with heavy chest and shoulders, with just the beginning of a pot belly and a faint sprinkling of gray in a beard that dominated his face. Federov's sheer size dominated the room, making even Governor Meandrov look small. Meandrov's holster was empty, but his hand still lingered close to it.

"Gentlemen," Envoy McCormick said. "There will be a time later when you can talk, to me if you prefer, or to each other. This is a time where I talk, and you remain silent."

He was shorter than either of the Russians and slender, but he spoke with such assurance that both men fell silent. "I seem to have misplaced my daughter. As provisional governors under the UN administration, you will use whatever resources you need to use to make sure she is home, safe, tomorrow morning." He paused. "I know that you both have enough control over the areas you govern that finding her should not be difficult." Envoy McCormick sighed. "Also, as valued allies, I want you to know that as part of ongoing readiness drills, a US force of no less than a brigade and up to five divisions will be airlifted into Fort Seminole for exercises tomorrow. B-29 bombers will fly into bases in Czechoslovakia, where they will be available as part of the exercise."

He paused and smiled coldly at the governors. "While the troops are here as part of a scheduled exercise, they can be available as part of a search if necessary. I trust that they won't need to get involved. They are trained as an occupation Army and their searches could be quite intrusive. They will be ready to join the search mid-morning tomorrow, if necessary. I hope I've made myself clear, gentlemen."

He turned and walked out of the office.

Federov opened his mouth. He looked as if he wanted to curse or run after the ambassador, but instead, he closed his mouth, face grim and walked out, followed by MPs. Governor Meandrov stood silently for a moment, then said, "I hear that you found Hannah. Thank you." He walked out too.

Colonel Rock turned to Captain Murphy. "You've heard of gunboat diplomacy. These days it's heavy bomber diplomacy."

Chapter Fifteen: Reinforcements

The next morning, Captain Murphy woke to the sounds of planes landing. The airbase was crowded with transport planes landing troops and vehicles by the time he got up. The flow of transports slowed, then Douglas Skyraider attack planes landed.

Hannah Reitsch showed up, looking fresh, seemingly unaffected by the kidnapping. She studied the attack planes. "I've heard a lot of good things about Skyraiders, but in an age of jets they are relics."

Captain Murphy eyed her. "A plane is just a way to deliver bombs or to keep the other side from delivering them. If a tool gets the job done, who cares how fancy it is?"

Hannah clasped her hands to her chest in mock horror. "You wound me, sir. Such blasphemy from a man privileged to fly helicopters."

"If Stalin comes across the border you'll see plenty of jets," Captain Murphy said. "But for now, we need bomb trucks and Skyraiders are very good bomb trucks."

"Maybe." Hannah turned to soldiers unloading their gear. "Looks like you brought in a brigade, plus bits and pieces. No tanks or heavy artillery. If you're starting a war, you're coming in way too light."

He glanced at her sharply. Her estimates were uncomfortably close to his. Fort Seminole's tank and artillery companies could supplement the rapid reaction force, but this wasn't a force that could take on warlord/Governor paramilitaries, much less the Polish army or, God forbid, the Soviets.

We need Shermans or better yet, Pershings. The M24 light tanks were probably here because some army bureaucrat thought light tanks would be better suited to the Marshes. They might be marginally better there, but Captain Murphy shuddered when he thought about them fighting T34/85s, Panthers, or even late-model Panzer 4s, some of which were undoubtedly lurking among the local paramilitaries.

Captain Murphy turned to Hannah. "A brigade and change? Good estimate. But is this everything the brass is bringing in?" He suspected the brigade was most if not all the reinforcements they were going to get. Envoy McCormick gave a brigade as the lower limit for the reinforcements, but even his upper limit of four divisions would barely be enough to deal with the warlords, much less the Poles and Soviets.

Hannah and Captain Murphy went to New Memphis and grabbed breakfast, with military police discreetly following them. "Your envoy is bluffing, against tough, war-hardened men who don't back down unless the odds are overwhelmingly against them," Hannah said while they ate. "The Nazis were wrong about Slavs. They are tough, smart fighters. We took Moscow in the fall of 1942 and that should have been the end for the Soviets. Moscow wasn't just their capital. It was where their communications and transport systems came together. Yet they fought on somehow, kept grinding us down year after year."

Captain Murphy wondered if Hannah really believed what she said about the Slavs. A lot of diehard Nazis didn't. They still thought they beat the Soviets, only to lose to treachery from their allies and to British and American armies. There was an element of truth to that, though Captain Murphy knew that the Soviets, after a disastrous start, fought a smart war. *We wouldn't be here if they were pushovers.*

He didn't push Hannah while they ate, just let her talk. If she was shaken by her kidnapping and escape, she showed little sign of it, though she said the expected words. Did that mean the kidnapping was fake? Maybe, but to be the kind of pilot she was, Hannah had to have nerves like steel cords.

"I hate intelligence work," he said. "Everything is lies, smoke and mirrors."

"My friend, if you are looking for truth, you're in the wrong business." She smiled ruefully. "You're also in the wrong part of the world." She touched his arm. "Strong. You Americans are strong when your enemy is in front of you, when you know who he is, and you can throw avalanches of metal at them. Those skills won't help you much here."

That was probably true of most Americans. Captain Murphy wondered if it was true of Envoy McCormick. The way he handled the governors last night hinted that it wasn't. *He played a bad hand perfectly.* Last night's meeting with the Governors was just an encounter though, not even a battle, much less the war.

They wandered back to Fort Seminole. If Envoy McCormick was bluffing in other ways, he wasn't bluffing about how fast the reinforcements would be ready to march. The first elements headed up the highway toward the Marshes well before noon, with light M24 tanks from Fort Seminole's tank companies leading a column of trucks and jeeps. The quick deployment put a smile on Captain Murphy's face. "We haven't completely forgotten how to fight."

"You haven't forgotten how to move troops around fast," Hannah said. "Fighting may be another story."

Captain Murphy hoped the men marching north were ready but based on what he saw among new recruits at Fort Seminole, he doubted it. The soldiers who won World War II and the Donets War were mostly civilians now, or dead. and if Congress wanted to keep getting elected, the survivors would stay civilians. A lot of experience at modern warfare went out the door after those wars and a lot of bad ideas about training soldiers came in. The new crop of soldiers seemed soft and overconfident. *If we fight a first-class army, we'll get our heads handed to us.*

He just hoped not too many young soldiers died before they learned how to fight again.

Hannah got called back to her plane. She asked Captain Murphy to stay with her until she was ready to go. US intelligence officers interrogated her again first but didn't pick up anything that Captain Murphy didn't already know. The only possible sign of mystery English prisoners was a narrow strip from a woman's dress wadded up and concealed in one corner of the basement, covered with dirt.

They were there. He knew that was wishful thinking, even as he thought it. He wanted to believe that his wife and daughter had been in the building with Hannah, though he knew it was unlikely. Even if American prisoners were there, thousands of American prisoners of war were still missing and were far more likely prospects. The Germans, Nazis or Communists, would hold Americans with skills or information they needed, not an army wife and her daughter. Were Americans or Brits missing from around Lvov? Probably. If civilians went missing in this wild, lawless area, nobody but their relatives would notice.

"I think the men in the tunnel were executed," Hannah said. She smiled grimly. "Sometimes the questioned learns more than the questioner."

"Someone released the poison gas on purpose?" He stared at her. "Are you sure?"

"No, but dead men tell no tales." She finished her preflight checks, then kissed him on the cheek. "Thank you for believing me."

I didn't completely, and I still don't. Aloud, he said, "Good luck working for the governor.

Governor Meandrov called Captain Murphy over before he left. The Governor was in a jovial mood. "I see you got a kiss from my prize aviatrix. I should be jealous." He grinned. "Thank you for finding her. Please remind your Colonel and the Envoy that I can help you find the young lady."

Captain Murphy nodded. "I'm sure they will ask if they need your help." *And they know your help comes with a price.* Aloud, he said, "Be careful on the flight home. Someone has a lot of anti-aircraft guns in the Marshes."

"You know who has the guns. The question is, what are you going to do about them?"

That question hung in the air. Meandrov's Luger was back in its holster. Meandrov's little fleet took off, the FW-190 fighter planes first, followed by the cargo planes.

"He was in a good mood." Sergeant Duncan strode over and watched the planes until they were out of sight. The Sergeant was back in uniform, with his hair cut.

"He probably hopes we'll take out his biggest rival," Captain Murphy said.

"Federov? Maybe. Why are we headed toward the Marshes?"

"Someone fired at a clearly marked US helicopter, with me in it, by the way." Captain Murphy paused. *Was that really just two days ago?* So much had happened that he wasn't sure. "What you're seeing is one part search for Amber and five parts a show of force."

"Make that six parts bluff that may backfire badly," Sergeant Duncan said. "Federov is a Communist bastard, but he isn't stupid. He also isn't weak. He is Stalin's man through and through. If Stalin tells him to send his men charging into machine guns until the guns run out of bullets, he'll do it."

"Meandrov has a lot to gain if the US gets into it with Federov and the Partisans," Captain Murphy said.

"You think he set up Hannah's kidnapping?"

Captain Murphy shrugged. "The thought crossed my mind. On the other hand, she led us to a genuine hideout of some kind. Maybe his intelligence knew about the building and wanted us to find it. What would that gain him, though?"

"Unless he's an idiot, he has nothing to do with kidnapping Amber," Sergeant Duncan said. "And he's not an idiot."

Whoever kidnapped Amber did it at the spur-of-the-moment, not as part of a plan, Captain Murphy thought. Nobody could have predicted that Amber would invite herself along, then use the jeep to search for a second hidden driveway.

"What was she thinking?"

"Amber?" Sergeant Duncan shrugged. "She probably thought she was on a grand adventure until someone grabbed her."

"Who grabbed her?" That was the crucial question. Whoever held her couldn't have known who she was when they took her prisoner. Her capture had to be opportunistic. An opportunity for what, though? Nazi diehards would try to manipulate the situation into a war between the US and the partisans, hoping it would grow into a war between the western Allies and Soviets. That was Hitler's hope when it became obvious Germany was losing.

"If we screw this up, we're looking at World War III," Sergeant Duncan said.

"We'll just have to not screw it up then," Captain Murphy said. But that depended on a worried father making the right decisions. *And I have no idea what the right decisions are.*

Chapter Sixteen: Dietrich Lang Contemplates World War III

Dietrich Lang enjoyed having hard men terrified of him, knowing that he could snap his fingers and they would die. He didn't indulge in that enjoyment often though. Convince a hard man he is about to die, and he might try something unpleasant, even deadly.

Lang kept a neutral expression. "You made sure they all died from the gas, but that it looked like an accident?"

Former SS Captain Fredberg nodded. "You didn't have time to figure out who let Hannah Reitsch go, so you made sure you got rid of the traitor."

Lang nodded. "But we didn't question the traitor, so we don't know when he started betraying us, or if he was working alone.."

Fredberg kept his face impassive, but Lang saw him tense subtly. "I saw no sign of disloyalty before we detained Hannah Reitsch. The men were probably unhappy about grabbing her."

"That's the problem with turning a pretty face and fast reflexes into a heroine of the Reich," Lang said. "People believe the crap."

What about his current prisoner? He should kill her. He should have slit her throat and left her in the thicket.

Still, she intrigued him. *She fooled me twice, had me thinking she was a peasant woman when I should have known immediately that she wasn't.* His shoulder still hurt where she clubbed him. A second slower and she would have had him.

Should I kill her? He didn't even know her real name. She claimed she was Sally Worth, a nurse who shacked up with a

95

sergeant on leave, then ran away in the jeep when their bedroom adventures got too rough. She claimed that the jeep was overheating, and she stopped to find water for the radiator. That was all plausible, but Lang didn't believe it. Having the jeep overheat at the gate when the Americans would have been coming stretched credibility.

But if the Americans came to attack the workshop, why bring a woman? He hadn't searched the thicket any further after he found her but had no evidence other Americans were near the second gate when he left.

Fredberg came back, his face a mix of fear and triumph. "I think I know who she is."

"A spy?" That fit. The woman had played a weak hand perfectly back at the gate and almost won.

Fredberg shook his head. "It's worse than that."

Lang listened to Fredberg's theory, then swore. "Amber McCormick?" He tried to debunk the theory, but it tied the pieces together entirely too well. *If it's really her, we have a huge problem and maybe a bigger opportunity.*

First, he had to prove that the woman really was Amber McCormick. What would Amber be doing alone in a thicket outside his workshop, especially so soon after Hannah escaped? He toyed with the idea that Amber McCormick was operating as a spy, but that seemed unlikely. Amber would know too many of her father's secrets for the Americans to let her risk herself.

He needed to question her, but carefully. He wanted to do it personally. Why not? She already saw his face. Did she know who he was? Probably not, but she had proven herself a good enough actress that he couldn't believe anything she said. He wondered if that would still be true under torture. Probably. Amber McCormick was quite good at coming up with plausible, but untrue stories.

They were in the basement of another truck repair building dating back to the Donets War. It was a setup nearly identical to the one compromised by Hannah's escape. He wondered if using the building was a mistake. If the Americans found the first workshop, they might search for similar ones. That was a problem for later though. Right now, he had to make sure he had the person he thought he did.

He wondered how to approach the woman, but decided a direct approach was as likely to work as anything. The woman was tied to a chair in a basement room, a hood over her head. He took the hood off so he could see her eyes. A single bare bulb lit the room, its light harsh. Not many women could look beautiful in that harsh light, with her face streaked with tears, but Amber McCormick, if that was her name, managed it. Lang stared at her, suddenly at a loss as to how to start.

Finally. he said, "I think your real name is Amber McCormick, which makes me sorry I ran into you."

"You're sorry? I'm locked up in a dungeon, guarded by trolls." Her voice gave nothing away, no hint of fear. "I hope you don't mind being called a troll. You're actually rather good-looking as trolls go, mostly wart free, and you might have a nice smile if you used it more. You don't smile much though. I can tell by the lines on your face."

"I notice that you didn't deny that you're Amber McCormick."

"I've told you so many things that you won't believe me one way or the other." She paused. "What would you do with an Amber McCormick if you had one?"

That was a good question. "Shoot her and dump her in a ditch unless she finds some way to be useful."

"That doesn't make me want to be Amber McCormick. Isn't her dad some big US government muckety-muck? Is it smart to cross a man like that? You look smart. Maybe you can figure out something smart to do with Amber that doesn't bring the full weight of the American government down on you."

Too calm. Too in-control. Lang wondered if the girl, whether she was Amber McCormick or not, had any idea how slim her chance of survival was. *I can't let her go.* She could tie his face, though not his name, to the workshop, to kidnapping Hannah and to the gas in the tunnel. Every minute she lived was a risk he couldn't afford.

"You can't unkill someone," the woman said.

And that was the problem. Lang could pull his Walther P38's trigger and the risk of the woman identifying him would be over. But then what? He had disposed of plenty of bodies. One more wouldn't be a problem. It was the aftermath he feared. *People are still looking for Amelia Earhart and they'll probably never stop.* That search would focus exactly where Lang didn't want the Americans to focus.

Presidential Envoy Eldron McCormick, Amber's father, wasn't just President Truman's messenger boy. He was effectively head of the Eastern European Provisional Federation, the organization the Americans used to finesse border issues in the Eastern European lands they occupied. Everyone in the lands the Soviets occupied in June 1941 that were now controlled by the Western Allies were part of the Provisional Federation, with boundaries between the Federation's provinces clearly labelled temporary. Nothing about those boundaries was supposed to matter in the final boundaries between countries. United Nations committees would set the final boundaries.

That was the way it was supposed to work, but boundaries hastily set up in the chaotic last days of the Donets War were hardening into permanence.

Envoy McCormick was the highest-ranking civilian official in the federation, theoretically outranking Omar Bradley, the top US military commander. McCormick controlled US aid to the Federation's provinces and strongly influenced Lend Lease and other US aid throughout the continent.

And I have his daughter. He was sure of that, despite their inconclusive verbal sparring. What should he do with her? If she hadn't seen his face, he would have let her go without conditions. Envoy McCormick couldn't let himself be influenced by his daughter's fate. Besides, what could Lang ask of the Americans that wouldn't shine unwanted light on his operations?

But she saw me. I have to kill her.

I could use her to trigger World War III. The thought intrigued him, but was it true? The search for Amber McCormick would probably trigger a war between the partisans and a coalition of Americans, anti-Stalin Russians and Ukrainian Nationalists. The search was bound to find the secret partisan buildup. It was too big to conceal, and the search for Hannah Reitsch already tore the veil off some of it.

The partisans would have to either give up their laboriously smuggled weapons or fight an open war with the Americans. *They'll probably fight.* If they didn't, he could trigger fighting anyway. He could easily bring in the Poles by staging attacks on ethnic Polish enclaves. He already had contingency plans for a false flag attack using a Ukrainian Nationalist splinter faction he supplied.

Would that bring in the Soviets and the Poles? It could, though he wasn't sure the Soviets would intervene now, while they were still recovering from war and famine. *Do I even want that?* His heart said yes. He was tired of waiting. Lang's head, though, told him it was far too soon. The allies would be appalled by how much he had built up, but if they found him out, they could crush him. They could probably beat any Soviet offensive too, though that victory would turn to ash if they tried to take more of the Soviet Union. His head said to wait. Germany would get an elected government in 1953 and an army eventually, carefully limited at first. The French and Poles would hang onto German territory they held, and the US and Brits would keep bases. The coalition that crushed the Third Reich would watch the Germans carefully, until the Soviets became, in their minds, the greater enemy. *Stalin won't give up. He'll keep rebuilding while the US grows wearier of the squabbles.* Eventually, the western allies would see the Soviet Union as the real enemy. *Then, World War III will come, and Germany will win.* This was still, much as he hated it, a time for patience, for small gains he could build on later, letting the big, inevitable trends of history play out.

That remained the long-range plan. *But what do I want now?* Ideally, the US should fight the partisans, become more suspicious of the Soviets, but not fight an open war with the Soviets yet. He couldn't make that happen, but he could influence it, and he intended to.

The wild, risk-taking part of his mind wanted to keep Amber as one of his playthings. That would be stupid, asking for disaster, but the idea fascinated him.

"Who do you think I am, Amber?" Lang asked.

The young woman shook her head. "You still don't know that's my name."

"It won't be hard to prove. I'm sure there are pictures."

The young woman sighed. "The cost of fame." She cocked her head, her eyes meeting his, apparently unafraid. "I think you got in too deep, got caught up in Hitler's madness and did things that you know are unforgiveable, that you couldn't forgive yourself for even if you believed in a God who could forgive you."

Lang laughed. "Do you really believe that?"

Amber shook her head. "No, I really don't. You might have been that guy once, but he's gone, replaced by a man obsessed with power and a mad dream, lurking in dank basements and kidnapping people when you want to go back to your life, watch your sons grow up, help them become good men."

"How do you know I have sons?"

"I didn't. Now I do. You miss them. That may be the only trace of the old you still left, but you want desperately to see them again." Her voice changed, not pleading, but softer. "I've seen your face, but I've never heard your name. If you let me go far from here, I can't lead anyone back. Dad will make me go back to Washington on the first plane. Then I'll be in a cocoon of bodyguards the rest of my life. Chances of us meeting again are almost zero."

That was probably true. The risk of her identifying him was low. It wasn't zero, though. Was it greater than the risks from the inevitable search?

"You haven't issued any demands or given the US military any indication who you are?"

Lang shook his head. "I'm not an idiot."

"Good. If you want out of this, make a call, maybe from near someone you don't like. Tell the Americans that I was caught up in some local fight and will be released unharmed. Then let me go."

"Just like that?" He laughed. "Is it okay if we question you first?"

Despite the laughter, Lang was tempted. Amber McCormick knew too much but killing her carried risks that could haunt him the rest of his life. *She's right. I can't unkill her.*

She had secrets locked in her head too, more than she realized. But she might learn too much from the questions. *I want the option of releasing her.* That was unlikely, but he needed to keep the possibility open. He had to carefully calibrate this, not just the risks of killing her or letting her go. Amber McCormack could give him something that pushed his plans forward by a decade. He didn't want to start World War III. *I want a shadowy, ambiguous war between factions no one in the US has heard of, over land the US doesn't want.*

Chapter Seventeen: Crisis

It felt weird to be headed for the Marshes in uniform, with other soldiers in the jeep and without Ruslana, but to Sergeant Duncan it also felt familiar, bringing back memories of World War II and the Donets War.

Before he left Fort Seminole, Ruslana pulled him aside and said, "All the provincial governors have far more heavy equipment then they let you know about, hiding in plain sight, in museums, supposedly not running, or hidden away."

Sergeant Duncan knew she was right, but a few dozen tanks, driven by inexperienced crews, wouldn't be a huge problem even if they were T34/85s or even King Tigers or JS2s against Fort Seminole's light M24 tanks. He was more worried about the partisans fading into the Marshes and doing hit and run attacks on US forces.

"It will take a lot more than a brigade to control the Marshes." He didn't realize he said that aloud until one of the other soldiers responded. The soldier, a Sergeant Emmet, didn't look old enough to have earned his stripes, a tall-gangling kid.

"Did you fight in the Donets War?" Sergeant Duncan asked.

"No. I was in the Pacific." Emmett didn't say where. The Pacific could mean tough fighting against Japanese holdouts in the Philippines, Indochina, the Japanese home islands or Manchuria, or it could mean easy billets on the Pacific islands. Sergeant Duncan guessed Emmett for an easy billet guy. He didn't instinctively scan his surroundings the way combat veterans did. Still, anyone in a quick reaction force had to be willing to fight if nothing else.

They were near the front of the US column now, with only a few scouts ahead of them and the M24 tanks a couple miles behind. A brigade might be small change in military terms, but it was still thousands of men, with their trucks, jeeps and artillery. They took up a lot of road.

The locals were probably hiding their livestock and daughters, while saying the Ukrainian equivalent of "I'm getting too old for this shit."

The highway was taking a pounding just from the columns using it, even without any fighting. Would there be fighting? Probably not here. This was strong Ukrainian Nationalist country and partisans weren't welcome here, as the locals demonstrated a couple times when the partisans sent in covert bands after the Donets War. Once they got to the Marshes, that might be different. The southern fringe of the Marshes was supposed to be Ruthenian territory, but the partisans controlled much of it. Last fall Ruthenian paramilitary forces tried to take control of 'their' territory and got their butts kicked in a bitter little war the US ignored. The partisans ruled the Marshes, whatever lines on the map said.

Governor Federov had been a partisan and was a strong Stalin supporter, but he let US and German traders do their business if they kept to areas he designated for trade. His province was a long way from the demarcation line between western troops and the Soviets, so he had to trade to survive. At the same time, Federov's secret police were everywhere, especially in areas that technically belonged in surrounding provinces. Federov's people probably assumed that Sergeant Duncan, in his other guise, was a spy, but then they thought all Americans who ventured into the Marshes were spies.

The sun was halfway across the cloudless sky now. Fort Seminole's P51 fighters were making their presence known along the column and in front of it. Sergeant Duncan wished they had more scout planes above them, or maybe the Douglas Skyraiders. Skyraiders built a reputation as an outstanding ground attack plane during the Donets War.

Sergeant Duncan's eyes swept the countryside. Western Europeans and New Englanders were often taken aback by the sheer size and emptiness of the Soviet Union, though

Midwesterners took it in stride. This had been, before the wars, well settled country, with neat, prosperous farms and towns. Further east, the countryside got emptier, with the already sparse population thinned by war, Soviet purges, Nazi atrocities and the Soviets taking millions of people east with them when they fled.

This area was already empty enough for Sergeant Duncan. The Soviets even took horses, mules and cattle east with them ahead of the Germans, and the Germans tried to do the same thing when the Allies invaded from the west. The US brought thousands of cattle and horses into the area after the Donets War, but herd animals were still scarce.

"Really think we'll see any fighting?" Emmett asked.

Sergeant Duncan heard artillery fire in the distance. "Yep. we'll see fighting."

Chapter Eighteen: War

Captain Murphy had his now mostly repaired helicopter up again. The US column looked impressive heading along the highway. This was a fully motorized force, with nobody walking or riding horses. If it had the heavy artillery of a normal US brigade it would have been a formidable force for its size, assuming the men knew how to fight.

The army has gone soft. Generations of soldiers said that about their younger counterparts, but this time it was true. A lot of families heard horror stories about abusive army training during the war and went to their congressmen. Army brass made the training easier, but less effective.

Individual officers like Colonel Rock quietly risked their careers to retrain new draftees, but saw their efforts overwhelmed by new, poorly trained men transferring in. At least Fort Seminole had a core of tough, well-trained soldiers. Was that true of the rapid-reaction brigade? Occupation duty or even combat against poorly trained diehard Nazis would weaken a force, teach them bad habits.

He heard distant artillery. The head of the US column was just reaching the fringes of the Marsh, but the firing wasn't coming from them, nor was it directed at them. *What are they firing at?* Who was doing the firing, for that matter?

That wasn't the most important question, he realized. Dozens of tanks emerged from the Marshes, maybe as many as a hundred, flanked by improvised armored cars built on truck chassis. He radioed what he saw to Fort Seminole, wishing he had a direct link to the rapid reaction brigade. The brigade was already deploying for combat, though. The reaction looked sluggish, but at least it was happening.

Captain Murphy wanted to get a better look at the tanks, but when P51s swooped over, the tank columns threw up formidable streams of anti-aircraft fire. *Where did those tanks come from?* Actually, US intelligence knew the partisans had quite a few tanks squirreled away. But how did they train tank crews and stockpile spare parts without the US detecting them? *Stalin.* He must have smuggled in parts and crews or trained local partisans in Soviet-controlled territory. Either way, the tank crews seemed to know what they were doing, and the tanks were in good repair, racing toward a US column that was slowly deploying for combat.

He got a look at the improvised armored cars. They were based on Russian-made Ford trucks, lightly armored, with light anti-aircraft/ground support cannons in swivel mounts at the back. There had to be at least three partisan divisions down there, with more emerging from the Marshes and they seemed well-equipped, though he didn't see much heavy artillery.

The partisan column slammed into the US rapid reaction force, moving fast. Whatever triggered the artillery barrages further east was still going on. Ruthenian Dewoitine fighter planes swooped in, strafing. Captain Murphy swore. The Ruthenian paramilitary probably triggered the fighting, using the US column as cover to grab parts of the Marshes they claimed. *And if we confront them, they'll claim they were helping with the search, on their own territory.*

Partisan and US scouts were fighting, with the partisan tanks and armored cars moving fast, tearing up fields barely dry enough to cross after the spring muddy season. He desperately wanted to see more but ran low on fuel and raced back to Fort Seminole. He circled briefly, spotting Skyraiders on the runway, but none taking off yet.

Captain Murphy reported directly to Colonel Rock, with Envoy McCormick sitting in. When he finished, Colonel Rock nodded. "We'll get Fort Seminole ready for an attack."

That seems premature. Captain Murphy stared at the Colonel. "Is it that bad already?"

Colonel Rock shrugged. "It can be. The partisans have sleeper cells nearby. They'll target the base."

106

The thump of mortar shells landing emphasized the point. They all ducked under the nearest furniture, with Captain Murphy stuck under a flimsy chair. Most of the base artillery was with the column, but somebody fired back, maybe with tank guns from the Franken-Shermans. *Do they know what they're shooting at?* He hoped so.

Colonel Rock crawled out from behind his desk and took command. He yelled to Captain Murphy, "Get your bird back in the air. We need eyes up there."

The crew checking out and refueling the helicopter went to ground when the mortar shells hit. Captain Murphy didn't blame them, but he had to get back in the air, so he browbeat the reluctant crew into refueling. The process took far too long, and the checkouts revealed a nagging engine fault that mechanics had to check, keeping him grounded. The mortar barrage faded to individual mortar bombs landing at irregular intervals, missing Fort Seminole entirely over half the time but still jangling nerves, almost more terrifying in their randomness than if they had been focused and professional.

He noticed that the Skyraiders were still on the ground, apparently undamaged, but showing no sign of taking off. *Our guys need those planes out there.*

Captain Murphy waited impatiently until the helicopter was ready, seething at the delay. He wasn't the only pilot waiting to get back in the air. An air force pilot on the other side of the fence motioned him over. "It's bad out there. We swatted a hornet's nest." The guy claimed that the partisan tanks sliced through the US lines as though they weren't there, routing the Americans. "They probably won't stop running short of the Romanian border."

Was that true? Captain Murphy hoped not, but the US troops were outnumbered more than five to one and outgunned.

"The Ruthenians are grabbing their heavy weapons out of storage," the Air Force guy said. "The Soviets are mobilizing all along the demarcation line. And Czech peacekeepers are pulling back to defensible positions. This got ugly fast."

Captain Murphy didn't comment. Wild rumors always raced through the ranks in fast-moving situations, and he knew not to believe them. He thought about reprimanding the man but didn't. What he said might be accurate and even useful.

An order came down to get the base ready for imminent attack. That drew the mechanics away, putting them on the perimeter with rifles until Captain Murphy got the order countermanded. Once he got the helicopter refueled, mechanics still had to fix the engine problem, leaving the helicopter grounded and Captain Murphy fuming. At least the base's P51 fighters were making flights, and hopefully giving Colonel Rock some idea what was going on.

Captain Murphy felt like he was walking through molasses, with simple, everyday tasks suddenly becoming nightmarishly slow. Colonel Rock called him to his office finally, giving him a break from cursing the delays.

"Your mission has changed," Colonel Rock said. He outlined new reconnaissance targets on a map.

Captain Murphy studied the map, fighting to keep his dismay off his face. The air force guy may have exaggerated some, but if the battle was happening where he was supposed to look, it was going very badly.

"We need those Skyraiders in the battle," he said.

"And they'll be in the battle," Colonel Rock said. "As soon as their munitions and spare parts show up."

They sent us ground support planes without bombs? "We need to knock the rust out of our warfighting."

"Federov is doing that for us," Colonel Rock said. "Meandrov was right about the partisan buildup. The buildup doesn't surprise me, but the size does."

"We knew we were headed for problems," Captain Murphy said. "We can't get by on bluff and past glories forever."

Envoy McCormick came to the door in time to hear that. He said, "US forces here are an economy of force operation. That may be false economy, but we work with what Congress gives us."

"I'm sorry your daughter is caught in this," Captain Murphy said.

An expression flitted across the envoy's face too quickly for Captain Murphy to know exactly what it was. Pain? Guilt? The envoy regained control immediately. "In my job, the public and private man have to be separate. For now, Amber doesn't exist." He stared at the map. "Governor Federov is being foolish. If he succeeds, he will become a hero, then Stalin will purge him as a threat. If he fails, Stalin will sacrifice him as the pawn he is. He probably won't survive."

Captain Murphy wanted to say, "You see a whole different map than I do." He kept that thought to himself, though. He said, "I'm hearing a lot of rumors."

"Of course," Envoy McCormick said. "And some of them are true. The Soviets and the Poles have mobilized and pushed armored divisions to the borders. The Soviets are doing military exercises along the border from the Black Sea all the way north. Our rapid deployment brigade ran into far more trouble than it can handle." He waved at the map. "The US looks weak, but we have resources Federov can't even imagine. Stalin is another story, but we can decide if his Soviet Union recovers or falls deeper into famine without firing a bullet. He can't feed his people without the Ukraine. Cut off the trickle of Dutch East Indies rubber we let him smuggle and his recovery stops in its tracks. Soviet synthetic rubber is a sad joke and they've used up their natural rubber. You can't run a modern war machine without tons and tons of rubber. Stalin knows some of the cards we hold and suspects others. He wonders if we have the will to use our power. He'll find President Truman is not a man to be trifled with."

Captain Murphy finally flew back to the battle. The US might look invincible from Envoy McCormick's perch, but the partisans were kicking the fast reaction brigade's collective butt. It wasn't as bad as the air force guy said, but a wedge of partisan tanks pushed down the highway almost as fast as the tanks could move, while more tanks pushed through the fields to outflank the Americans and lightly armored trucks jolted across the fields ahead of the tanks, their automatic cannons blazing. The partisans were acting as though they had already won, bypassing US resistance to cut off retreating American forces.

Were the US troops panicking? Not really. They were retreating fast, but it was a fighting retreat. Several pockets risked getting cut off though, far behind the partisan spearheads and he saw little chance US forces could stop the partisans before they reached Fort Seminole.

The locals scrambled to get out of the way of the onrushing war, moving with practiced speed. Captain Murphy felt a wave of sympathy for peasants and merchants caught in the middle. How many times did armies rampage through here in the last decade? Far too many. He also thought about Amber McCormick. All the old money confidence in the world wouldn't save her from a bomb or artillery shell or her kidnappers killing her to keep her from slowing them down.

The helicopter came under partisan fire twice, with the flak way too accurate. He wanted to scout deeper but fixed wing planes could fly behind the partisan spearheads with less risk.

Ruthenian paramilitary forces streamed back from the marshes too. Their retreat threatened to become a rout, though they had reinforcements moving up, including tanks and artillery 'liberated' from UN heavy weapons warehouses or hidden from inspectors until now. Captain Murphy spotted six ex-German Panthers among the tanks and a couple possible King Tigers, along with tank destroyers. *How did they hide King Tigers?* For that matter, how did the Ruthenians keep the ex-German tanks running?

He flew back to Fort Seminole, his mood somber. Despite Envoy McCormick's confidence, the situation was bad. *And if he is still at Fort Seminole he may get a close-up view of how bad it really is.*

Chapter Nineteen: Dietrich Lang Makes a Choice

Dietrich Lang stood at a large window in a second-story warehouse office of his salvage company. He saw the entire warehouse floor from his office, a godlike view. He watched Amber McCormick below him, tied to a chair, blindfolded, but still conveying unshakeable self-confidence. Lang felt an overwhelming urge to break that self-confidence. He wobbled back and forth on the decisions he had to make.

"I can start World War III." Tensions in the borderlands were so high that he could use Amber to cause fighting to spiral out of control. A mangled corpse with her clothing and purse at the right place could jar Envoy McCormick into actions that would force Stalin and the Poles into the fighting. *And the corpse wouldn't have to be hers.* He could make sure there wasn't enough left of the corpse to identify. *Then I can play with her all I want, with no one even looking for her.*

When he was younger, he would have made that choice in a heartbeat, confident that he could use the resulting chaos to make his business interests and his underground army stronger. Now, he hesitated, wondering if memories of his wounds from a nearly fatal day seven years ago had made him a coward. *It's too soon.* He had already made that decision before he talked to Amber and logic told him to stick to it, to act quickly. With the partisans and Americans tearing at each other, he would soon lose his ability to influence the situation.

Finally, he turned to Fredberg. "Tell her that you are taking her to New Memphis and that you'll let her go there. Don't let her see anything on the way and make sure you make enough turns that she won't be able to retrace her route."

Fredberg looked as though he was about to protest but nodded and turned to go down the stairs.

"I'm not finished," Lang said. "Take her to the edge of partisan territory, find a secluded spot and shoot her. Make sure she's dead, then get to a phone they can't trace back to us and report finding the body."

Fredberg nodded. "It's a shame. She's quite a package." He turned and walked down the steps.

Lang stared after him. *I wonder if you know how close you are to dying.* The former SS captain probably did know, Lang thought suddenly. Lang wouldn't let Fredberg live after he killed Amber McCormick. Too much chance of betrayal if Fredberg got caught for something else. The man who ordered Amber McCormick's death would be a big bargaining chip for an underling heading for the hangman's noose.

I'm getting paranoid. But something in Fredberg's expression when he turned away worried Lang. Killing the men at the workshop might have been necessary, but it had to raise questions among Lang's men. They were all guilty, someone of letting Hannah go, the rest of negligence for letting whoever it was get her out of the building. Fredberg wasn't at the workshop when it happened. *But he will be a loose end if he kills Amber, and he knows it.* Hannah didn't worry Lang at the moment. Another kidnapping would raise questions, but planes crash, even when piloted by famous test pilots. *I'll have to stay away from Governor Meandrov until I can arrange a crash.*

Lang watched Fredberg walking to the door with Amber. His instincts screamed at him to stop the man. Amber was smooth, persuasive. She had almost convinced Lang himself to let her go. What if she had already gotten her hooks in Fredberg's mind? Had she been alone with the man at all? Lang wasn't sure. *I have to do it myself. That's the only way to be sure.*

He tried to talk himself out of it, but the logic seemed inescapable. Anyone who killed Amber McCormick would be a loose end, and he knew from his brief contacts with her that the girl had an instinct for finding and exploiting men's fears and weaknesses. Part of his mind chastised him. *I've become a coward and I'm letting a once-in-a-lifetime opportunity slip through my fingers.* He ran down to Fredberg, smiled and said, "I changed my mind. I'll take her myself."

Fredberg tried to control it, but his face showed an overwhelming relief. He nodded. "She's all yours."

I was right. She got to him somehow, or maybe he just thought it through the same way I did. Lang resolved to be careful around the ex-SS captain. He chose two bodyguards and ushered Amber into a jeep.

He knew the woman really was Amber McCormick now, through a picture in one of the magazines. He thought again about using her in a more decisive way, of putting all his influence into pushing the factions of Europe into World War III now and keeping the girl while the powers ground each other to pieces. *I'm thinking like an old man, avoiding risks.* He couldn't win, couldn't become the power behind the politicians of a new Germany, if he didn't take risks. He resolved to kick his preparation into high gear. There would be other opportunities to set Europe ablaze.

As for Amber, no matter how persuasive the young lady could be, he would shoot her once to the back of the head and leave her in the ditch. A pity. He would have liked to see that self-confidence and poise gradually disappear once she realized she was totally in his power, with no one coming to rescue her. Once he controlled the secret services of a renewed Germany, he could acquire a young lady like her at his convenience and add her to his collection of playthings. *Maybe she has a sister.*

Chapter Twenty: Ground Truth

Sergeant Duncan manned a heavy machine gun, trying to separate a T34/85 tank from its accompanying infantry. If he pinned the partisan infantry down, some poor saps could work their way around to the side of the tank with a bazooka and maybe knock it out. He sensed panic in the men around him and tried to keep it from infecting him. His missing finger throbbed, giving him an urgent warning that he didn't need now. *I know I'm in a world of shit.*

His jeep was further back, hopefully out of range of the partisan tank's cannon. They weren't going to stop the partisan tanks this way but forcing the accompanying infantry to deploy slowed the partisan advance. *We're mosquitos pestering an elephant.* This elephant had an 85-millimeter gun and could slap the human mosquitoes pestering it from beyond the range of either Sergeant Duncan's heavy machine gun or bazookas.

At least his heavy machine gun forced the tank crew to button up, reducing their vision. The partisan tank crews seemed appallingly well-trained, using their tanks like veterans. Fortunately, the partisans on the armored trucks weren't well-trained, spraying light cannon shells across the battlefield enthusiastically, but not accurately. He recently knocked two partisan trucks out with his heavy machine gun, though their light cannons outranged him., and someone nearby knocked one out with a bazooka.

Using bazookas against trucks was overkill, he thought, a waste of scarce ammunition. Speaking of ammunition, he was running low, and so were the bazooka teams. Their supply lines seemed to have collapsed.

At least he was with men from Fort Seminole, men who knew what they were doing, though nobody did well fighting tanks without heavy artillery or anti-tank guns. The rapid reaction force wasn't much help on the antitank front and lacked the experience and training of the Fort Seminole men. It didn't have much antitank capacity beyond bazookas, though lightweight towed 105-millimeter howitzers could at least harass the partisan tanks.

After a few disastrous encounters, US M24 light tank crews tried to avoid taking on the partisan T34/85s directly, using their speed to maneuver for side shots, or snipe at the heavier tanks from long range, trying to take out their tracks.

We need Shermans. Sergeant Duncan would have settled for tank destroyers. *Hellcats would work.*

The bazooka team fired at the oncoming T34/85 three times, hastily shifting their position each time as the backblast marked their position for the tank. Two of the rockets hit the tank, but by some malign trick of fate nowhere vital, though hopefully they forced the crew to change their underwear.

The breeze shifted, giving him a brief whiff of something fishy smelling. Sergeant Duncan had a brief, absurd thought that the smell was from the tank, then it was gone. His team scrambled back, pushing through brambles and saplings growing tall in an abandoned field, the thorns grabbing at them and making the retreat a nightmare of tearing away clinging weeds. They used what little cover there was on the too-flat ground. Partisan cannon-fire thumped around them, overwhelmingly powerful and random.

Partisan armored trucks sprayed the field with their light autocannons, cutting through the weeds like chainsaws through tall grass, the shells buzzing like giant angry hornets.

Planes shrieked by, low overhead, strafing. *Skyraiders.* One fired rockets, one of which scored a direct hit on the nearby T34/85, then bounced off without exploding. A bomb slammed down no more than ten yards away. The others dove for cover, but Sergeant Duncan just squatted. *This is when you kiss your ass goodbye.* The bomb partially buried itself among the thistles. *A dud?* Apparently.

He took a deep breath. "Rest of our lives are because somebody was hungover when they built that oversized firecracker." If anyone heard that, they didn't react. They kept moving back. The tank crew blazed away wildly with their machine gun, probably trying to flush them.

Sergeant Duncan kept tearing through thorns, bent double to keep his head from showing. He was in good shape, but the pace left him gasping for air, his knees and back aching. Then, without warning, he was clear of the thistles, running in the open through heavy mud in a low, weedless spot about thirty yards wide and several hundred yards long, still muddy from the spring rains. The tall weeds hid it until Sergeant Duncan and his crew were slogging through it.

That ends our bonus round. They couldn't get across the mud before the pursuing tank crew spotted them and there was no cover until they reached the other side. *This calls for running like hell.* He did, tempted to ditch his equipment, but knowing that would leave them defenseless. A couple guys dropped their packs and rifles, sprinting ahead of the others. One slipped in the mud, doing a spectacular faceplant and sliding halfway across the open spot with his chin plowing mud. No one stopped to help him. He staggered to his feet, far behind the others and wiped mud out of his eyes. Sergeant Duncan turned, ready to run back despite the guy's cowardice, but a tank shell hit way too close, spraying mud over the Americans. The tank advanced through the thistles, seemingly unstoppable.

A cannon roared nearby, from the side of the clearing they were running to. The tank abruptly spouted flames, then lost its turret in a muffled explosion.

Sergeant Duncan slogged the rest of the way across the mudhole, wondering where the antitank gun that saved them came from. A squat, turretless armored vehicle eased backward, surrounded by Ruthenian paramilitary men. *A Hetzer.* The ex-German assault gun had its German markings blotted out and a prominent US star painted on its top with Ruthenian markings on the side. He spotted seven more Hetzers nearby. *Not enough to stop the partisans, but something at least.*

A paramilitary captain stopped briefly. "We saved your asses. You can keep quiet about how."

"I didn't see a thing," Sergeant Duncan said. "Mud in my eyes."

He heard tanks rumbling and clanking behind them and muttered, "Oh crap." The tank sounds were different from either the US M24s or the partisan tanks. He glanced at the paramilitary captain. "Yours?"

The captain indicated his Hetzers. "That's most of what we can spare. Federov is attacking the oil fields."

Sergeant Duncan risked a glance over the brambles. "Franken-Shermans, the ones from Fort Seminole. How did they keep them running this far?"

Eight of the pieced-together tanks joined the fight. They fired rarely, probably short of ammunition, but forced the partisan tanks to slow, giving Sergeant Duncan and his men much needed breathing space.

A deep roaring came from the west, planes and a lot of them. The planes flashed overhead. Sergeant Duncan recognized the shape. B-29 bombers. "Where did they come from?"

The big US bombers unloaded, their bombs falling far too close to Sergeant Duncan and even behind him. The rapid reaction brigade was back there, showing that it could rapidly retreat. *Unless we're lucky, they hit guys back there.* Bombs also hit among the partisan columns and pounded a lot of thistles and empty fields into muddy chaos. It was an impressive, ground-shaking display of firepower, if nothing else, leaving the Ruthenian paramilitary guys staring, their mouths hanging open and their ears undoubtedly ringing.

Sergeant Duncan had seen B-29 raids before, during the Donets War, but this one still left him wobbly and confused. He stumbled back to the jeep, unmolested by surviving partisan tanks, and joined a quick, but reasonably orderly retreat toward Fort Seminole. He saw no sign of pursuit. The highway was taking a beating under the tanks and heavy trucks. They only had to detour around one bomb crater in the highway, but craters and knocked out trucks and jeeps in nearby fields showed where bombs landed among friendly forces. Further back, Sergeant Duncan spotted seven more Franken-Shermans along the highway, with their crews trying to get them going again.

"They got over half of them to the battle," a soldier said. "I'm impressed."

"I just used up my seventh and eighth lives," Sergeant Duncan said. He noticed that his missing finger no longer throbbed.

Chapter Twenty-One: Amber McCormick & The Dewoitine

Dietrich Lang wasn't squeamish, unlike many other top Nazis, who couldn't handle watching real-life deaths from their decisions. He didn't particularly enjoy killing. It ended any power he had over the victim. Maybe they even went to a better place in the afterlife. Lang very much doubted that, but his Catholic upbringing meant that the idea of an afterlife lingered. *If there is a hell, I've long since condemned myself to it.* He grinned. The devil himself might be impressed by Lang's work.

He wasn't squeamish about killing women either. He didn't do it often, but he wouldn't hesitate to pull the trigger when the time came.

He *was* concerned that he was driving in a war zone, not in the path of the warring forces, but movement became more dangerous with the forces gearing up for war. Partisan secret police would be out in force, mopping up spies and shooting deserters. The US and its allies would have planes up, trying to determine the size and shape of the partisan offensive. There was a very real risk of getting caught up in their actions.

He kept up a pleasant conversation with Amber McCormick, who sat in the passenger seat beside him. The hood was off now, wind from an open window playing through her hair and making her look years younger. Many men would have felt a surge of protectiveness seeing her like that. Lang wondered if the affect was calculated. *It won't work on me.* She chatted back casually, as though it was normal to ride with her hands tied behind her back. Lang wondered if he should tie her feet too. She might sense that something was wrong and try to run. *But tying her legs means we have to carry her.*

"Amber McCormick is worth a finder's fee of a hundred thousand dollars," he said. "We'll go our separate ways, and you'll never see me again, unless there is an afterlife, and you end up in hell. I'll be there, though at a much deeper level than you could aspire to."

The finder's fee was a lie. Trying to ransom her was too risky. Hopefully, the story would lull her. It didn't matter much, but Lang instinctively reached for the little edge.

"An afterlife? I bet you were raised Catholic," Amber said. "Then the Nazis hijacked your need to believe. But when you rose high enough in their ranks, you stopped believing in them too."

"Still trying to figure me out?" He grinned. "Still trying to manipulate me. You don't need to."

"You started a war when you grabbed me," Amber said. "Was that what you wanted?"

"I would have been far happier if we never saw each other," Lang said. "I'm taking a huge risk in letting you go."

"Not as big as not letting me go. You can't imagine the hell my dad could bring down on you, no idea how smart and ruthless he is. Sometimes I worry that he'll lose track of who he is and become like you."

"Like me?" He glanced at his watch. Almost there. "What do you think I've become?"

"Empty except for ambition. No room for what makes life worth the effort."

"Actually, I quite enjoy my life," Lang said. He glanced back at his bodyguards in the back seat. They didn't know what he had planned for Amber McCormick and wouldn't see what happened to her or have any direct knowledge of it.

Lang had a specific place in mind as Amber McCormick's final resting place. They would reach the spot soon. The road was empty except for them. The locals knew to disappear when trouble loomed.

Motion in the sky drew his gaze. He tracked a plane idly, mostly looking for the spot he had chosen. The plane got closer, and he identified it as an early World War II French-built Dewoitine, probably from the Ruthenium provincial air force. What was it doing way out here? They were far from any fighting. Maybe the pilot was lost. Provincial air forces didn't get much flying time.

The plane dived sharply, way too low and heading toward them. Lang swore when he saw a line of dirt puffing up along the shoulder. Strafing? What the hell did the pilot think he was doing? The impacts stitched toward the jeep, most of them hitting the road, but a few hitting the shoulder. Lang felt a burst of adrenaline and realized he was laughing with the sheer thrill of danger. He tensed behind the wheel, waiting while the plane's strafing stitched toward him. At the last moment, he twitched the wheel, sending the jeep onto the downward slope of the road ditch. The steering wheel wrenched at his hands, with the jeep on the verge of overturning or spinning out. He held it, kept it going straight, then eased back onto the road when the plane roared past. It barely cleared the treetops at the end of its run, then clawed its way up and out of sight.

Lang let out a deep breath. "There is nothing like getting shot at and barely missed."

He saw his spot ahead of them and drove his jeep into a clump of trees that shielded it from the road. He felt exhilarated. "I need to get out more. I have no idea what the pilot thought he was shooting at, but he's going to crash that plane."

He got out, still feeling the rush, a huge grin on his face.

"I'm going to take you far enough from the road that nobody will find you unless they know where to look," he said. "I'll tie you to a tree, then go call the Americans. I know the place. It has a great view. The Americans will find you and this unpleasant episode will be over." He paused. Amber didn't respond. "You will then get out of Europe and stay out. If we meet again, you will die."

She nodded. "I never liked Europe. Too soaked in blood."

"Unlike America where your Indians simply died instead of getting in your way."

"We had our wars, and they were bloody enough," Amber acknowledged. "But I have no love for Europe."

"Good."

He helped her out of the jeep. Her posture still looked calm, in control. *I should make her beg before I shoot her.* Lang shook his head. If she went to her death still in control, she would win at some level and ruin this perfect day. *I'll just shoot her.*

That wouldn't be as satisfying but would deny her a chance at winning a last inconsequential victory. "You'll need to walk now."

She grimaced. "My leg is asleep. Could your men steady me?"

"Sure." He nodded to a bodyguard. Amber took one step, stumbled, and then her hands were loose. A knife flashed in her hand and a bodyguard grabbed his inner thigh. The knife flashed again, and the other bodyguard had a long red gash from the top of his stomach to his belt. Lang grabbed for his Walther P38. Amber had one of the guard's sidearms now, pointed at Lang. He paused, his hand on his sidearm.

It all happened so fast that Lang still felt the euphoria from dodging the strafing run. He tried to make himself take the escape attempt seriously but found that difficult, despite his wounded men. The stolen Walther P38 looked far too large for the woman.

"Why did you stab my people?" Lang asked. "I told you we were going to let you go."

"And I didn't believe you," she said. " I didn't just stab your men. I killed them. Well, actually just one so far, but the other will die wishing he died right away." She jerked her head toward the guy with the leg wound. "Major artery sliced open. Only seconds before there isn't enough blood left. You wanted ruthless. You got ruthless. And no, you weren't going to let me go."

The guy with the leg wound collapsed, bright red blood pooling around him and suddenly Lang's euphoria went away, replaced by a hard focus. "I still don't intend to let you go. This will end with you dead."

"Actually, at best it will end with you putting your P38 on the ground, along with your keys, then walking away."

"And I suppose you expect to drive away in my jeep."

"Why not?"

Because my fingerprints are there. That might not be a total disaster. e had destroyed the few sets of prints from his previous identity and from the real Dietrich Lang. Still, having his prints tied to this scene would be a loose end.

Lang pushed down a roller-coaster mix of emotions and thought coldly. Amber McCormick had to die here. How could he make that happen? The bodyguard with the stomach wound still stood, hands clasping his stomach, moaning. He was tough, though. He eased back, further from Lang. Lang took a step the other direction, eyes fixed on Amber.

Lang still had his hand on his sidearm. If she glanced toward the wounded man he had her. He wouldn't hesitate when he got his sidearm out. Even if she fired, she would probably miss. He wouldn't.

The wounded bodyguard made a lumbering charge. Amber turned and shot him in the head, then had the Walther P38 aimed at Lang again before he could move, before the bodyguard fell, unmoving.

"I don't like guns but I'm good with them," Amber said. "Dad made his bodyguards teach me."

Lang felt a sudden wave of despair. The shot was bad enough, but her stance and quiet confidence was worse. He had been a fencer once, and he knew the feelings that come before defeat, though he had rarely felt them. He was going to lose here. He could feel it.

The euphoria of minutes ago turned into a growing hopelessness, depression, desperation. This pampered shallow little girl was going to ruin everything, end his dreams of power, end his life. He gathered himself to make his move, keeping his face expressionless.

"They say to aim for the center of mass," Amber said. "A good enough marksperson can be more selective. I would go a little lower. The first shot might not kill you, but it would make you wish you were dead. In the scrotum, just like Herman Goering in the Beerhall Putsch. He survived, of course, but the wound got infected. That would be painful, wouldn't it? I would have to shoot you in the head afterward to spare you the pain."

She seemed calm, matter of fact.

"Where did you get the knife?" Lang asked. He looked desperately for some way to turn this disaster around. The bodyguard with the slashed thigh lay still, a pool of bright red blood spreading beneath him. The other man also lay still, sightless eyes staring at his stomach as if fascinated by the wound.

"One of your men gave me the knife," Amber said. "He told me to remember what he did if I got away." She smiled. "I'll let you figure out who did it."

Lang didn't doubt her. The girl was too good at finding reasons for men to do what she wanted. "I should have cut your tongue out." He smiled, hoping the expression looked natural, confident. "The best you can hope for is killing me while I kill you. I've lived a long life, done things that will make the history books. You've barely started living."

His hand was still on his sidearm. Part of him wanted to get this over, to make his play, win or lose. *She's just a girl. She can't beat me.* Another part. remembered the blurs of motion when Amber stabbed the bodyguards and took the sidearm, then killed the wounded bodyguard. That part told him to wait for an opportunity. One would come. Lang got where he was by being the first to see opportunities, then ruthlessly exploiting them. Opportunities always came.

A faint sound in the sky made him want to pull his eyes away from Amber, but he resisted. "Are we going to stare at each other all day or is one of us going to do something?" he asked. "Most times when a man and a woman stare at each other this long, they're about to have sex."

"That's not in the cards. I'm giving you a chance to get out of this alive," Amber said. "You'll either try to draw your gun and die or take it out gently and set it on the ground. You decide. I'll wait."

The sound in the sky got louder. *A plane.* He laughed. "That idiot Ruthenian pilot is coming back." He wasn't sure it was true, but the sound was right. He had a sudden surge of hope. The plane was his opportunity. He just had to take advantage of it.

Chapter Twenty-Two: Dietrich Lang Tells a Lie & Sends a Sniper

It really was the same plane. Either that or the Ruthenian Provincial Air Force had two idiot pilots flying over a nearly deserted patch of road and randomly strafing. The plane wasn't strafing yet. Lang saw it over the treetops, flying barely over them, not missing the treetops by much. Was the pilot looking for the jeep he had so narrowly missed minutes ago? That made little sense, but then neither did the plane's first attack.

"In wars, sometimes things just don't make sense," he said. "The plane is back. It's behind you."

"I hear it," Amber said. She remained poised, focused on him.

Why don't you blink or scratch an itch or glance away? Lang felt anger and impatience rise in him and forced both emotions away. This was a time for patience. He moved his hand a little, watching her hand. Her finger tightened on the trigger a fraction of an inch. She held the Walther P38 in a two-handed grip, the grip looking practiced and professional. *I'm a fraction of an inch from dying.* He studied her arms, looking for any hint of a tremor. Holding a Walther P38 on a target this long couldn't be easy, he thought, but he saw no sign of impatience or fatigue.

The plane kept getting closer. Maybe the pilot would shoot her. Instead, it veered toward the jeep. "He spotted us."

Lang stayed focused on Amber. *She'll look.* The plane was behind her. It would fire and the urge to look would be overwhelming. He mentally rehearsed what to do when she did. Just draw and fire at the center of mass, Keep shooting until she was clearly dead. Then put another round in the back of her skull to make sure. Then this nightmare would be over.

The plane made a strafing run toward the jeep. Lang watched her eyes, but they didn't flit away. He saw the jeep burning in his peripheral vision. It was going to explode. *That will be my chance.* Something exploded, but not the jeep. Something behind him. He turned, with his inner voice screaming at him not to. The Dewoitine fighter was lodged in a tree, wrecked and burning. He turned back, saw the barrel of a sidearm flash toward him, then lost consciousness.

#

Amber McCormick showed up at Fort Seminole's main gate late in the evening. Captain Murphy spotted her when MPs escorted her to Colonel Rock's office. She smiled at him, seemingly as composed as ever. He nodded but didn't smile back. *She started a war by being stupid.* That wasn't true. She pushed up the timing, but a war was brewing here, Amber or no Amber.

Can we stop it before it gets a lot more guys killed? He was working with drill sergeants, getting ex-servicemen who lived in New Memphis back into the army routine. They had been volunteered into a scratch unit. Some *were* volunteers, ready to defend their new homes here. Others were reluctant, drafted through some technicality that made them reservists, whether they knew it or not. Few seemed to remember much of their training and Captain Murphy wondered if it would come back quick enough to help.

He got called to Colonel Rock's office. Amber sat outside the office. "I'm sorry I got you in trouble."

"What happened?"

"I had an adventure or two with a Nazi bigwig. I knocked him out and left him tied to a tree, but he got away before the MPs got there. I should have shot him, but I thought our intelligence people would want a chat, maybe get him to give up their entire network."

He stared at her. "You're kidding, right?" She seemed too calm for any of that to have happened, but then she seemed far too calm for any kind of kidnapping.

"I'm still holding it together," she said. "I have to until the intelligence guys get every shred of what I remember written down. Then I can collapse into a quivering mass of hysterics or try to sleep and have a fine time in nightmare land."

"I'm intelligence. I should be in on what you tell them," Captain Murphy said.

"I think I got you in enough trouble that you won't be in on it," Amber said. "Have they talked to you?"

"We're too busy for them to tell me how much trouble I'm in," Captain Murphy said. "A lot, probably." He dismissed that thought. Nothing he could do about it now. "A Nazi bigwig? Hitler? Himmler? Goering? Borman? One of the missing scientists?"

"They're all dead."

"I know. At least they're supposed to be. Tell me what happened. Every detail."

She shook her head. "Sorry. I can't. I will tell them it wasn't your fault."

"I was in command, so you were my responsibility." He shrugged. "If they kick me out of the army, I'll go on with my life."

"You would never find out what happened to them, though."

"My wife and daughter?" He took a deep breath. "I already know. Not a hundred percent certain, but ninety-nine with a bunch of nines after the decimal point. I'll never fill in that last tiny bit of doubt. I should just go home and build a life."

He stopped himself, annoyed that he said so much. "My tongue is wagging too much. Ignore everything I said."

"I don't think you should ignore it." She smiled again. "I can't tell you much, but I can tell you that while I saw the man who kidnapped me, I have no idea who he is, other than that he spoke German. I assume he's a Nazi and a big name one, but what that name is I have no idea. He didn't hurt me, though they intended to kill me. They made sure I couldn't trace them back the way Hannah did, assuming she really did figure out where that building was from memory. I'm not sure she did." She stood and hugged him. He stood awkwardly until she released him and said, "Good luck in there."

He turned and went in, braced for anything from an evacuation order to a dressing down for Amber's kidnapping.

Envoy McCormick was there. He nodded to the captain. "I hear the partisans handled our rapid deployment force rather roughly."

Captain Murphy nodded. "What I saw wasn't good, though it could have been worse. Occupation duty takes the edge off armies, even the parts that run around fighting fires. The partisans have been building up, and those tank crews know what they're doing."

"Stalin took boneyard tanks, smuggled in spare parts to make them work and slipped in crews to use them. Voila. Instant tank divisions," Envoy McCormick said. "We should have seen it coming. The Soviet role is all deniable. The tank crews will be ex-Red Army volunteers and Germans captured the tanks long ago." He sighed. "Stalin risks very little and makes us look weak. He isn't ready to take us on directly, but he wonders how much iron is in President Truman's spine. He hears Congress debating cuts and hears how war-weary Americans are and wonders if we'll fight for territory we never really wanted."

That pretty much summed it up. *Your daughter thinks you're a magic man. Show me your magic.* Aloud, Captain Murphy said, "We need armored divisions. Push Federov back into the Marshes." He paused. "But that just kicks the can down the road. We should take the Marshes and root the partisans out."

"That is one way to do it," Envoy McCormick said. "We couldn't get US armored divisions here before the partisans took Fort Seminole, but we could bribe the Czechs or Poles or Hungarians to help us until we got forces here. They would help, but we would pay a price." He smiled wryly. "Everybody wants something for their help, even after we spent blood and treasure rescuing them from two mad dictators. Sometimes I think the isolationists were right. Let Europe drown in its hatreds. Then I look at the consequences." He adjusted his tie and stood, like a teacher in front of a black board. "In the borderlands, nobody can afford gratitude or loyalty. That's where Federov has it wrong. He is loyal to Stalin, but Stalin sees Federov as a tool to be used. How do you think Stalin is using Federov?"

"You already explained how," Captain Murphy said.

"Not the key part. Stalin wants us to do exactly what you suggested, fight Federov and his partisans in the Marshes, in perfect guerrilla country, taking casualties and spending dollars until America gets sick of it. We won't do that." He sighed. "The next seventy-two hours will be tough, dangerous. I wish you didn't have to go through it. I wish my daughter wasn't here, but I can't fly her out now. She wouldn't go and the press would make it the lead story if she did. Good luck, gentlemen, and I sincerely regret what we'll have to endure."

He nodded and walked out. Captain Murphy turned to Colonel Rock, but the Colonel shook his head. "I have no idea what he's up to, but we have nothing to stop Federov this side of Lvov, and that includes us at Fort Seminole. Normally I would evacuate the base, but my orders say hold Fort Seminole at all costs."

With what? Aloud, Captain Murphy asked, "Does the envoy know we can't hold the fort against three tank divisions."

"Make that four tank divisions, and I was quite clear on that. The bad news, as if we need more, is that he isn't bringing in the Poles or asking the Czechs or Hungarians to send heavy forces. They have claims on some god-forsaken sliver of land we haven't decided to give them and if we call them in, they'll grab it. So, beyond the peacekeepers, we're on our own until more US troops get here. The good news, such as it is, is that Envoy McCormick plans to stay here. He'll have a personal stake in getting us reinforcements fast."

"And you have no idea what he is up to?"

"Not the faintest idea," Colonel Rock said. "But whatever it is, Fort Seminole is at the center of it."

#

"I let her go," Dietrich Lang lied. "She was trouble, and she knows nothing useful. A pretty face, but spoiled and empty-headed." He touched his forehead. "On the way back, a crazy Ruthenian pilot strafed the jeep and killed the others, then crashed his plane into a tree." That was mostly true but was probably the part of his story his men found hardest to believe. *It doesn't matter what they believe.* Actually, it did matter. He led these desperate men because he had a reputation for winning. Take away that aura and his power would subtly but dangerously diminish.

Lucky. He didn't feel lucky right now. Actually, he felt quite the opposite of lucky. *That girl took my power away, had me helpless, outsmarted me and left me tied to a tree.* She also might have left him with a concussion. His head ached and he felt sudden bouts of dizziness when he moved quickly. He hid all that, determined to show no weakness. At least he got out of the ropes and talked a Ukrainian trader into dropping him off within walking distance of one of his warehouses connected to his quite-legal salvage company.

The girl also left him with a time-bomb of a question: Who gave her the knife? Maybe nobody did. Maybe she concealed it somewhere in her clothes. *We should have strip-searched her.* That they hadn't showed how badly they had underestimated the girl.

Lang felt one small bit of vindication after his defeat. Before he left the scene, he traced Amber's tracks. After she tied him up, she had, if he read the footprints right, stumbled away, leaned against a tree and cried. *She held it together just long enough, then collapsed.* Was that really what the footprints showed? He pushed any doubts away.

Coming back alone and weaponless raised questions, though not ones his men dared ask. That was a problem for later, though. Now, he had to keep his businesses from getting crushed by the onrushing war. He also had to kill Amber McCormick. Would killing her be enough? He could have it done unless she left the

131

borderlands. He could even have it done in ways that put the blame on whichever faction he wanted to receive the brunt of the American wrath. He had men, snipers even, infiltrated deep among the partisans, men in a position to, if necessary, kill Governor Federov. He could get a Polish militia group faction to do it, or a Ukrainian Nationalist splinter group. Both factions hated the Americans for not ruling in their favor in the boundary disputes.

Amber McCormick was a dead woman when he gave the word. She knew too much, not just his face but insights into his character. At the same time, he felt as though a bullet from the distance would be an empty victory. *I need to get her in my power again and break her.*

A part of his mind knew that was stupid and dangerous. The woman needed to die in a ditch, with his hands far away. That was the mature way to handle it, the way the leader of a movement to restore a great nation should handle it. At the same time, he felt the need to personally avenge his defeat, to wash away the humiliation of her escape, of getting pistol-whipped by a spoiled brat of a girl and waking up tied to a tree. He shrugged. He would have to deal with that humiliation some other way.

"In the long run, I lost nothing." He said that aloud and glanced to see if anyone heard him. Apparently not. The more he thought about it, the more he realized that was true. Amber was the only other witness to what had happened. Even if she told someone about her victory before she died, no one other than maybe her father would believe her. She didn't know his name or where he took her. Amber McCormick was going to die in the coming fighting, just the most prominent corpse in a welter of them. That was for him, to wipe out the defeat in his own mind, not because she could hurt him any further if she survived.

Lang laughed. *A minute ago, I had to kill her. Now it's just a whim.* Which was true? He decided it didn't matter, set her death in motion, then leaned back in his chair, not satisfied, but with the matter no longer in his hands.

Chapter Twenty-Three: The Battle of Fort Seminole

Amber McCormick sat outside Colonel Rock's office when Captain Murphy walked out. She looked as though she had been crying but stood up and smiled at him. "You must wonder what dad is thinking."

"Actually, I wonder if you're okay. Nobody can walk away from what you went through without it doing something to the way you think." He checked to make sure the door to Colonel Rock's office was closed. "I also wonder what your dad is planning, but if you knew, you couldn't tell me."

"Am I okay? No," Amber said. "I came within seconds of ending up dead in a ditch." Her eyes looked haunted for a second. "I don't know what Dad is doing, but he knows his decisions get young men killed. He has to make big decisions, but he also wants to always know that young men die, people, not statistics."

"A noble sentiment," Captain Murphy said. "But it will mess up his head. The nature of war is that people die, and wartime leadership means sending people to die. During the Donets War, I sent people on missions I knew most wouldn't come back from. You come out of a war walking a line between seeing those men as expendable and letting each one haunt you. Or you pour yourself down a bottle."

"Your decisions are about battalions or brigades," Amber said. "Dad's decisions are about countries and armies. If he draws a line on a map, this is part of The Ukraine, and it may stay that way for two hundred years. If he draws a different line, there may never be a country called The Ukraine. After Napoleon, the victors put together a settlement that mostly stopped major wars in Europe for fifty or arguably a hundred years. After World War I, the settlement barely lasted twenty years. If Dad isn't careful, the peace after World War II won't last five years. The stakes are high enough that Fort Seminole or New Memphis don't seem to matter much. Most people in his position would never come here. They would be dots on a map. He came here. Remember that, whatever happens."

"That sounds ominous," Captain Murphy said.

"Stalin built a sledgehammer in the Pripet Marshes and aimed it at Ukrainian nationalists," Amber said. "We're in the way."

That summed it up, Captain Murphy realized. "If the Ruthenians protect their oil fields, they'll lose Lvov. The Poles will jump in because if they don't they'll have to fight entrenched pro-Stalin forces. So, the Ruthenian paramilitary will shift forces to cover Lvov and the partisans will wipe out the progress we've made on getting the oilfields working, or Polish militias will take the fields."

She nodded. "I'm not just a pretty face. I can read a map."

"And the map says Federov needs to take Fort Seminole if he plans to threaten Lvov because we control the highway." Captain Murphy nodded. "We need more troops here fast."

When he said that, he realized reinforcements couldn't get to the fort soon enough. The US had armored divisions in Europe and quite a few mechanized ones, but the nearest substantial forces were either at the demarcation line or in the US occupation zone in western Germany, at least five days away. *The rapid reaction force is what we had in ground forces that could get here fast.*

"The partisans may just leave a screen and bypass us," Captain Murphy said. That would be smart, though the base dominated a long stretch of highway and planes based there could make life difficult for the partisans. *If we get enough spare parts and working bombs.*

Outside, the base bustled with activity. Cargo planes landed, unloaded and took off with precision, though what happened after they unloaded was a confused mess. Men rebuilt defenses they had allowed to decay and added new lines of trenches and barbed wire outside the wire fences that enclosed the base, leaving too few people to move unloaded cargo where it needed to go.

Women and children from New Memphis filled sandbags, while men shifted between digging defensive lines and sorting unloaded cargo. The transports brought in light artillery--anti-tank guns and 105-millimeter howitzers, though Captain Murphy wondered if the base had enough trained men to use them. Some of the planes brought in soldiers, though nowhere near enough. They also brought in rations, enough for a siege. Did the quick reaction brigade plan to make a stand here? That made a little more sense than having the garrison fight it out alone, but it would immobilize the only major US force around. *We can't stop the partisans from surrounding us.* A fighting retreat made more sense, slowing the partisans and giving the US time to bring in more troops. *Why aren't we doing that?*

The merchants and bar owners in New Memphis didn't share the army's reluctance to leave, though they boarded up their windows, apparently hoping to return. Restaurants sold food at cut rate prices, so they didn't have to move it. Bar owners tried the same thing with booze, but the army shut them down.

P51 fighters took off, made their runs and returned, pilot faces increasingly grim. Colonel Rock spotted warehouse manager in Captain Murphy's background and assigned him to untangle the chaos of getting spare parts and equipment where they needed to be. The clear summer day blurred into evening while he pushed his exhausted body and those of his men. How close were the partisans? He thought he heard artillery rumble in the distance when the wind was right, but that could be US forces fighting infiltrators or partisan advance scouts. The last time he was up in his helicopter, the partisans were very aggressive with their light armor, using the trucks' speed and light automatic cannons to harass US forces. Those tactics would get them shot to pieces against a normal US brigade, but against light US forces they could get away with it.

Two or three US infantry divisions could probably stop this offensive, but the US didn't have those divisions anywhere close.

The Czech and French peacekeepers were more police forces than armies, with only a few battalions each having much combat power. *We're on our own.*

The Skyraiders were taking off more often now, but their tempo was still far too low. Darkness was coming, which would limit them even if they got their logistics unsnarled. Aircraft mechanics searched crates and grabbed parts that were in short supply without waiting for the warehouses to catalogue them, screwing up record-keeping. The mechanics probably grabbed more than they needed so they could barter for other essentials they couldn't find. The military police would normally stop that semi-looting but were overwhelmed by dozens of other demands.

The partisan mortars that hit the base earlier became more sporadic through the day, as accurate US artillery fire killed or intimidated their crews. Dozens of US artillery spotter planes arrived, dwarfed by the transports, but at least as important as the artillery and ammunition the transports unloaded. During late World War II and the Donets War, spotter planes, along with advanced US artillery tactics, made US artillery uniquely deadly.

MPs spent much of their time screening people from New Memphis who wanted to come inside Fort Seminole. They sent most people south, though they allowed US ex-soldiers in, along with their Ukrainian wives and kids. The road south was choked with wheezing, overloaded Studebaker trucks and Russian-made Ford trucks, used by the Red Army, captured by the Germans and now in civilian hands, taking peasants and their possessions away from this new war. *How many times have they had to run while armies ravaged their way through?* Too many. How many times did armies march through, only to have peasants disrupt their supply chains and force them to divert troops to fighting hit and run raids? The US wanted to end the wars. *But we won't spend the money to do it.*

Those thoughts flitted through Captain Murphy's mind, disjointed. His knees and lower back ached from a long day on his feet, constantly moving.

How long before the partisans got to Fort Seminole? Maybe sometime in the night. More likely around dawn. The all-out effort to get ready for them left everyone inside Fort Seminole exhausted. Captain Murphy gave his soldiers brief breaks, but when darkness fell, they kept working under the base's harsh electric lights, sleeping in four-hour shifts. Cooks pushed carts around with sandwiches and water instead of stopping for meals.

In the clear night, Captain Murphy saw flashes on the horizon—artillery firing, while a continuous dull rumble filled the night. With nightfall, partisan mortar bombs hit the base again. The electric lights made Fort Seminole an easy target and night kept the artillery spotter planes grounded. The mortar bombs weren't very accurate, with most landing harmlessly outside the fort, but the thought of one landing among unloaded ammunition waiting to be secured made Captain Murphy's skin crawl. Stowing ammunition had priority, but so did finding Skyraider parts and getting newly arrived artillery in position.

Ambulances rushed in, dropped off wounded and rushed back to the front. One part of Captain Murphy's mind noted that there weren't many wounded yet, while another part insisted on putting faces on mangled young men.

He spotted Envoy McCormick and the reporters briefly. The Envoy was pushing a cook's cart, distributing water to warehouse workers, while reporters clustered nearby, getting comments from anyone who would talk to them.

MPs broke up any extended conversations and kept the reporters away from the wounded.

A truck veered from a refugee column on the highway and crashed through an outer gate. Sentries fired heavy machine guns at it as it raced toward the inner defenses. It detonated halfway between the inner and outer defenses, spraying shrapnel and pieces of truck. Captain Murphy wondered if the driver expected to jump out when the truck got closer to the inner gate. He hoped so. *Brave we can handle. Kamikaze is tougher to stop.*

Either way, the explosive laden truck was a reminder that the battle for Fort Seminole would be brutal.

Chapter Twenty-Four: The Retreat

Sergeant Duncan's mind told him to move fast. In combat you move fast or die. His body didn't cooperate, not after long hours of retreat toward Fort Seminole. He squatted at the edge of a newly planted field, dug in among nettles that framed the field and sucked in tired breaths. He was in a decent position, not in contact with the enemy, but he had orders to take his little scratch force south again.

That became routine through the evening and into the night. He moved south, dug in, sometimes skirmished with partisan trucks, but more often just moved south again. His men now worked with an M24 light tank company. The M24s weren't directly confronting the partisan T34s. Instead, they focused on partisan light trucks that were trying to flank the American column or cut pieces off from Fort Seminole. Towed 57-millimeter anti-tank guns, newly arrived, were supposed to stop, or at least slow down the partisan tanks. Maybe they made a difference, though Sergeant Duncan would have preferred Sherman tanks or something with even more punch, like Pershing tanks.

The armored trucks were much faster than the partisan tanks and their crews ranged ahead, acting like light cavalry, trying to disrupt the Americans and destroy logistics units. The M24s weren't as fast as the trucks but were almost invulnerable to them. The truck crews tried to draw American tanks into range of nasty bazooka-type weapons. The partisans had a lot of "bazookas" and used them against any US vehicle they saw, not just tanks. They even used them against infantry, like extra-light mobile artillery or long-range grenades. Those were good tactics for a force without much heavy artillery, though like many partisan tactics they would get the partisans cut to pieces if they tried them against fully equipped US divisions.

We could sure use a US division. Sergeant Duncan blinked sleep out of his eyes and stared into the darkness. His group of men from Fort Seminole was dwindling, with one dead and a couple others rushed back to Fort Seminole with wounds. The tanks they worked with dwindled too, mainly from mechanical breakdowns rather than combat.

How far were they from Fort Seminole? Sergeant Duncan wasn't sure. He knew this road, had driven it dozens of times in his undercover role, but everything looked different in the dark. He had no idea where he was. He hoped the company's commander knew and had some idea where the enemy was.

They lost contact with the Ruthenian paramilitary and their Hetzers shortly after the Hetzers knocked out a partisan T34/85. The Ruthenians were good fighters, but their best units were tied up defending the oil wells further east, from what Sergeant Duncan heard. His world narrowed to the field in front of him, with the rest of the war a dangerous distraction.

His little force abandoned their positions as ordered, marched back to their battered jeep and drove further south.

It had to be well after midnight. He was running on adrenaline and barely awake. Two soldiers in the jeep with him fell asleep and snored, an ear-grinding duet punctuated by snorts. Sergeant Duncan's eyes kept drifting shut despite the noise and the ever-present fear. Boredom punctuated by terror. That pretty much summed up his day and night so far.

US light howitzers fired nearby, the roar from three nearly simultaneous shots startling him fully awake and their blasts briefly lighting the night. Their targets could be four or five miles away, but from what Sergeant Duncan knew about US artillery, someone would have a very bad night at the other end. US artillery tactics were very effective, slamming fire from multiple artillery positions down on a single target simultaneously. *We just need more guns to make it work.* The light howitzers helped, but they needed heavier, more modern artillery.

The howitzers woke the two sleeping soldiers briefly, but they quickly went back to sleep. Sergeant Duncan didn't bother them. His missing finger was itching, not throbbing. He shook his head at how much he relied on the missing finger to gauge danger. *If I start really believing that crap, it will get me killed.*

The howitzers fired again, in near unison. The sleeping soldiers didn't even wake up. The missing finger suddenly throbbed, jolting Sergeant Duncan fully awake. He mentally replayed the seconds around the howitzer flash. He must have seen something that flitted by too fast for his conscious mind to catch it. What though?

He poked the sleeping guy beside him. "Get everyone awake. Something out there I don't like."

They were in a convoy with a dozen trucks and a couple light M24 tanks. The convoy moved at the speed of the M24 tanks, fast for tanks, but much slower than jeeps or trucks. They were on the highway, every third vehicle driving with headlights on, the danger of driving the unfamiliar road without headlights outweighing the risk of revealing their position. Maybe his finger was warning him about the headlights, but the headlights went on long before his finger throbbed.

Ambush! That was the only thing that made sense. He must have caught a glimpse of partisans moving when the howitzers flared. Where were they, though? Eight partisan bazookas lit up a nearby field, sending their lethal little rockets into the convoy. Sergeant Duncan frantically slammed on the brakes, though the rockets were inaccurate enough that he was as likely to put the jeep into one's path as to avoid one. A rocket carved a path inches in front of the jeep. The other guys in the jeep blazed away at the bazooka teams, their fire guided by backblast from the rockets that ignited brush behind the bazooka teams, making blazing arrows pointing to them.

"Did we get them?" One of the soldiers asked. He kept firing wildly. A tank opened fire with its machine gun.

Did they get the bazooka guys? Sergeant Duncan didn't know. At least there was no more bazooka fire.

"Bad tactics," a soldier said. "Bazookas at night are suicide."

Sergeant Duncan nodded. "They're a mix of professionals and brave but stupid amateurs."

Those amateurs knocked out one truck, he realized when he heard shouts behind him. A truck near the rear of the convoy burned, the rear of its suspension gone. The smell of burning meat told Sergeant Duncan the truck carried rations. "At least that's better than ammunition."

His stomach rumbled, reminding him that he hadn't eaten for too many hours. The rations were beyond salvaging already, though, with meat grease stoking the fire. He sighed, tried to put the burning meat odors out of his mind and muttered, "Long time until morning."

Chapter Twenty-Five: Siege

Captain Murphy grabbed a few hours of sleep between midnight and first light. He woke to artillery fire and planes screaming into the air. The sun was still behind the eastern horizon, but its light reflected off low clouds, dispelling the darkness.

More cargo planes landed and unloaded, adding to the chaos, though some were combat loaded, set up so that, theoretically, everything needed for an artillery unit was on board and could be unloaded as a unit. Combat loading reduced cargo capacity but got the cargo to the front faster.

A lot of artillery was coming in, heavier stuff along with antitank guns, The planes also carried a lot more bazookas. The new artillery and ammunition added to the backlog. The base didn't have enough vehicles to tow the weapons into place, so soldiers had to manhandle them.

Colonel Rock called Captain Murphy into his office, along with several other officers. The Colonel's jaw clinched. "We're going to hold the fort or die trying. Orders from the top. The partisans are already pushing past us. The rapid reaction force is about five miles out from the fort, falling back. They'll be the outer ring of our defense." He gestured toward the airport. "We're not completely on our own. US army headquarters is sending us anything that will fit in a cargo plane, including dribs and drabs of soldiers, mostly artillery units." He smoothed his uniform down, looking surprisingly fresh, though he probably hadn't slept much more than Captain Murphy. "The artillery will help, but we'll be outnumbered ten to one if the partisans put their main effort against the fort and that assumes they don't bring up more troops."

Captain Murphy studied a wall-sized map behind the Colonel. It showed seven partisan divisions, four of them tank divisions, advancing along the highway. If the Ruthenian paramilitary or the French and Czech peacekeepers were around, the map didn't show them.

"Sending this much of their military south leaves the partisans vulnerable to Governor Meandrov," Colonel Rock said. "He mobilized and asked us for tanks, but isn't doing anything, not even air strikes."

He knew the partisans were up to something. Why wasn't he ready? Based on his record as a Red Army commander and a warlord, Meandrov was a good soldier. *Probably wants us to do the hard fighting before he jumps in.* That assumed the US won here. *That's not a safe assumption.* Fort Seminole wasn't well-placed to hold out against a siege, though it did cover a chokepoint along the highway. The partisans could bypass it on both sides, but the fort's artillery and aircraft could dominate their supply lines.

"We'll be within their artillery range before long," Colonel Rock said. "We're moving command to bomb shelters. I wish we could send the civilian workers south, but we need them to unload the planes." He shrugged. "More mouths to feed. We can feed them if we keep the runways open. If partisan artillery closes the runways, we'll have more urgent things to worry about."

Artillery roared, close enough that Captain Murphy barely suppressed a twitch. One of the other captains jumped. Colonel Rock grinned ruefully. "We'll get used to that sound again."

Captain Murphy nodded. The partisans could push within artillery range of Fort Seminole. No way to stop that. They would pay a price, both from the fort's artillery and from ground attack planes if the air force could unsnarl their logistics.

Last time he was outside, a few Skyraiders took off, but most still sat on the runways, easy targets for the partisans if they got artillery close enough.

The meeting ended. Captain Murphy relieved an exhausted officer who was trying to get unloading procedures under control and get unloaded ammunition to units or into storage. That wasn't easy because transport planes kept adding to growing, precariously stacked mountains of goods--mostly food and ammunition. The nightshift warehouse guys were falling asleep on their feet, but he kept them moving until the next shift arrived.

The combat-loaded transports were welcome breaks, but they held bulkier items, like heavier artillery and heavier ammunition. Much of the unloading was by hand. The few vehicles available were already spoken for.

Artillery fire kept getting closer, marking the rapid reaction force's retreat. Partisan artillery fire, other than sporadic mortar rounds, wasn't hitting the fort yet, but it was getting closer too. It wasn't heavy compared to the outgoing fire and Captain Murphy hoped it would stay light, though he didn't expect it to.

This is going to get bad. He redoubled his efforts, trying to get vulnerable supplies dispersed under cover before the partisans got within range. The heavier artillery should slow them down if he could get it to the front. There simply weren't enough men or machines to do everything he needed done though, even with the slow march of artillery fire toward the fort spurring their efforts.

The flow of transports got heavier. Captain Murphy tried to focus on unloading planes and distributing what came off them but couldn't tune out the approaching battle. He ruthlessly refocused on his task when his attention drifted. He wanted to be up in his helicopter, seeing the battle from above, rather than grinding away here. *I want to see what's about to hit us.*

Artillery along the new defense lines outside the fort's fences fired, though only the heavier guns. That probably meant the enemy main body was still five or ten miles away. *Getting close now.*

Captain Murphy kept fighting logistics snarls. The mountains of offloaded supplies shrank slowly, reluctantly, the progress barely visible. The Skyraiders were still mostly runway queens, with rumors of what they were missing ranging from tires to some engine gizmo. Whatever it was, the missing parts might already be at Fort Seminole, buried in the mountains of other crap.

The fast reaction force was getting more firepower, with antitank guns and heavier artillery rushed to the front when vehicles to tow them became available.

Captain Murphy half-wished the partisans would hurry up and attack, though every minute they didn't made the fort stronger. The waiting grated on his nerves, especially with no idea what was happening outside his tiny sliver of the war.

The artillery on the outer lines of defense fired more often now, with lighter-weight howitzers joining in. Partisan artillery rounds started falling among the outer defense lines, but it was still sporadic and not particularly accurate. *They must not have a lot of ammo.* At least Captain Murphy hoped so.

How much could the partisans have captured from the Germans or smuggled in? The tanks were a nasty surprise, but Envoy McCormick was probably right about how the Soviets got them in operation. Boneyard tanks were common, and all the provincial paramilitaries had a few running tanks squirreled away. The Soviets must have smuggled a lot of spare parts and mechanics in to turn salvageable tanks into running ones. Did they do something similar with artillery and artillery crews? Maybe. *They couldn't have smuggled an entire army through our lines.* At least he hoped not. Even if they did smuggle in men and equipment, they couldn't smuggle enough ammunition and spare parts to keep up a war for long, not against a modern army. *But they aren't up against a modern army.*

And ready or not, the siege of Fort Seminole started. The rapid reaction force retreated into the outer defense lines, the process only visible in brief glimpses.

Partisan artillery fire got heavier and more accurate, though it was aimed at the outer defense lines.

"They got the bastards with the mortars." That rumor spread around mid-morning. Captain Murphy didn't know if it was true. The fire had been so sporadic that a long pause didn't mean much. The increased US artillery and artillery spotter planes made firing the mortars more dangerous and maybe the partisans were laying low until dark.

Captain Murphy finally got a break from warehouse duty to get his helicopter up around noon. The partisans were all around Fort Seminole, though not in strength. The rapid reaction force could probably still break out to the south. He didn't see much partisan heavy artillery, but they had a crapload of light anti-aircraft guns and plenty of ammunition, as they proved by blazing away at him whenever he got close to their lines. The light anti-aircraft guns were hard to spot until they fired, cunningly camouflaged. If partisan heavy artillery was concealed as well, the partisans would be hard to root out once they dug in.

We need those Skyraiders in the air while they're on the move. He felt guilty for being up here while the logistics problems were still unsolved, but the US needed trained observers in the air too. He gathered what information he could, radioing back positions of partisan heavy artillery he spotted and anti-aircraft guns that fired at him.

When he landed, he reported to Colonel Rock, who was now commanding from a bunker. Envoy McCormick was there. He nodded to Captain Murphy. "I'm cleared to hear your reports, but I'm an observer. If the base needs anything I can help you get it, but I'm not in the military chain of command."

Those were the right words, but Captain Murphy wondered if the envoy would stick with them. He could intervene if he wanted to. Would he stay out of decision-making when the battle got hot? *He already pushed us not to evacuate Fort Seminole.* Letting US ground forces get surrounded might be politically necessary but was militarily questionable.

McCormick and his daughter need to be gone. Amber started the chain that led to this whole fiasco with her insistence on going to Lvov with him, though the partisans had obviously been preparing for this attack for months. The search for Amber precipitated the attack, but only because the search would have revealed the buildup. Maybe it was better that the war happened now instead of when the partisans were completely ready.

Captain Murphy went through what he saw, adding, "They are good at camouflage once they dig in. I probably saw only a fraction of what they have out there."

He studied the map behind Colonel Rock. It showed the rapid reaction brigade in a loose circle around Fort Seminole, with two partisan infantry divisions surrounding the fort and the bulk of the partisans heading toward Lvov.

"What's between them and Lvov?" Captain Murphy asked.

"A couple Ruthenian brigades, a Ruthenian reserve division if they get it mobilized fast enough and a battalion each of Czech and French peacekeepers who may not fight unless they're attacked," Colonel Rock said. "They're occupation troops anyway, not much use in combat."

"If the partisans get close to Lvov, the Poles will jump in," Captain Murphy said. "They won't let Russians take Lvov without a fight, whether they're partisans or the Soviet army itself."

"And the Soviets know the Poles will jump in," Envoy McCormick said. "They have already mobilized and moved armored divisions up to the border. If Stalin thinks he's ready to take back his 1939 borders or even his June 1941 borders, the partisans will try to beat the Poles to Lvov. If Stalin isn't ready for total war, it will be interesting to see what he does."

"Do you think he's ready for World War III?" Captain Murphy asked.

"I don't think he's decided," Envoy McCormick said. "'Probe with bayonet.' That's an old Bolshevik tradition. Push your opponent, test them, but don't commit to war. See if they're weak or strong." He smiled wryly. "You already have enough to worry about, but I'm being honest with you. How Americans fight the next few days around Fort Seminole may decide whether he launches World War III."

Chapter Twenty-Six: Stalin's Test

When she was a prisoner, Hannah Reitsch heard a guard give orders to prisoners in English. Captain Murphy hadn't thought about the faint possibilities those orders represented lately. Logic told him the supposed prisoners had nothing to do with his wife and daughter. There were so many other possibilities.

Now, with a last chance to grab sleep before the approaching battle, with thousands of American troops trapped in Fort Seminole, Captain Murphy's mind flitted back to the mystery prisoners. They weren't the only mystery in the building where Hannah was held. US troops who searched the building found no firm evidence of who kidnapped Hannah. Diehard Nazis? German Communists? Some strange combination of the two?

Defeat made strange bedfellows and Captain Murphy remembered how Stalin let Germans test new tank designs and theories, in exchange for access to the designs. Then there was the infamous pact that divided Eastern Europe between Communists and Nazis before the Nazis invaded the Soviet Union. There were rumors of a new Nazi/Communist collaboration, with the Soviets helping diehard Nazis fight the Allied occupation of Germany.

And none of that was urgent. He could usually sleep at will, but now sleep refused to come. Sleep deprivation was a soldier's lot, but it also got men killed. Command required decisions made fast and hopefully well. *Which is why I have to go to sleep.*

Putting that kind of pressure on himself often led to sleep fleeing, but his exhausted mind finally pushed him into a sleep punctuated by half-remembered dream fragments.

He woke at noon, with the siege of Fort Seminole under way. The shelter's thick, concrete walls muffled artillery fire, but he still heard US guns firing and occasionally partisan return fire. Captain Murphy climbed to the surface, blinking in the sunlight.

The sounds of battle were suddenly loud, mostly artillery firing. Dozens of huge B-29 strategic bombers roared in from the west, heading south. The strategic bombers packed a huge, lethal punch, but they weren't very accurate, a crude club to hit cities and factories rather than fast-moving tank columns.

The Skyraiders, if they lived up to their reputations, were what the fort needed, but the Skyraiders were still mostly grounded.

Envoy McCormick rushed by, looking grim, but paused briefly. "Stalin consistently outsmarts himself." The Envoy rushed on without explaining.

Artillery rumbled all around Fort Seminole now, with sounds of automatic weapons drifting in on the breeze. Was the artillery fire getting closer? Probably. The rapid reaction force didn't have enough men to hold the outermost defense lines against determined attack. They would hold that line as long as they could, then fall back to a smaller, denser circle.

Captain Murphy wanted another look at the battle from his helicopter but was back supervising logistics. The mountains of unsorted crates were smaller now, and most of the ammunition was secured or dispersed to the front. Warehouse operations now had some of the rapid reaction force's trucks and prime movers. *I wonder how they managed that.* He also wondered if the brigade would get their vehicles back. *Possession is nine points of the law here too.*

The ground shook in a series of explosions. At least fifty planes Captain Murphy didn't recognize swooped in from the north. "Hostiles!" He ran for the nearest bomb shelter while air raid sirens blared. As he ran, he identified the incoming partisan planes. P39s. The Soviets got thousands of the American-built planes in Lend Lease. He dived through a bomb shelter door that slammed shut behind him.

"They hit us with planes we gave them to fight Nazis." He felt a wave of hatred for Stalin while bombs shook the shelter, too close. Captain Murphy hoped all the ammunition was stowed away but doubted it. Most, yes. All, no. There were too many crates for munitions to hide among.

A rapid string of nearby explosions confirmed his doubts. He swore. They needed the ammunition that was cooking off. They needed the food and spare parts that the exploding ammo was probably destroying too.

When a siren sounded the all-clear, the situation was better in some ways than he had feared. The secondary explosions were confined to one end of the smallest supply mountain, in pockets of ammunition among ration crates. Firefighters worked to keep the fires from spreading to the rest of the supplies, especially threatened jerry cans of gasoline. Lines of soldiers spontaneously formed to pass cans away from the fire.

Someone said, "Our Mustangs got all the bastards on their way out." That probably wasn't true, though Captain Murphy saw seven wrecked enemy P39s south of Fort Seminole and another had crashed in a New Memphis restaurant.

One catastrophe: a third of the Skyraider attack planes were burning wreckage, destroyed on the ground.

"Well, crap." Captain Murphy went to work salvaging what he could from the mountains of spare parts and food. At least the attack interrupted the flow of cargo planes, letting the logistics people catch up a little, though that was only good in the short term. Fort Seminole needed what the cargo planes could bring in before partisan artillery made the runways too dangerous. As the partisans closed in, their light antiaircraft guns would make landing here perilous. When they got closer, when their artillery could hit the runways, cargo flights would be restricted or stopped entirely. *Then we live on what we have here.*

Hundreds more US B-29s thundered over, flying high and heading southeast, toward Lvov. That made sense. Hit the tank columns while they were on the move and hopefully give the Ruthenians time to mobilize to save the city. The big strategic B-29 bombers weren't ideal planes to stop tank columns, but if they were all the US had in range, they were better than nothing. If nothing else they could turn the highway US engineers worked so hard on into a cratered mess. *And they'll kill a lot of Ruthenians in the process.* Collateral damage. That was what the air force called it when they hit friendly civilians.

The afternoon melted into a blur of warehouse work. The sheer amount of material coming in overwhelmed Fort Seminole's limited number of fork trucks. Midway through the afternoon a cargo plane filled with fork trucks arrived, but without drivers. Captain Murphy combed through personnel files to find anyone with fork truck experience. *This is where wars are won. Shuffling paper and moving crap around in warehouses. Finding spare parts that get planes in the air.* It was also hard to focus on when the battle raged within easy earshot, when casualties flowed back, and enemy artillery salvos got closer.

Finally, late in the afternoon, the brass pulled him off warehouse duty and Colonel Rock ordered him to the command bunker. The Colonel looked even more exhausted than he had earlier. He said, "The partisans aren't quite ignoring us, as you can hear, but they mostly screened us and headed for Lvov. They could have taken Lvov hours ago but stopped a few miles outside the city."

"Why?"

"Probably afraid the Poles will jump in. They're right to be afraid. The Poles would kick their butts, grab the territory up to their 1939 borders and maybe further. And then we'll be in World War III because the Soviets won't let the Poles grab that territory without a fight." He shook his head, looking old. "Envoy McCormick handles the politics, which is fine. I just wish I knew what he was doing."

Something that puts a huge target on Fort Seminole. What was it? The partisan offensive didn't make much sense. This was an all-out offensive that could take a major objective, but then they paused, letting their enemies gather strength. Why would Stalin organize and push the offensive and not follow through on it? Captain Murphy understood probing for weaknesses, but this offensive went both too far and not far enough. The US couldn't let

Federov's partisans remain in control of the Marshes after this. *We'll root them out unless the Soviets come into the war.*

He remembered what Envoy McCormick said about the Marshes. *Does Stalin want us to follow Federov into the Marshes?* How could the US go from where they were now, with most of their forces trapped around Fort Seminole to attacking the Marshes?

The irony was that US allies had plenty of forces close enough to help, but every one of them had territorial ambitions in the area. *We can't call on them without setting off a scramble for territory, with more brushfire wars than anyone can count.* Maybe that was what Stalin wanted, to make all those squabbles more intense, to make the US take sides and make enemies of whoever they sided against.

"I want an enemy I can smash," Colonel Rock said. "Not endless intrigues."

They did have a smashable enemy, as muffled artillery fire around Fort Seminole testified, but were they the ones that mattered? While the partisans surrounding Fort Seminole outnumbered the garrison five to one, the bulk of partisan power was focused on the drive to Lvov, or at least had been.

"The partisans are trying to take the Ruthenian oil fields too," Captain Murphy said. "The drive on Lvov is probably a diversion, trying to get the Ruthenians to pull their forces to Lvov." The ground shook as he said that. "It's one hell of a big diversion if that's what it is." He took a deep breath. "Are they putting more force into the oil field drive or this one?"

"This one from what I hear," Colonel Rock said. "And that doesn't make a lot of sense. They might grab the oil fields without the Poles intervening, but not Lvov. The Poles won't let the Russians take it."

That took them back to the lurking questions. Would Stalin start World War III to keep the Poles out? Was this attack a probe or the beginning of World War III? If Stalin was starting World War III, why didn't the partisans drive into Lvov when they could easily take the city?

"How long can we hold out if the partisans shut down the airfields?" Colonel Rock asked.

Despite Captain Murphy's focus on logistics, he had to say, "I've been so worried about getting supplies sorted that I don't have the big picture." Fort Seminole had multiple deep wells, so water shouldn't be a problem. Food? Soldiers could live for weeks on short rations if they had to, though it cut their fighting ability. Ammunition? There were mountains of ammo even after the Soviet air raid, but modern warfare consumed ammunition frighteningly fast. Fuel? Not as vital as ammunition but moving forces quickly to seal off breakthroughs was a force multiplier. Medical supplies? Again, he had no idea. The fort was well stocked for its own garrison, but the rapid reaction brigade and added artillery companies multiplied the men drawing on supplies at least five-fold.

"We can keep the soldiers fed two or three weeks," he said. "I can't vouch for ammo or medicine, or enough doctors to treat the wounded."

How long would it take for the US to shift heavy divisions from Germany or the demarcation line in the Soviet Union? It shouldn't take more than a week to ten days at most.

"If the partisans want Fort Seminole, they'll have to fight for it," Captain Murphy said. "They won't have time to starve us out."

That wasn't necessarily a comforting thought. The partisans, if they concentrated on the fort, would outnumber the Americans close to ten to one and they were sneaky, as the P39 air raid proved.

"Reporters are comparing Fort Seminole to the Alamo," Colonel Rock said. "We're getting a lot of press."

"All of the Alamo's defenders died," Captain Murphy said.

"And the odds could be just as bad here," Colonel Rock said. He pointed to a stack of reports. "This claims that one of their tank divisions turned back. They'll be here before dark. Another tank division never left. It'll be an interesting night."

Chapter Twenty-Seven: Nowhere to Retreat

Summer days at Fort Seminole were long, with twilight lingering. Sergeant Duncan and his men spent much of that long day on the outermost defense line around Fort Seminole. They were miles away from the fort's outer fence and their line was thin. Sergeant Duncan knew the commanders didn't expect to hold this line long. They were there to slow the partisans and spot for US artillery. Deploying so far forward had its disadvantages. The partisans could infiltrate through the lines and attack from the rear if the US wasn't careful. So far the partisans were cautious, probably waiting for nightfall. They hopefully would get a nasty surprise. Some rapid deployment soldiers had infrared scopes, capable of seeing in apparent darkness. Sergeant Duncan got one of those scopes in a complicated set of semi-larcenous transactions. *Following the rules is a good way to make everything grind to a stop.*

Sergeant Duncan was within partisan artillery range. So far the enemy artillery was more a nuisance than a threat. It was more accurate than he expected but didn't fire often. The partisans fired a few shots, followed by long pauses. Maybe they were short of ammunition. They might also be wary of US artillery, which was very good at taking out enemy artillery when it revealed itself. Time on target. That's what the US artillery guys called a devastating US artillery tactic where widely separated US artillery pieces coordinated their fire, so their barrages all slammed down at a target at once. Hopefully, the tactic hadn't been lost when the US military shrank so much after World War II. *We'll need every edge we can get.*

Time on a battle's front lines had a weird rhythm. It combined constant danger, where one careless move could get you killed or maimed for life, with long periods where nothing

154

happened. Some people sheltered their minds from fear of sudden death by constant routine. Others focused intently, looking for openings to kill the enemy. Still others grew reckless, lulled by routine that hid constant threat. Sergeant Duncan's mind split during times like these, with part monitoring constantly, ready to react to incoming artillery rounds or attacks, while part relaxed, replaying snatches of half-remembered songs in his head.

He rarely talked about time on the front line, but from what he heard from other combat veterans, the way they reacted varied wildly. For him, time flowed quickly, but in a peculiar pattern, with beads of action widely separated on a necklace of boredom. His mind didn't track the long stretches of boredom, or didn't remember them, though he was aware of their passing. It was mid-afternoon. A partisan artillery round kicked up dirt too close to him. Then the sun was low on the horizon and partisan snipers fired, too close for comfort.

Through all of that, his missing finger itched, but didn't throb. He was careful not to let that make him complacent. *The finger is not magic.*

With twilight falling, the finger throbbed. Sergeant Duncan also heard tanks clanking in the distance. He tried the infrared scope briefly, then decided he could see more without it. *I'll try again when it really gets dark.*

They had more to fight tanks now, with 57-millimeter anti-tank guns scattered along the defense line, and a lot more bazookas. A 57-millimeter gun could take out a T34/85, though the anti-tank crew had to be good. The tanks' main guns outranged the antitank guns, making the guns vulnerable before they could get in a kill shot. *We have heavier stuff.* The airlift probably just grabbed whatever could get here fast. A US artillery barrage hit around where he heard the partisan tanks, shrieking overhead like malignant train whistles, the sound reaching him after the shells were already past and exploding among the enemy position. It was like a movie with the audio running behind.

Did the barrage get the tank or tanks? He didn't hear secondary explosions, so probably not. Plenty more tanks were headed their way even if the first ones were out of the battle.

The battle heated up, with partisans trying to infiltrate the American positions, supported by hastily dug in tanks. Sergeant Duncan figured US command would pull back to the next line any minute now, was surprised that the order hadn't already come. Retreats were notoriously hard to control, especially with inexperienced troops. Finally, he got the orders and led his men back to the next line. They took tank fire before they got there. Maybe thirty partisan tanks pushed through where they had been and tried to take the next line without pausing. US machine guns pinned down partisan infantry, though, leaving the tanks vulnerable. Antitank guns picked off a couple partisan tanks, and the rest went to ground, dueling with the machine guns, trying to pin the crews down so partisan infantry could catch up.

The partisan offensive continued into the night, pushing through US defense lines, each line stronger than the last. The partisan tankers were good, concentrating quickly to break through, then dispersing their tanks to make them less vulnerable to US artillery.

The infrared scope showed Sergeant Duncan blocky green images not much better than what he could see in the darkness, but it helped him shoot two partisan infiltrators he might not have spotted. He didn't react to the deaths, not now. They weren't people. They were enemies. They had to be, or he would hesitate, and they would kill him. They would have faces in his nightmares.

He was living in a nightmare now. He couldn't remember the last time he slept, and his muscles ached in a way that told him he would pay for what he was doing for days after he stopped.

His men dwindled away through the night, carried away by corpsmen, some dead, most wounded. A few replacements arrived, men he didn't know and wondered if he could count on.

Sergeant Duncan remained uninjured as far as he could tell. He checked himself out occasionally. In the adrenaline of combat, it was possible to get hit and not feel it for long enough to lose a lot of blood.

The partisans took defense lines way too fast. The outermost line was token, a way to force the enemy to deploy. The second line should have held through the night, but it didn't last more than an hour. The partisans had too many tanks and deployed them too skillfully. They didn't have to have a lot of skill at ten-to-one odds, but the tank crews were well-trained, professional soldiers. The partisan infantry wasn't as good, but they had some training. They were, he was pretty sure, taking far heavier casualties than the Americans, though probably not a ten to one ratio. *At this rate, we'll run out of space long before they run out of bodies.*

The fighting came like ocean waves, subsiding between waves. The quiet intervals were tense, but welcome. He had his men catch brief naps in shifts because if he didn't they would fall asleep or make stupid mistakes. He even managed a brief nap himself despite the ongoing artillery duel over their heads.

The moon was up now, a faint sliver that went in and out of clouds, giving weak light, then fading out. The partisans timed their attacks for when the moon was hidden, but it didn't make much difference.

His unit moved back again, this time to within sight of Fort Seminole's outer fence. The engineers hadn't had time to set up minefields in front of the outer defense lines, but they had in front of this one. That should slow and channel the partisan attack. *We need to stand and fight somewhere.*

The latest retreat put New Memphis outside the defenses and engineers blew up the buildings to keep partisans from using them. Sergeant Duncan watched the distant explosions. *That's a lot of peoples' livelihoods gone.* It had to be done, though.

The partisan attacks intensified. Each US retreat seemed to give them more confidence, despite the price they paid, steeper each time as the defense got denser around smaller circles.

How was US morale? Sergeant Duncan wondered how many retreats these green troops could take. The replacements were slower and softer than the Fort Seminole men, but they weren't as bad as the horror stories about American infantry indicated. The rapid reaction force was an elite force compared to normal occupation troops, he realized. *If these are our best...* He didn't want to think about how the rest would stack up.

How deep into the night were they? Sergeant Duncan had no idea. The partisans were acting as though the night was nearing an end. They were also acting as though they were close to victory, moving more aggressively. Were they right? Would their self-confidence and aggressiveness win the battle?

"We have to get through the night," he said softly. "Then our planes can get back in the battle. Hang on a few more hours."

Chapter Twenty-Eight: Last Flights to Fort Seminole

Fort Seminole's air raid sirens wailed just as the eastern sky lightened with the coming sunrise. Captain Murphy was working another shift as a logistics officer. He ducked into a bomb shelter as P51s roared off to counter the raid. This time, no bombs shook the shelter, though he heard distant explosions. Hopefully, that meant US air cover drove off the enemy planes before they got to Fort Seminole.

Captain Murphy mulled his next moves while he waited for the all-clear.

Additional fork trucks made warehouse operations faster. He assigned inexperienced fork truck operators to loads that wouldn't go boom if the drivers did something stupid, but inexperienced drivers still snarled things up enough that he thought about weeding out the worst drivers, despite leaving fork trucks idle when they were vitally needed.

The flow of cargo planes slowed for the night, giving warehouse workers a much-needed chance to catch up, but the flood of cargo would resume soon.

The Fort needed experienced warehouse guys. It needed tanks or mobile antitank guns even more. The partisan tank division gave them unmatched mobile firepower that was picking apart US defensive lines.

The partisans were one defensive line away from bringing the airfields under artillery fire. Once they broke through that line, the fort would be cut off, except for quick landings braving artillery fire. US artillery could try to suppress partisan fire while transport planes landed, but that was iffy. The partisans, if they had heavy artillery, could outrange the US. With heavy artillery, they could also hit the airfield from their current positions. *A few captured German big guns could shut us down now.* So far, there was no sign of partisan heavy artillery, though they had a lot of medium caliber guns.

The sirens finally told him it was okay to go back outside. Not much had changed except the sun was peeking above the eastern horizon. It was a cloudless mid-summer morning, marred by a haze of dust from artillery strikes. Birds flew overhead, though they stayed high in the sky. Insects buzzed, though ants swarmed around their ant hills, probably disturbed by the ground shaking. Soldiers rushed about their business, most of them on foot. Vehicles and gas were reserved for vital tasks.

Colonel Rock called Captain Murphy and several other officers to his office. The Colonel looked tired, but with an edge of excitement that left him almost vibrating with energy. "I hope you enjoyed the sunrise. We may not be outside much for a while." He pointed to a map. "The partisans concentrate their forces briefly for breakthroughs, then disperse before our artillery hits them. They are in heavy artillery range of the airfields and barracks. They ringed the fort with anti-aircraft guns and that ring keeps getting stronger. Resupply is getting harder, and help is a long way off. Reporters are comparing Fort Seminole to the Alamo. They may be right." He paced. "The hell of it is that we don't have to be trapped here. The Poles have four armored divisions and several motorized ones at the border, a day or two away. The Czechs and Romanians have forces they could send if we asked. But if they come, no matter who we ask, we set off a scramble and a multi-sided war. The partisan offensive only makes sense if they understand we can't call on our allies and they want US soldiers in coffins, tiptoeing up to the line where we'll call for help but not crossing it. We're in for a rough time, but we're also keeping millions of people from getting caught between warring armies again. We have to prove that tackling us isn't smart, no matter what the odds."

It wasn't the most inspiring speech, but Captain Murphy nodded. *We have to make the cost so high that nobody tries this again.* If congress gave the military enough troops and money to dictate borders and make them stick, they could fix these issues permanently. Or could they? The US was trapped in a web of disputes that went back to the Middle Ages and still got young men killed. *How do you end that?*

Captain Murphy pushed those thoughts away. American soldiers were fighting as their officers talked, learning lessons they should have learned in boot camp. They were doing better than he expected, given their performance when they first met the partisans on the highway, but learning lessons in battle meant watching comrades die when they shouldn't have.

He wondered where Envoy McCormick and Amber were. He saw the Envoy in the distance occasionally, but McCormick no longer attended officers' meetings, maybe to resist micro-managing the battle. *Or maybe he is putting distance between himself and the men he is using.* Captain Murphy remembered Amber's words. *He wants to remind himself that the people he sacrifices aren't faceless pawns.* Did he expect Fort Seminole to fall? If so, why would he stay, especially with his daughter? To prove his bravery? McCormick didn't seem like he would need to prove anything to himself or anyone else.

Colonel Rock said, "The partisans have offered us a ceasefire if we stop air raids and artillery fire on them. They will make sure our troops know about the offer."

Crap! The reasonable-sounding offer had fangs. The only substantial US force in the region could sit in Fort Seminole and give the partisans a free hand in Ruthenia or endure a bloody siege and maybe get killed or captured. *We have to reject it or nobody in the region would take us seriously.*

The Colonel said, "Be ready to counter their propaganda. Morale is shaky after so many retreats." He looked around the room. "Stakes are high, gentlemen. We have to win this."

Partisan heavy artillery hit well inside the fort a few minutes after they left the meeting, sending them scrambling to air raid shelters.

More crap! The partisans probably rolled heavy artillery in during the night and concealed it well enough that US planes didn't spot it until it opened fire. The landing fields quickly emptied as half-unloaded cargo planes hastily took off. The airworthy Skyraiders took off too, along with the base's P51s. The planes searched for partisan big guns and strafed where they found them, though partisan anti-aircraft guns made that risky. US artillery hit back savagely at the big guns they could reach.

What do we do now? The partisan big guns were a game-changer, their power and range overriding the US skill at using artillery. Shells slamming into the heart of Fort Seminole made resupply iffy, made basing planes there difficult and would tear the heart out of the American defenses if the barrage wasn't stopped.

The bombardment went on sporadically over the next hour, never many shells at once and not very accurate, but unnerving. The US had no way to hit back except bombing raids and the P51 fighters weren't the ideal plane for that job. The plane for ground support was the Skyraider and the Skyraiders remained mostly on the ground, still unable to do their job due to some logistics snafu Captain Murphy still didn't understand, though he heard at least three explanations, none of which made sense to him.

About an hour after the heavy partisan guns started their bombardment, the sky filled with B-29s, at least two hundred huge four-engine bombers. The giant American planes plastered the partisan lines, sending dirt and debris flying in close-set bomb craters. Carpet bombing? Captain Murphy had heard the term but had never seen it. Was this it? He wasn't sure. He did know that the partisans were getting the crap bombed out of them. The huge bombers roared away, leaving a brief interval of stunned silence. The artillery duel started back up almost tentatively, as though both sides wondered if it was worth firing their popguns after the big planes did their pass. The partisan big guns came back to life a little later than their other guns, leaving Captain Murphy with a brief flicker of hope that the B-29s had knocked them out.

How did anybody live through that? Captain Murphy surveyed the battlefield through binoculars and shook his head. There shouldn't be anyone alive among those craters, but partisans survived, still full of fight.

The partisan big guns weren't firing as often now. Were they short of ammunition? If they were, they would probably have to wait until nightfall to get more. US planes scoured the highway for partisan supply trucks. Not all the planes were from Fort Seminole. They must be flying in from Poland or Czechoslovakia. Captain Murphy wondered how many arms Envoy McCormick had to twist to get basing rights. Probably a lot. The Central and Eastern European countries were prickly about their independence, though they still depended on US aid.

The partisans probably weren't getting much food down the highway or along secondary roads. Civilians who needed to move around were out of luck too. The planes would be less effective at night though, giving partisans a chance to sneak in supplies.

The partisans got noticeably less aggressive as the afternoon wore on. They breached the last US line of defense outside the fort's outer fence but didn't follow up the breakthrough before a US counter-offensive restored the line. They cratered a landing field with their big guns, but work crews filled in the holes.

The evening wore on. Captain Murphy overheard soldiers saying that the B-29 strike took the fight out of the partisans. He wished he believed that. *They're waiting for nightfall.*

Another B-29 raid came in around supper time, even bigger than the earlier one. This time, cargo planes flew in shortly after the raid, timing their arrival so the partisans would still have their heads down. There was another twist to that strategy. A smaller B-29 strike came in after the transport planes landed, apparently trying to catch any partisans targeting the cargo planes.

Did any of that make much difference? Captain Murphy didn't know. *Typical air force. Too clever by half.* The cargo planes got mostly unloaded before partisan big guns started firing. Most of the planes got away, but partisans hit two on the ground, sending ground crews fleeing and wrecked planes spewing secondary explosions. *That's a lot of ammunition we don't get to shoot at them.*

The cargo planes burned far into the night.

Chapter Twenty-Nine: Tightening the Screws

Captain Murphy grabbed sleep a few hours at a time through the night. As an intelligence officer he wanted to be figuring out what the enemy was up to, but the army kept him working logistics. He tried not to resent being so out of the loop. Colonel Rock brought him in a couple times for updates, but how accurate was the information? Colonel Rock confirmed that US fighter-bombers were flying in from Czechoslovakia to strafe and bomb partisan supply columns. A couple partisan divisions were still inexplicably poised outside Lvov, though the Ruthenians had enough mobilized divisions now that the partisans probably couldn't take the city without the forces currently attacking Fort Seminole.

Governor Meandrov was still mobilizing, but not much else. Colonel Rock didn't know why he hadn't sent his paramilitary south into partisan-held territory. Part of that territory was officially in his province, and this was an ideal time to grab it. Why wasn't he moving? Colonel Rock didn't know. "Maybe he's holding out for more aid."

"He's being short-sighted if that's it," Captain Murphy said. "We'll remember what he does."

Colonel Rock had a lot of unanswered questions. How much ammunition did the partisans have for their big guns? Was the heavy artillery currently hitting the fort just a first installment, with more arriving every night? That was a nightmare scenario that might easily lead to the fort falling.

Those were questions Captain Murphy should be trying to answer but couldn't in his current position. "Any idea how many partisans the B-29 strikes killed?"

"I know how many the air force claims they killed," Colonel Rock said. "And if they really killed that many, the partisans won't bother us tonight."

"Taking bets on a quiet night?"

The Colonel grimaced. "I can guarantee we won't see one."

The artillery duel went on, muffled in the bomb shelter but a constant background.

"Have you talked to Envoy McCormick lately?" Captain Murphy asked.

Colonel Rock shook his head. "He has a plan and we're part of it, but what part I don't know. If he takes a plane out we'll know we're in trouble."

The Envoy didn't strike Captain Murphy as a man who would fly out of a fight unless he was directly ordered to. *What is important enough here for him to risk his life?*

"The press keeps calling this a second Alamo," Colonel Rock said. "God, I hope they aren't right."

"If we go down, I hope we take an Alamo-sized bunch of them with us," Captain Murphy said.

After the meeting he went back to a crowded bomb shelter to grab a little sleep. When he woke, it was to a wild crescendo of artillery bombardment, though the explosions didn't seem closer, just heavier and more frequent. *They're pounding the front lines.*

He grabbed his sidearm and a rifle, then made sure the weapons were loaded, hoping he was being paranoid. He cautiously emerged from the bomb-shelter and looked around with his binoculars, his instincts quivering. Night-shift warehouse workers moved food and spare parts in and out of warehouses. Their speed was improving as inexperienced or rusty drivers got better at their jobs.

He prowled the base, trying to gauge the fighting. MPs eyed him suspiciously but moved on when they saw his insignia. He needed to go back to the bomb-shelter and get what was left of his sleep time. The battle was too close and bitter though. He calculated how long it would take partisan tanks to get from a breakthrough to the center of the base and shuddered. The base had contingency plans to issue rifles to the warehouse workers and organize a defense, but the only drill he saw turned into a fiasco, with armory personnel insisting on issuing each rifle to a specific soldier, at a time when, if the drill scenario had been real, that delay would have probably seen the base overrun.

He had the nightshift logistics officer issue rifles to select men. Rifles wouldn't stop tanks, but they could strip away accompanying infantrymen. Hopefully there were contingency plans to issue some warehouse guys bazookas, but if there were he didn't know the details and he would have to implement the orders if the partisans broke through during his watch. And his watch would be coming up entirely too fast. He wanted to head back to the bomb shelter and assume someone had contingency plans to protect the warehouses from a breakthrough, but the problem kept buzzing around in his head. You didn't just throw bazooka teams together. The weapons were simple but did take some training.

The clatter of tank treads made him jump, then sprint toward the nearest bomb-shelter. A tank rounded a corner. He relaxed slightly when he recognized the shape. Franken-Sherman. What was it doing out in the middle of the night though? He started toward the tank, but four more rounded the corner, moving fast. He flattened himself against the side of a warehouse as the tanks rolled by, not just the first five but nine more, with an ex-German King Tiger sputtering along behind them. Do they have ammunition for that monster? This was the first time he had even seen it moving.

The Franken-Shermans fired in near unison, the blast lighting the night. The King Tiger fired a few seconds later. Captain Murphy stood uncomprehending for a second, then swore. *Partisan breakthrough.* Someone sent the salvaged Shermans and the King Tiger against the partisan tanks as a last-ditch defense.

He couldn't see partisan tanks or know for sure that they broke through, but from the direction the Franken-Shermans fired he had a pretty good idea. Warehouse and other service troops raced to form up defenses, some of them, he noted with approval, already armed with rifles, *My contribution to the war effort.*

A journalist and cameraman jockeyed for a good shot, ignoring MPs until the MPs dragged them to safety. The Franken-Shermans kept firing. How good were their crews? Pretty good. The mechanics who put them back together were tank enthusiasts who had probably used Shermans in World War II or the Donets War.

He finally saw partisan tanks and his stomach clinched. *Way too many of them.* There had to be at least a hundred T34/85s heading for the core of the base, with hundreds of armored trucks flanking them. Where were the defenders from the front line? He saw no sign of them. The partisan tanks and trucks headed for the core of the base, for command bunkers, warehouses and airbase runways, with very little to stop them except Franken-Shermans and warehouse workers armed with rifles.

That wasn't entirely true, he realized. The base's anti-aircraft crews turned their rapid-fire cannons on the partisans, knocking out trucks and forcing tank crews to button down, slowing their assault and reducing their vision.

The Skyraiders still sat on the runways, vulnerable on the ground. They weren't just targets, though, he realized. They also had a lot of firepower, Captain Murphy tried to figure out how to get their machine guns and rapid-fire cannons into action, but someone had already thought of that. The Skyraiders taxied into position and fired at the attacking trucks. It was an awful way to use airplanes, but sort of worked. The partisan attack slowed.

Partisan infantry caught up as the unequal fight raged, making it even more unequal. A few hundred US frontline troops joined the fighting from some mobile reserve. They had bazookas and a few anti-tank guns, which helped, but there were nowhere near enough of them. The partisan infantry kept coming and turned the fight hand-to-hand. More partisan infantry swarmed toward a nearby warehouse.

Captain Murphy rallied a dozen nearby warehouse workers and ran to the warehouse, plowing into around twenty partisans at the door.

The Americans had momentum, hitting the partisans from the side. They were outnumbered nearly two to one though. Captain Murphy fired his sidearm until it was empty, hitting maybe half the time despite the short range. The fight moved too fast for accurate shooting and the sides were too intermingled. His were the only shots fired by either side. Both sides were too busy clubbing or knifing their enemies.

The fight turned into a running, swirling melee, spilling into the warehouse, among startled fork truck drivers. Captain Murphy was in the thick of it, fists flying. He grabbed a giant wrench from beside a fork truck and swung it at the nearest partisan, a huge guy with a graying beard and thick arms. The guy got a hand up, but the wrench slammed both itself and the partisan's hand against the guy's skull. The guy wobbled, his eyes crossed, but he kept lurching forward. His arm lashed out in a huge roundhouse like a tree trunk. Captain Murphy ducked and shoved the wrench into the partisan's face as hard as he could. Blood gushed from the partisan's nose, but he kept coming. Captain Murphy backed away, wishing he had saved at least one bullet. *Not even sure bullets would stop him.* That flashed through his mind, then a fork truck slammed its forks into the huge partisan's back and drove him into a shelf full of heavy engine parts. A carton of parts crashed down on the partisan's head, sending him to his knees. Captain Murphy swung his wrench like a baseball bat, full into the partisan's unprotected face. The huge guy finally went down. A heavy metal engine part slammed down on the back of his head.

That should have killed at least three or four normal men. Captain Murphy still wasn't sure the guy was dead, but two more partisans ran toward him, knives flashing, the rifles slung over their backs apparently forgotten. Captain Murphy wondered briefly where his rifle was. He had it shortly before the fight but had no idea where it had gone. He backed against some shelving so the partisans couldn't get behind him and swung the wrench back and forth, hoping the partisans weren't good with their knives. He studied the way they held their knives and figured they knew what they were doing. *Crap!*

168

Two to one and they had better weapons. He had a reach advantage but had to swing the wrench in long arcs, which would give skilled knife fighters openings to get inside his guard. Captain Murphy wished he had more unarmed combat practice. He mentally rehearsed a couple moves before the partisans reached him. They spread out, coming at him from both sides. He yelled and raised the wrench high to distract them, then kicked one to the side of the knee, knowing the trick could only work once at most. His heavy work boots crunched into the side of the guy's knee.

The other partisan lunged in with his knife at the captain's exposed side. Captain Murphy slammed the wrench down, the momentum brushing the partisan's hand and knife down, then crashing into the top of the guy's front knee. The partisan grabbed his knee briefly, then came in with the knife again. The knee collapsed, and he crashed to the floor moaning. The first partisan balanced on his uninjured knee, trying to get close enough to use his knife.

A sharp, metal grinding sound echoed through the garage. Captain Murphy wanted to look up but had to stay focused on the partisans. The rest of the fight spread through the warehouse, leaving him and the two partisans isolated. He was faster than them now and he took advantage of that to run between them. Both partisans had injured knees. Hopefully he could run fast enough to keep them from cornering him.

He ran a few steps, then glanced toward the metal-grinding sound. A partisan tank sat half in the warehouse, one of its treads mangled. Shelving and engine parts partially buried the tank, but its turret rotated, the tank's gun briefly pointed at him, looking huge. He ducked. The tank gun moved on, the crew apparently not considering him a worthy target if they even saw him.

The tank fired, the blast echoing. It hit a fork truck, igniting the vehicle's fuel tank. The driver bailed, leaving the fork truck to crash into a shelf, dumping carefully cataloged parts on the floor. Someone ignited a gas-filled Jerry can on the tank's engine deck, spewing flames over the back of the tank. The crew bailed before the tank's ammo exploded, sending the turret six feet into the air, then crashing down on two of its crew.

Captain Murphy lost track of the two partisans he had been fighting. Were they still in the warehouse? He didn't see any fighting. Was the fight over? Was he the only American survivor in the warehouse? He fought down a brief burst of panic, then saw US MPs combing the warehouse for partisans.

What was going on outside? A firefight, based on the sounds, with artillery and tank guns firing at short range. He felt like an ant in a buffalo stampede and wanted to keep his head down until it was over. He reluctantly poked his head out of the warehouse though.

The King Tiger was thirty feet from him, its crew stalking partisan tanks. There were a lot of partisan tanks out there, though he counted a couple dozen knocked out. The King Tiger quickly added two more to that total, its long 88-millimeter gun effortlessly blasting through enemy tanks. At least five Franken-Shermans were burned out wrecks again. *Will they fix them again?* That thought flashed through his mind, absurdly. *First we have to win.*

He wasn't sure how to help when his only weapon was an empty sidearm. He found a rifle and a few clips on a dead partisan. That was marginally better than nothing. With tanks battling outside, the rifle didn't make him much more than a slightly bigger ant.

Was command still operating? He hadn't heard anything from them since the partisan breakthrough started. *I could be the senior surviving officer.* That thought shocked him. What was going on with radio communications? Nothing that he had heard. He noticed that the radio at his belt was gone, lost sometime during the fight.

Someone did seem to be directing the US side of the fight. Troops poured back from the front lines to seal off the partisan breakthrough and push them out of the fort. He recognized Sergeant Duncan among soldiers setting up barricades in the streets, using fork trucks to shift pallets of sandbags. Soldiers man-handled anti-tank guns into position.

The King Tiger still prowled, the ex-German heavy tank rolling up an impressive score of partisan tanks. *How did we take those suckers out?* Probably bombed or bypassed them.

Dawn was coming, with the eastern sky getting lighter. The battle raged on, with tanks and artillery dueling, US soldiers and partisans firing rifles at each other at close range or fighting hand-to-hand. The warehouse was a temporary island of relative peace, but Captain Murphy got workers setting up barricades in front of the doors, using boxes of engine parts.

US firepower was having an effect. The partisans had tanks and trucks, but US troops had more machine guns, automatic rifles and artillery pieces, especially light anti-aircraft guns, many of them firing point-blank into the enemy. The partisans had to be taking horrendous casualties.

US light tanks still avoided the heavier partisan tanks when they could, but Captain Murphy saw them draw a dozen partisan tanks into mass artillery fire that left most of the partisan tanks flaming wrecks.

The sun rose, and with it came US bombers, hundreds of smaller two-engine B-25 bombers, specialized strafers with an ungodly number of heavy machine guns and sometimes 75-millimeter cannons in the nose. The B-25s swept over the partisans again and again, leaving chaos and burning vehicles behind. They didn't strafe close to the front line, probably unable to distinguish friend from enemy, but they were devastating where they attacked.

Why didn't we have those things yesterday? Probably basing issues. The B-25s didn't have enough range to fly in from Germany with much fuel left when they got to Fort Seminole. It took time to get permission to use allied bases and move needed supplies. *It's surprising they got here this quick.*

The B-25s dueled with partisan anti-aircraft guns and didn't always win. Three B-25s went down that Caption Murphy saw, one of them landing hard on a Fort Seminole runway.

171

Sunrise and B-25s turned the tide. A US counter-offensive threatened to cut off partisans inside the base fence, and sent them scrambling back, strafed by B-25s until the retreat became a chaotic rout.

A wedge of partisan tanks and armored trucks made it back to their main lines, leaving much of their infantry behind. Partisan tanks and trucks littered the base, probably half the vehicles in the breakthrough.

With the crisis over for the moment, Captain Murphy got back in touch with base command, just as Colonel Rock called an officers' meeting. A couple officers looked as though they were going to fall asleep in front of the Colonel. *I probably look like that too.*

"The partisans broke through with one tank division, plus another one to exploit," Colonel Rock said. "They kept their third tank division back, threatening another breakthrough if we brought too many men back. Not great generalship, but not bad." He closed his eyes and looked as though he didn't want to open them again. "They hit us hard, but paid a price for it, four or five bodies left behind for every American dead or non-walking wounded. They probably lost ten thousand dead or captured. You can do the math and know what our losses were."

He sighed. "You can also figure out that we can't take many victories like that. We'll fly the wounded out once we get the runways cleared. We'll get replacement troops if we keep the runways open. The B-25s are our only way of hitting their heavy guns, so we hope the air force knows what they're doing for once. It would also help if the partisans stayed short of ammunition for the big guns, but we can't count on that."

The briefing went on, not telling Captain Murphy much new. The US casualty figures appalled him. Two thousand or more dead or seriously wounded. That was a lot from a US force of no more than six or seven thousand total. *If we don't get replacements, we won't hold out another night.*

172

He dreaded going to sleep as much as his body craved sleep. Sleep was when his mind processed the horrific scenes of battle, when the dead stopped being statistics and grew mangled faces and bodies. Despite probable nightmares, Captain Murphy was asleep within seconds after he got back to his bunk in a crowded bomb shelter.

Chapter Thirty: Dietrich Lang Lurks in the Shadows

Dietrich Lang had a very good intelligence service, far better than the bumbling German efforts during World War II. His connections in French intelligence helped, but he didn't depend on them. His intelligence service kept him invisible or nearly so to the other powers. The Brits were vaguely aware of fragmented diehard Nazi cells and the Americans knew at some level that someone was operating in the background. He was pretty sure neither country knew much about him. He had men deep inside Federov's partisans, enough to anticipate their actions and motives. Stalin, on the other hand, was a mystery. Lang couldn't infiltrate the Soviet spy agencies, so he knew little about what they knew or guessed of his activities.

His intelligence service kept him informed about the partisan/American mini war, but left a lot of mysteries, some of which he gradually unwound. Why did the partisans stop when they could have taken Lvov? The Soviet top leadership ordered them to. That made sense if the Soviets didn't want to unleash an uncontrollable descent into World War III. Why did the partisans drive on Lvov in the first place, if they didn't intend to take the city? They were trying to pull the Ruthenians away from the oil fields so they could destroy the wells, reversing progress US engineers had made. The whole drive down the highway and the siege of Fort Seminole was a large-scale feint, as far as he could tell. It should have worked. The Ruthenians should have pulled forces over to defend Lvov. They didn't. Why? Their inaction remained a mystery.

174

The feint down the highway had a secondary purpose of exposing US weakness, while inflicting casualties the partisans hoped would strengthen antiwar sentiment in the US. They certainly managed to inflict US casualties, but whether they were exposing US weakness remained to be seen.

Was there more to the partisan strategy? The current battle was the wrong fight for them, a slugfest against US forces that could call on far more firepower than them, rather than hit and run raids that avoided US firepower while inflicting continuous pinprick casualties. Stalin was notoriously willing to spend Soviet lives for important objectives though. Maybe he was willing to pay the price in partisan blood to inflict US casualties.

Why was Meandrov staying out of the war so far? Lang's intelligence gave an intriguing but difficult to understand answer. The Americans were, so far, quietly and deniably urging him to delay any attack. That made little sense. Was it true? Why would Americans want to keep Meandrov out of the war? That mystery nagged at him, making him think he was missing something important.

What did the mini war mean to Dietrich Lang? His salvage business would profit from picking up after the fighting, while battles let his embryonic military preview tactics his enemies had developed since the Donets War.

He didn't see much downside unless the war escalated further, though in the short-term the US looked stronger now. Unless the partisans took Fort Seminole, US prestige would rise, especially with local powers getting a reminder of what US air power could do. In the long-run though, victory at Fort Seminole would deny the US a needed wake-up call. From Lang's point of view, that was good. An easy US victory at Fort Seminole might also tilt Stalin toward a cautious, arms-length relationship with Lang's network. That didn't make sense after the way Nazi/Soviet alliances worked out for the Soviets in the past, but Stalin, ruthless as he was, was ultimately a fool, blinded by his successes inside the Soviet Union and thinking the outside world was as easily manipulated.

Another Nazi/Soviet pact? Lang smiled. Why not? The Soviets needed to keep the US off-balance, and Lang's network needed more weapons and places to train.

He glanced down at a picture on his desk. Amber McCormick, blindfolded and tied to a chair, but seemingly calm and in control. *I had her in my hands, and she beat me.* That bothered him, nagged at his mind, though he tried to push thoughts of her away. *When I control Germany, I can have a dozen like her.* He wished that Amber herself could be among them, but that decision was already made. Amber McCormick was a dead woman walking.

Chapter Thirty-One: Fort Seminole Days and Nights

The siege of Fort Seminole went on, day blending into night and then into the next day. Captain Murphy didn't see much daylight, though what he saw was beautiful, nearly perfect summer days with lazy white clouds. The days would have been perfect without the gunpowder smell and the dust from artillery strikes. The risk of sudden death if a round hit nearby was an issue too, of course, but after a while people tuned it out more than they should have. The partisan big guns didn't fire much during the day. B-25s orbiting the battlefield were too ready to swarm any partisan artillery that revealed itself and too effective at taking out the gunners.

US artillery and aircraft ruled the days, making partisan movement difficult and deadly. At night, the partisans came into their own, rushing trucks down the highway with food and ammunition for the siege. Then, in the wee hours of the morning, partisan heavy artillery opened up, followed by attacks along the front, with reserves ready to exploit any breakthrough. In other words, every night was a replay of the strategy that had almost overrun Fort Seminole.

Three nights. Three attacks stopped cold.

The US had too much firepower, even at night with the planes mostly grounded. US transports brought in men to replace the casualties. They brought in enough anti-tank and anti-personnel mines to create ever thicker belts around the front. They brought in more anti-tank guns and bazookas. They even managed, through some logistics wizardry, to bring in heavy artillery to match the partisan big guns.

As intelligence officer, Captain Murphy supervised prisoner interrogations and sorted through the notes from them. There were enough prisoners from the first night's attack that some had to be transferred to POW camps in Germany. Captain Murphy tried to get a sense of the partisans from the interrogations. They mostly fell into three categories. Many were veterans of partisan fighting against the Germans, Red Army men cut off by the Germans or locals. More than half were new recruits, trained since the Donets War. Maybe ten percent were Soviet soldiers or KGB agents sent to stiffen partisan units or provide specialists—logistics and artillery guys, combat engineers and tank crews.

He didn't see either of the men he fought in the warehouse. Nobody with the injuries he inflicted came through the prisoner of war lists, which probably meant they were dead.

The press remained in Fort Seminole, still sending breathless stories comparing Fort Seminole to the Alamo, but tension noticeably eased. US firepower, along with the constant airstrikes, had to be bleeding the partisans white. Despite the tanks and heavy artillery, they weren't trained or equipped to go toe-to-toe with a modern army.

On the fourth morning, Colonel Rock called his officers together. "We're seeing signs of desperation on the partisan side. This isn't the kind of war they can win. Federov is looking for a way out, offering to withdraw if we agree to stay on base and not bother his convoys. They should have withdrawn after they didn't overrun the base. I don't understand why they are fighting our kind of war, but I'm glad they are."

They have cards they haven't played. Captain Murphy was sure of that.

When the meeting ended, he walked out into a nearly cloudless late morning. The artillery was briefly silent, and nothing was flying right now. The rations and ammunition were mostly in the warehouses, with enough progress that he was officially released from warehouse duty, a huge relief.

Envoy McCormick strode down the street, with two MPs escorting him and reporters following at a respectful distance. The Envoy motioned for Captain Murphy to come over. "I need to ask you something."

Captain Murphy hesitated. "Does Colonel Rock need to be in on this?"

"You can tell him about the conversation, but I'm looking for an intelligence guy's opinion."

Captain Murphy nodded. "I've been on warehouse duty lately, but what's on your mind?"

"As you know, the partisans are fighting our fight, in the open where our firepower can hammer them. I think I know what they want. I just don't see how this kind of fighting gets it for them."

"I can't even figure out what they're trying to do," Captain Murphy said.

"Stalin wants to make us chase them back to the Marshes and get bogged down in a nasty, death of a thousand cuts war." Envoy McCormick shrugged. "Taking the fort would do it, but their chances of doing that go down every night, and if they lose enough men here, it doesn't matter if we chase them into the Marshes because we'll win there anyway."

Captain Murphy nodded. Goading the US into fighting for the Marshes made sense from Stalin's point of view. "Causing US casualties here makes a certain Stalin kind of sense."

"It does, but how do they plan to get from here to pulling the US into the Marshes after them?"

That was a good question. "Maybe they figure that if they do the same thing with more men, tanks and artillery they can break through again." He realized he didn't believe that. The partisans, up through the breakthrough night, fought a smart war. "Maybe they think that if they kill enough Americans we'll give up."

"Chances of that happening soon ended when reporters compared Fort Seminole to the Alamo," Envoy McCormick said. "The partisans may not understand Americans enough to know that, so they could be trying to cause as many casualties as they can, with nothing else in mind, but I don't believe that. Stalin likes to think he's the smartest, most ruthless man in the room. He has something up his sleeve. I wish I knew what it was."

Captain Murphy nodded. The Envoy's concerns reinforced his. "They're up to something. If I figure out what, I'll tell you." He scanned the horizon, watching US artillery systematically pounding the partisans. "You're up to something too. Ready to tell me what?"

The envoy grimaced. "Moving US armored divisions here would be nice, but the Poles claim they don't have enough railroad or highway capacity to do it fast. They may even be right. The Germans did a lot of damage on their way out and the Poles don't have the money to fix it. We've been trying to shake money loose from Congress to help them, but the Poles haven't made themselves loved there. Too many border issues. We may have options, but don't get your hopes up."

"I'm sure Stalin noticed how long it's taking to get US ground reinforcements here," Captain Murphy said.

The envoy nodded. "Along with everyone else in Europe. We'll have to fix that." He sighed. "The Poles are probably stalling because we came down hard on them. They have a militia of Polish exiles from Lvov and were gearing up to send it in. Save the city from the Russians, then stay and make it part of Poland, all without formally bringing in the Polish army. They hand Stalin a fait accompli and hope he doesn't come across the border to kick them out." He shook his head. "We threatened to cut off all aid and so far that has stopped them but getting US divisions across Poland suddenly got much harder."

"Polish militia might be a decent answer," Captain Murphy said. "Proxy army versus proxy army."

"Except the Czechs have been quietly training a Ruthenian army in eastern Czechoslovakia. The Czechs want an independent Ruthenia or Ukraine, whichever you want to call it, because it would give them access to the oil, which they won't get if the Poles grab the oil fields. If the Polish militia goes in, the Ruthenians would go in too, almost certainly beat the Polish militia. Then the

Polish army would go in and draw in the Soviets. Three-cornered war with us in the center of it. No thanks."

"Sometimes I hate this part of the world," Captain Murphy said.

Envoy McCormick nodded. "We're the guy in the ring with tigers. One wrong move and they all pounce on us, or each other. Welcome to my world." He smiled grimly and walked on. "Keep thinking about what the partisans are up to."

Captain Murphy took that as a dismissal and walked away. What *were* the partisans up to? What could they gain by keeping their troops in this fight? Maybe Stalin didn't trust the partisan leadership and wanted Federov's forces ground down. Could the Soviets be planning to send more warplanes to challenge US control of the air? The Soviets had thousands of US Lend-Lease planes they could send to partisan airbases, and plenty of "volunteer" pilots to loan. But US jets would meet any such challenge and drive hostile planes from the sky. A massive sneak air attack might work, but the US was better prepared for partisan air raids now, and undoubtedly had planes standing by in neighboring countries if Fort Seminole's airfield was unusable or if partisans sent more planes than the base could handle.

What are they up to? He spent hours at a cramped desk in the command bomb-shelter poring over prisoner interrogation notes, looking for clues,. He typed a report summarizing the interrogations, then sat and stared at it. Was Envoy McCormick right about Stalin's motives? Was this siege intended to lure US forces into the Marshes? Maybe that was part of Stalin's plan. Testing, and maybe humiliating the US had to be part of it too.

The other provisional governors weren't acting as expected. The partisan threat to Lvov should have drawn Ruthenian forces away from the oil fields so the partisans could wreck them. The Ruthenians had to have nerves of hardened steel plate to leave Lvov undefended and dare the partisans to take the city. Captain Murphy wouldn't have believed the Ruthenian government could call the partisan bluff. Then there was governor Meandrov. Why was he staying out of the fight? He couldn't expect Stalin to forgive him. His inaction would look disloyal to the Americans and holding out for more aid now would backfire.

Then there were the Poles. They wanted their 1939 borders back, everything that had been Polish between the wars. The drive on Lvov gave them an excuse to send in forces and refuse to withdraw. Of course, the Poles sending in their forces would probably start World War III, but Captain McCormick's sense of the current Polish government was that they would risk war for the disputed lands. A lot of exiled Poles wanted to come home, which meant intense pressure on the Polish government to seize border areas.

Opportunity. Pressure from exiles. Yet the Poles remained on the sidelines. That was good, but it didn't fit with Captain Murphy's view of them. The discrepancy bothered him like a jagged hangnail. He turned in the report, then realized that he had a strange ten pm to two am duty officer shift. That meant he had the afternoon off, hopefully to catch some sleep.

He stepped outside and was shocked to discover it was already mid-afternoon, and hot. He hurried to the bomb shelter and slept, hoping the many mysteries of the siege would seem less mysterious when he woke up.

He woke with time to spare before his shift and took the walk he intended to take in the afternoon. It was twilight but still warm. Partisan artillery would probably start shelling soon. The base seemed almost deserted and for a second he had a weird thought that he might be the last American survivor of some clever partisan attack. The more rational side of his mind told him that the heat, plus risks from partisan big guns, made wandering around outside dangerous.

He strode back toward the bomb shelter but paused when Sergeant Duncan waved, then pulled his battered jeep over. "Nice night for a stroll, sir."

"That it isn't. What are you doing here?"

"Mail run." Sergeant Duncan stared up at the captain. "Any idea what the partisans are up to? I drove back from the front and my finger started itching. I got here and it started throbbing." He

182

held up his hand and pointed to where the finger should have been. "Itching means I'm missing something dangerous. Throbbing means 'You're about to get yourself killed, you idiot'."

"And you take this seriously?"

"It works. Some trick of my mind, things I sense but can't put in words."

"Sort of like the 'I'm forgetting something' feeling," Captain Murphy said. "Could be useful."

"It has saved my ass more times than I can count," Sergeant Duncan said. He waved the hand. "I only have an ass left to put in this seat because of the finger."

"Can your phantom finger tell you why you're in danger?" Captain Murphy felt silly for asking, but he took old soldier hunches seriously.

"It's not magic," Sergeant Duncan said. "It's something I can sense. Something is deadly wrong."

"Their heavy artillery getting ready to fire? A partisan air raid coming?" Artillery fire remained sporadic. A breakthrough would have meant an upsurge. *Unless the partisans used gas.* He mentioned that possibility, but Sergeant Duncan shook his head.

Captain Murphy sighed. "I want to take you seriously, but you make it tough."

"Want a ride somewhere?" Sergeant Duncan asked.

"I'm just restless."

"Me too. Hop in."

Sergeant Duncan drove around the base, seemingly at random. He drew suspicious looks from MPs but didn't get stopped. The drive took them deep among the warehouses.

"Throbbing is getting worse."

Captain Murphy felt something too. *Something wrong. Something I'm missing.*

Sergeant Duncan abruptly turned toward a warehouse, sending the jeep toward the huge front door. A sentry should have challenged the vehicle, but no challenge came. The front door was closed, but it abruptly opened. A guy in an ill-fitting US uniform started to wave them through, then abruptly grabbed for his sidearm.

Sergeant Duncan slewed the jeep around and raced away. "Partisans!"

The guy at the warehouse door didn't fire at them as they raced away.

"I've worked in warehouses at night. There is something off there."

Captain Murphy tried to remember what was in that warehouse. Not explosives. "It's mostly rations." What else? Fuel maybe. The transports brought more fuel than they could store properly, but the excess was dispersed in jerry cans to minimize chance of fire.

What could the partisans do with gasoline? *I don't want to find out.* He radioed the MPs, directing them toward the warehouse. "I hope your finger knows what it's doing."

"That's probably the only time I'll hear those words in a sentence."

"It's the only time I'll say them."

Did the partisans infiltrate men into the base tonight or during previous nights? Did they come in during the earlier incursion and hide out? Neither possibility was reassuring.

"What are they planning?" He asked that aloud, though he didn't expect an answer.

"Has to be something big," Sergeant Duncan said. "They're taking a pasting out there. We broke out the special sauce--artillery shells with proximity fuses."

MPs were converging on the partisan-occupied warehouse. Captain Murphy shook his head. Sabotaging or burning down a warehouse would hurt, but it wasn't big enough. The partisans had something else in mind.

"It's a distraction," Captain Murphy said. "They're drawing the MPs away from something else." Did that make sense? *The MPs are going in because we caught the partisans.* Maybe the partisans had intended to draw the MPs in some way, starting fires in the warehouse.

"If you were the partisan commander and you wanted to make the US come after you, what would you target?" Captain Murphy asked. "What would hurt the most?"

"Kill Envoy McCormick?" Sergeant Duncan steered the jeep down a street, apparently randomly. "Kidnap him back to the Marshes? He shouldn't be here. He knows too much."

McCormick as the main target made some sense, but Captain Murphy didn't buy it. "Anything else?"

The partisans inside the base had to be specially trained men, Red Army commandos instead of local partisans. *What would I do with men like that inside Fort Seminole?*

A firefight broke out behind them at the warehouse. The firing should at least wake everyone in Fort Seminole up. He wondered briefly if that was the point. Get people outside when the partisan big guns could hit Fort Seminole without interference from US B-25s. That still didn't feel big enough though.

Captain Murphy's mind kept circling back to what was coming. It had to be big, or it wasn't worth doing, not at the cost of the partisan casualties over the last three days. *What is that big?* Something that delivered the fort to them? That would be worth the casualties, but how could the partisans pull it off with a few dozen infiltrators or even a hundred?

The fighting intensified behind them, drawing his attention back to the warehouse. Maybe burning the warehouse was all the partisans planned. Maybe their leadership was being stupid when it left the partisans fighting US firepower the partisans couldn't match. Maybe whatever plan they had depended on them capturing the warehouse undetected.

Amber McCormick strode out of a bomb shelter in front of them, looking as calm and in control as ever. She smiled and held up a thumb in the classic hitchhiker's gesture. Sergeant Duncan stopped the jeep, started to tell her to go back inside, then she was in the jeep.

"Active night," she said.

"Too active," Captain Murphy said. "You need to be inside."

"Actually, I need to be out here." Her smile went away. "The partisans will make their move tonight, go for broke. No place in Fort Seminole is safe. I might as well be where I can see what is coming."

"What do you think is coming?" Captain Murphy asked. "Do you know something I need to know?"

That didn't seem likely, though Envoy McCormick could have sources of information he didn't share with base command. But would he share them with his daughter? That would be unprofessional but having her here was unprofessional too.

"I don't know anything you don't," Amber said. "But the partisans are running out of time. Every day they don't take Fort Seminole, they get weaker. We will have US armored divisions here within a week, and those divisions may not find much to fight if the air force keeps pounding the partisans. Fort Seminole is the Air Force's chance to show that it can win wars on its own and it is pouring everything it has into the fight. The air force is wrong about winning wars on their own, but they can cause a lot of havoc. The partisans have to move before they can't."

"Okay, that I knew," Captain Murphy said. "But what are they going to do that's worth the pounding?"

"Something the US can't ignore. Something that forces us to follow them into the Marshes and gut ourselves trying to root them out. Something like the Berlin bombings."

That made sense as far as it went, but Captain Murphy still couldn't see what would do that. "We know the goal, but what are they planning to do? What would force us to do that? It has to be something big. How can they do something big with a few dozen infiltrators?"

"It doesn't have to be big," Amber said. "It just has to look big to reporters."

"Crap!" That made entirely too much sense. Captain Murphy's mind flitted through the possibilities. Something spectacular. Something that killed a lot of reporters? No. They had to be alive to report whatever it was. Maybe the partisans would capture the reporters and make them watch something horrific.

His mind kept spinning through possibilities and finding no reason the partisans kept fighting here, to his growing frustration.

"Maybe they're just trying to kill as many Americans as they can," Sergeant Duncan said. "Maybe they want our attention here while the Soviets do something in Germany or Asia."

Those were all possibilities, but the partisans planned something here, tonight. Captain Murphy could feel it, his old soldier instincts warning him like Sergeant Duncan's finger did.

"Your dad is a huge prize," Sergeant Duncan said. "He knows too much to be here."

"They wouldn't capture him alive," Amber said. Her face tightened. "None of us need to know the details."

"He still shouldn't be here," Captain Murphy said. "You shouldn't be here." He barely controlled the urge to say more. Amber had already experienced the risks and Envoy McCormick understood them. The Envoy, at least, had an incentive to make sure Fort Seminole held out, and he certainly spurred the military to give the fort maximum support. That triggered an idea that quickly flitted away. "Crap! I almost had something." Captain Murphy circled back. Envoy McCormick was here, making sure the fort got what it needed, communicating with top brass. "Coding machines. He has them here. If they can grab them…" He thought through the implications. The US could change its codes, but if the partisans captured the Envoy's coding machines they could work through past intercepts, giving them insights into US thinking and logistics. The machines would be a major prize, but even if the partisans grabbed the machines, how could they get them out of Fort Seminole?

They had a narrow window tonight. *How would I do it?* Create a distraction. Have infiltrators seize Envoy McCormick and the coding machines. Put everything they had into opening a corridor long enough to get the coding machines out.

The attack would have to be fast. The US had procedures to destroy code books and machines if they were threatened.

Amber looked worried. "And they wouldn't take dad alive. They wouldn't expect to, but if the attack was sudden enough they might get the code machines."

Was that the partisan plan? It felt right. The infiltrators would be scrambling after being discovered in the warehouse. The attack had to happen soon though, because a breakthrough in daylight, with B-25s overhead, was unlikely.

"Get base command on the radio," Amber said. "Tell them what you suspect." She winced. "That's a suggestion, not an order."

Captain Murphy shrugged. "It needs doing." He tried, but the frequency was jammed. That was new and unwelcome. He tried alternate frequencies but couldn't get through. "The partisans must have a Soviet electronics warfare team here." That was a major escalation. How far was Stalin willing to go the take Fort Seminole? Massive jamming was pushing deniability further than it would stretch. "Head to wherever the code machines are." He wasn't sure where that was. Envoy McCormick, he realized, kept his base location a secret. But the partisans must have figured it out. *And Amber probably knows.*

"They may not know where he is," Amber said. "We could lead them to him."

That seemed unlikely. If code machines were the partisan objective, they would have scouted the base thoroughly. Still, she might be right. "Okay. We'll go to base command."

Sergeant Duncan steered the jeep to the command bunker, where they roused Colonel Rock. Captain Murphy explained what he suspected.

"We can check it out," Colonel Rock said. He turned to the radio, then swore. "Jammed. Something big is about to happen." He sent runners to the base's electronic warfare team. "Maybe they can find where the partisan transmitters are so we can hit them. They have to be close."

The base radar was also 'jammed', with the sky full of mylar strips that made it nearly impossible to spot aircraft among the reflections. "Jamming and radar busting," Captain Murphy said. "They're going all out." A massive partisan air attack? Maybe, but could the partisans pull off a night attack? "The jammer is also a radio beacon. Their pilots are homing on it."

That meant the US had to get planes in the air but that meant lighting up the airstrips, making them better targets for partisan artillery. Colonel Rock had apparently already figured out the trade-off. He called on the base phone to get planes in the air. They weren't night fighters, but at least they wouldn't be caught on the ground.

Did the partisans have dedicated night bombers? The Soviets did but sending those planes would be a blatant intervention. US Lend Lease planes or captured German ones were deniable. Actual Soviet-built planes felt like they would step over a line. But maybe Stalin was willing to cross that line too.

The radio jamming was persistent and thorough, making mobile communication within the base nearly impossible and getting messages to the outside world iffy.

Envoy McCormick showed up at the command bunker, looking grim. "We know why they sacrificed those partisans. It was a giant electronic warfare operation."

That was a new slant on the attacks. Were they designed so the partisans could ferret out US radio and radar frequencies? Maybe.

"That's probably not all they're planning," Captain Murphy said. He glanced at Colonel Rock. "Mind if I tell him my theory?"

"Why not?"

The Envoy listened, then nodded. "They might try grabbing the coding machines and settings, but we should be ready for them. We already had a drill when they broke through earlier. We weren't far from destroying the coding machines before the counter-attack."

The radio and radar jamming didn't fit with the code machine raid idea, Captain Murphy thought. *Maybe I was overthinking it.* Maybe the partisans figured they could take Fort Seminole with the jamming and an air raid, along with disruptions from their infiltrators.

"The jamming takes out a lot of our advantages," Captain Murphy said. "Using interior lines to shift forces, sophisticated artillery tactics--it all takes communications, and ours just went back to foot runners."

That wasn't quite true. Jeeps could help some. Motorcycles would help more, but Fort Seminole didn't have enough. In the core of the base, phones would help too. Still, switching forces to seal off a breakthrough would get slower. *We don't have room to be slow.* A partisan tank division could slice through from the front lines to the command bunker in fifteen minutes if it kept rolling, probably less.

"We can lose this in a hurry," Colonel Rock said. "It's do or die tonight."

A heavy rumble shook the bomb shelter, almost as though his words were a signal. The rumble continued, got heavier. The lights flickered, then came back up, probably on generator power now.

A soldier knocked on the door. "Phones are out, most of them."

"Crap! That's what the infiltrators were after." Captain Murphy thought through the implications. The fort's phone network couldn't substitute for radios, but would have helped, especially if the defenders got pushed back to the center of the fort. *And now it's gone.*

They had to repair the lines, but partisan infiltrators would snipe at the repair people. "We need to hunt down the infiltrators before they screw up anything else."

That was stating the obvious, Captain Murphy realized, but Colonel Rock simply nodded.

A partisan air raid was going on above them, heavy and continuous. *How are they finding the fort?* Homing on the partisan radio jamming, then looking for fires the infiltrators set for final coordinates. It all made sense.

How accurate could night-bombing be, even with the jamming source as a beacon and the fires as terminal guidance?

190

Hopefully not very accurate. The pilots, at least some of them, would be Soviet air force "volunteers."

"How far can Stalin push us before he sees B-29s over his bunker?" Captain Murphy asked.

"He's close," Envoy McCormick said. "This is an invasion in everything but name."

The bombs kept shaking the ground, wave after wave of them, mingled with partisan heavy artillery.. With the radios useless and most phone lines cut, the command shelter was largely cut off. A few runners brought news from the front, along with a few calls from the remaining phone lines. Partisans were attacking all around the front lines where commanders were still in contact. Which attacks were decoys, and which were attempts at a breakthrough? Reports were too fragmented to tell.

"It's down to our guys fighting them at ten to one odds," Captain Murphy said. He felt useless cowering in the command shelter. Partisan tanks could already have broken through, could be rounding up survivors in the fort and gathering to attack holdouts in their bomb shelters. He might not hear small arms fire among the near-continuous explosions or even know if partisan tanks were systematically taking out bomb shelters. Breaking into the bomb shelters wouldn't be easy, but they wouldn't be easy to defend either.

Finally, the bombing stopped. Captain Murphy cautiously stepped out to get a look at the damage. He couldn't see that well in darkness punctuated with fires, but what he saw looked in rough shape, with runways and streets cratered and warehouses and barracks burning. About half the Skyraiders were apparently knocked out, though air force guys swarmed around them, salvaging guns and munitions. Partisan big guns still pounded the fort, but their fire now seemed concentrated on the front. An MP yelled, "Keep your heads down. Snipers."

Five MPs sprawled on the dark street, emphasizing the point. Firefighters braved artillery fire and snipers, trying to salvage what they could from flaming warehouses.

A truck with heavy machine guns mounted in the back raced by, with MPs firing the machine guns at a warehouse. When the machine guns went silent, a rifle cracked, the shot whining by where Captain Murphy's head had been seconds earlier. He swore. The MP machine gun fired at the muzzle flash, probably too late. The sniper would have moved as soon as he shot. And the sniper could have been a woman, Captain Murphy reminded himself. The Soviets used a lot of women snipers against the Germans.

At least the fort's loudspeakers still worked. The air raid siren stopped but was quickly replaced by a double pulse followed by someone saying, "Incoming partisan tanks. Emergency deployment stations. This is not a drill."

Captain Murphy didn't recognize the voice and for a second he wondered if partisan infiltrators had seized the loudspeaker network. They could be trying to get men out of their bomb shelters for the snipers or for another air raid. *And if I keep thinking like that I'll paranoid myself to death.*

Men deployed, setting up barricades around the core of the fort. The moves looked chaotic but went a lot faster than the first night. US anti-aircraft guns were still set up for ground support as well as anti-aircraft roles.

Several Soviet planes were shattered, flaming wrecks, burning in the remnants of barracks. Captain Murphy spotted what looked like a B-29, but with partisan markings. "Where did that thing come from?"

Captain Murphy didn't expect an answer, but Envoy McCormick said, "The Soviets reverse engineered one of ours that had to land in the Soviet Union. We'll want that wreckage."

I can think of things we need more. Aloud, Captain Murphy said, "If the fort holds out, I'm sure we'll send it off." He turned to the envoy. "How is sending strategic bombers to raid a US base not an act of war?"

"It's an act of war when it's in the US interest that it be an act of war." Envoy McCormick looked grim. "But what does winning a war with the Soviets look like? Do we want to still be here twenty years from now? Do we want to add ten times as many square miles to what we hold now? Cold, nasty, harsh land that turns to swamp half the year and into Antarctica the rest? Do we want to occupy the largest country in the world, full of people who hate each other and us? Once we took more, how would we get out? We break it, we own it. We already own too much of it. Hitler was a fool for invading this place. President Truman isn't a fool." He stopped abruptly, looking as though he regretted the outburst. " Stalin will pay for what he does here, but we'll decide how."

"Did your plan include them jamming us, bringing in a mass night air raid and infiltrating elite Soviet snipers?"

The envoy shot him an angry glance, and Captain Murphy shut up. *If this is part of a plan, the plan sucks.*

"As the military says, no plan survives contact with the enemy," Envoy McCormick said. The words were mild, but with an angry edge to them.

I may have just ended my military career. Captain Murphy found it difficult to care, with the fort in ruins, maybe minutes from being overrun.

He turned away. Someone was firing off a lot of heavy artillery on the north side of the line. Where was the partisan breakthrough? If they broke through they would be here in minutes. Was the breakthrough even real?

The snipers were certainly real and dangerous in a sporadic, nerve-wracking way, though the darkness kept them from being as devastating as they could have been. Captain Murphy had been under sniper fire before, but this brought back his visceral hatred of them. *Not many snipers make it to POW camps.*

Where did Amber get to? He lost track of her when he went into the command area of the bomb shelter and didn't see her when he came out. *I hope she has enough sense to stay under cover.* That was hope, not a realistic expectation.

"She'll get herself killed." Captain Murphy said that aloud, then hoped Envoy McCormick wasn't close enough to hear. Or maybe it would be better if he heard it. *She shouldn't be here. He shouldn't be here.*

He saw Sergeant Duncan crouched behind an improvised barricade built from a wrecked truck and sandbags. Amber was beside the Sergeant, barely recognizable in a too-large helmet, holding a rifle. She popped up and fired at a muzzle blast from a warehouse, the action quick and smooth.

Captain Murphy unslung his rifle and ran to the improvised barricade. Communications were so screwed up that he couldn't command anything, even if he knew enough to issue meaningful commands. *Sometimes it comes down to being a rifleman.*

He glanced at Amber. "What are you doing here?"

"Hunting snipers." She shrugged. "Nowhere safe here anyway." She glanced at him. "Keep your head down. One of their snipers is making it personal."

Two shots thudded into the sandbags near her. "Okay. Two of them are making it personal. You may not want to be around me."

"Got my missing finger throbbing," Sergeant Duncan said. "Not that I needed warning."

They fell silent. The truck's heavy machine guns kept firing at a warehouse and taking return fire, but the artillery fire paused briefly, leaving what felt like silence, though it was filled with rifle fire, shouts and moans. Corpsmen rushed past with stretchers, though the fort's hospital was on fire. Captain Murphy popped up and shot at a recent sniper muzzle flash, not expecting to hit anything.

A US light tank trundled up the street and fired its main gun at the warehouse where the snipers were holed up. The sniper fire stopped, but the tank kept firing, shredding the warehouse wall, tossing pallets into the air and setting something with pork in it afire, sending frying meat smell across the fort and reminding Captain Murphy that he couldn't remember the last time he ate.

Three partisans ran out, on fire. The tank crew shot them.

Captain Murphy pulled his thoughts together. The infiltration had other motives, but Envoy McCormick's coding machines would still be a tempting target.

Colonel Rock was trying to pull command back together. Some snipers were out of the way, letting jeeps and runners send commands. Nobody had a clear picture of where the partisan pressure was greatest. Was there a breakthrough? If so, what was the priority? Protect base command? Secure the code machines?

"Colonel needs your bird back in the air," a runner said. That made sense, though Captain Murphy wasn't sure how much he could see tonight. Muzzle flashes maybe? That would be better than what they had. *Flying the helicopter at night, though.* That made his hands grow clammy. *I can do it, I think.* It didn't help that the moon was behind high clouds. He nodded anyway, told Sergeant Duncan where he was going and threaded his way through the wreckage to the helicopter.

#

Sergeant Duncan felt forgotten at the improvised barricade. He wanted to get back to the front but had been ordered to provide security here. Right now, that meant a sniper duel with snipers who for some reason had zeroed in on Amber or Sergeant Duncan. The sniper was remarkably focused, passing up clearer shots for long moments after the tank destroyed another snipers' nest, then missing Sergeant Duncan by inches when he moved. Amber fired back. She looked competent, though he couldn't tell if her shots were hitting near the muzzle flashes.

A sniper duel on a moonless night. It felt nightmarish. Only the fires spread through Fort Seminole made it possible and the flickering fires sent shadows dancing, making it hard to tell movements from tricks of light.

Human eyes adapted to low light remarkably well though. He had been inside, in light and his eyes hadn't completely adapted. *And their eyes have.* That advantage could easily get him killed. "I'm on my nineth life here. None left to spare."

His missing finger kept throbbing, becoming a background ache.

Two more shots thudded in, way too close. "Did you spit in their vodka or did I?"

"I guess I did," Amber said. "They were gunning for me before you came."

Sergeant Duncan knew that good snipers were loners, quirky. They might not know who they were shooting at, but once they selected a target they could obsess on taking it down. *And she may have killed one of their team.*

He had trouble seeing the Amber he met earlier in the version beside him tonight, quiet, patient and apparently quite good with a rifle.

"You ever shoot before?"

"A rifle? Of course. I have five older brothers."

He wasn't sure why that mattered. He circled back to Captain Murphy's theory about partisans grabbing Envoy McCormick's coding machines.

"Know where your dad was headquartered?"

She nodded. "Code machines, right? I'll take you there."

He opened his mouth to protest, then realized he had no idea where to go. "We need permission."

"They assigned you to protect command assets, right? They didn't say where."

That was true and a dozen guys were milling around the improvised barricade. At least going would get her away from the snipers. They shouldn't know one shadowy figure from another. That reminded him that he was still carrying the night vision scope. He tried it out again and found that it helped, but the infrared beam didn't reach the warehouse the snipers were holed up in. "Not useless, but not a sniper-killer."

They slipped away, treading carefully along the wreckage-strewn street until they put a barracks between themselves and the warehouse's snipers. *They need to send a tank against that nest too.*

The barracks also cut them off from the flames that gave them some light. The darkness was deep enough that Sergeant

Duncan slid his feet along the ground to keep from tripping on wreckage. He lost track of Amber, then thudded into her.

"Careful," she said. "Guards will be jumpy." She paused. "Why aren't you using your night scope?"

That was a good question. He turned it on and got a blurry greenish view of the street. "I didn't want to kill my night vision," he said, then added, "Or maybe I forgot."

She nodded, the motion a green blur. "Tell me if I'm about to fall in a crater."

They picked their way down the street. Sergeant Duncan got used to the night vision scope, though it looked as though he was shining a flashlight that turned everything blurry green. He felt exposed, which he would be if partisans had night scopes too. That wouldn't surprise him, though the gadget might be too bulky for infiltrators to bother with.

"We should be seeing MPs," Amber said.

Sergeant Duncan swept the street with the night vision scope. "No sign of them." His finger had subsided. Now it throbbed again. *Just tell me what I need to know, you imaginary piece of shit.*

He spotted a body on the ground in front of an open door. "No MPs, unless one is dead in the street."

She pulled the scope down so she could look through it, then swore. "That's the place. Infiltrators must be here, or maybe already left."

He saw no sign of partisans or anyone else. This section of street was an island of calm in the battle, though shots and explosions echoed around them, muted by the buildings.

"There is a bomb shelter under the building," Amber said. "Dad took it over."

Sergeant Duncan listened, trying to sort sounds from inside the building from the battle sounds. Nothing. They crept closer. The dead guy was an MP. Two more MPs were sprawled inside the door, in puddles of blood, then a scattering of MPs who took refuge behind desks and died there. No sign of whoever killed them. The battle here probably went unnoticed among the sniper fire, bombing and artillery.

Were the partisans gone?

"The bomb shelter would have been closed when the partisans attacked up here," Amber whispered. "It might already have been locked because of the air raids."

How would the partisans break into the bomb shelter? Would bazookas do it? Military grade explosives against the walls? Sergeant Duncan wasn't sure. Maybe guards were still holding out down there. He stopped again and listened. Still silence, then muffled voices. Russian? He thought so but wasn't sure. *We should have brought more men.*

Something heavy thumped below them. Truck engines sounded outside. Amber stood by the hatch to the bomb shelter, while Sergeant Duncan crept back to the door. Two Russian armored trucks eased up, their lights off. A dozen men deployed to cover the street in both directions, while six more headed for the door. *Eighteen to two, plus more in the trucks. I wasn't planning to live forever.*

Sergeant Duncan tossed a grenade under one of the trucks, then fired as fast as he could pull the trigger until his rifle emptied, swapped clips and went through the second one. The partisans heading toward the door fell, several of them yelling in Russian, apparently thinking they were under friendly fire. The grenade under the truck cut down partisans closest to it and the remaining guys in the truck scrambled out.

Sergeant Duncan tossed his last grenade into the biggest cluster of partisans, then slammed the door and ducked away. Pinpricks of light appeared in the door when the partisans shot through it. Sergeant Duncan swore. The building wasn't built to fight from. Rifle bullets could go through the walls and heavy machine guns or bazookas would cut through them like a chainsaw through cheese. They did offer concealment, but that went both ways. He had no idea where the partisans were.

"How many?" Amber eased back from the hatch, her rifle still pointed at it.

"Two truckloads. Maybe twenty. I got some of them." How many? Not enough. "The trucks broke through. How many more behind them?"

That was the real problem. Even if they could hold out here, Fort Seminole was probably getting overrun.

"Three hours to daylight," Amber said. "That's our only hope."

Sergeant Duncan nodded. The short summer nights might help, but three hours was plenty of time for the partisans to finish taking the fort. After that, US air force firepower wouldn't help much. The partisans might even use their captives as human shields. "It would take armored divisions to help us now."

"That may happen," Amber said. She bit her lip, the motion barely visible through the night vision scope. "Something I shouldn't have overheard but did. Forget I said anything."

"Unless it happens fast, any rescue will just give us a proper burial." He wondered if Ruslana would ever know what happened to him. He didn't have much family left in the states and what there was wouldn't miss him.

He hastily overturned heavy iron desks, making improvised firing positions. Would the desks stop a rifle bullet? He didn't know. They wouldn't stop a heavy machine gun, or the twenty-millimeter light cannons mounted on the truck.

Bullets stopped coming through the door. Why? Maybe because the partisans had people inside, trying to get the coding machines out. That was another complication. Partisans in the bomb shelter would come out eventually. Was the hatch the only way they could go? Probably not. Bomb shelters always had an emergency exit. Too easy to get trapped without one.

"They can get the code machines out without coming through us," he whispered. He felt a brief guilty flash of relief. *We don't have to die.* But the partisans could wreak havoc with the code machines and if they overran the fort they would capture Amber and him. Locals whispered about camps deep in Siberia where the Soviets worked prisoners to death in the deadly Siberian winters.

The partisans would smuggle Amber to the Soviet Union and torture her, hoping the envoy let something important slip in front of her. "You might want to save a bullet for yourself."

If her face changed, he couldn't tell it in the nightscope's fuzzy green light.

Chapter Thirty-Two: Night Sky Over Fort Seminole

Both sides were blazing away at any noise from the sky, as Captain Murphy quickly discovered. He tried to stay oriented by focusing on the warehouse fires but had trouble figuring out where he was, much less seeing the battle. He wanted desperately to set the helicopter down as soon as he figured out how difficult flying it was, but dreaded landing even more than flying. He had flown conventional planes at night, though rarely, and flew the helicopter on one emergency mission with a full moon, but this was horribly different.

I'm going to kill myself and not even see anything before I die.

He took a deep breath and tried to orient himself. The partisan jammer and big warehouse fires helped. *But can I figure out anything about the fighting?* Muzzle blasts sparkled like stars below him, though he wasn't sure if he was seeing rifles or heavier weapons. If the blasts were artillery, was he really seeing muzzle blasts or explosions when the shells landed? Either way, artillery might not tell him where the front lines were.

He studied the blasts, pairing muzzle blasts and explosions. Hopefully that gave him the shape of the front lines most places, though not how far from the fort they were. Could US troops fall back to new lines without fast communications? He doubted it. The partisans moved too fast.

What would a partisan breakthrough look like? He looked for differences and found a stretch where fire from the US side was light to nonexistent.

Tracers rose to greet him when he flew closer. The helicopter abruptly got harder to handle. *Crap on a stick!* He turned toward the air bases and hoped he could maintain control long enough to set down. *I'm not even sure I'm headed the right direction.*

That doubt grew in his mind. The fires and jamming gave him the right direction but only a vague idea how far he was from the runway. The helicopter got even less controllable. At least the space around the airbases wasn't cluttered by buildings, so he only had to get close to stick a landing. He reached what he thought was the edge of the airfield and descended, only to have a building loom in front of him. He veered to the side, coming down hard in the street, the helicopter tilted, partly on top of some piece of wreckage or half in a crater.

Captain Murphy grabbed a huge breath, half surprised to be alive. He pried his hands off the controls, his arms and legs feeling like rubber, then froze. Someone flashed a light in his face as he turned off the engine. They yelled in Russian-accented English for him to get out.

He swore and struggled out of the helicopter, hands away from his sidearm. He promptly fell into a bomb crater. The Russians fired. He ducked the rest of the way into the crater, realized it was only about two feet deep and yelled, "I fell! I'm not trying to escape."

The shots kept coming. He swore and tried to get his sluggish muscles moving. He fired back, not knowing what else to do, not sure how many partisans he faced or if they were in range of his sidearm. *I'm trying to surrender, you commie bastards.* He remembered stories of Siberian work camps and decided to keep fighting.

He had a rifle in the helicopter, out of reach now. He tried to cram his body into the crater while shots ricocheted off the helicopter and something blazed across his calf, leaving a burning path. He fired back blindly with his sidearm, just blazing away in the right general direction. More shots hit near him. Four people shooting? It could be more. He fired again. This time there was no return fire. He poked his head up cautiously, hoping the partisans could see as little as he could. He could barely even see the helicopter, only a few feet away. That gave him an idea. He pushed himself up to grope around in the helicopter, feeling for his rifle, while expecting to get shot. He didn't find the rifle in the dark, but his hand closed on an emergency kit. What was in there? He dropped into the dubious safety of the crater and fumbled through the kit. A flashlight, which would be worse than useless now. Rations, which would be great if the partisans let him take a snack break. Medical supplies. And a flare gun.

He closed his eyes and fired a flare, keeping them closed until he dimly saw it go off through his closed eyelids. He put a hand up to shield his eyes and opened them. Where were the partisans? He spotted two crouched three yards away and fired at them. They both grabbed their chests and fell, one moving feebly. He didn't have time to congratulate himself. Where were the others? He finally saw three guys running away. Was that it?

He jumped up and kicked the partisan rifles away. One partisan rolled over, waving empty hands and yelled, "I surrender." The partisan added in heavily accented English, "Hungry. Done with fighting. Looking for spam."

A bag of rations, probably scavenged from an overrun field kitchen, sat beside the guy, while open ration tins littered the ground nearby. *These guys are stragglers, and I interrupted their meal.* That made sense. The partisans could only get supplies in at night and probably gave ammo priority. He remembered how a late World War I German offensive lost momentum when hungry German troops overran Allied field kitchens and looted them. The siege of Fort Seminole was only a few days old, but the partisans had to be hungry.

The other partisan he shot was dead. He couldn't tell how badly wounded the hungry one was. He also had no idea where the front lines were.

"I can't take you with me," he said. "And I'd probably kill you if I try to patch your wound in the dark. I'll leave a first aid kit and the food. Then I'll take your weapons and walk away. Don't move until you're sure I'm gone."

He grabbed the partisan rifles, found his own rifle, then strode toward the airfield. When he thought he was far enough from the partisan, he paused to listen for the sounds of battle. There was plenty of rifle and artillery fire, but the sounds echoed, and he wasn't sure where they came from. He tried to match what he saw around him with his mental map of Fort Seminole and what he saw from the helicopter. If the partisans did break through, he was probably behind their lead elements. They would move fast, not stopping to mop up US resistance. That meant that he could run into partisans, trigger-happy US remnants or both.

The night just keeps getting more fun.

He heard tanks nearby, probably partisan T34s. He thought he could tell the difference between Soviet tanks sounds and US ones, though he wouldn't bet his life on it. Machine gun fire sounded a block ahead of him, then an explosion. A bazooka? Apparently. The tank noises stopped, followed by secondary explosions. *So, there are US troops up there. I just need to get to them without getting shot.*

#

Sergeant Duncan crouched behind his heavy desks and wondered what to do. The partisans would get away with Envoy McCormick's coding machines if he stayed here, assuming they captured the machines intact. That shouldn't have happened. The MPs should have given technicians in the bomb shelter enough time to destroy the machines. This whole adventure was probably pointless. Still, the partisans wouldn't put this much effort into trying to capture the machines if they didn't think they had a chance. What did that mean? A man on the inside? But if the partisans or Soviets had a spy close to Envoy McCormick they would want that spy to stay in place so he could continue to feed them information.

If they didn't have an inside man, how did the Soviets know where to come? How did they get into the bomb shelter, assuming they did? The infiltrators could have figured out which building Envoy McCormick worked from, but that didn't get them into the bomb shelter.

And none of this gets us closer to saving the code machines or getting out alive.

He glanced back at Amber. She was crouched behind two nested overturned desks. That made sense. Two layers to stop bullets instead of one. It probably wouldn't make much difference, but it was clever.

"Did you check the hatch?" he whispered.

"Locked from the inside."

What did that mean? Partisans would lock the hatch behind them, but so would Americans under attack. The dead MPs meant that partisans raided the building but didn't mean they got into the bomb shelter. Maybe they left to get reinforcements. He couldn't count on that though. If there were partisans in the bomb shelter, could they communicate with the partisans outside? The partisan jamming was across a range of frequencies. Did they leave some frequencies untouched for their use?

Sergeant Duncan crouched in the darkness with no way to answer those questions. Oddly, after the first bunch of bullets through the door, he heard nothing outside the building, at least nothing close, though artillery kept firing. No bullets or rockets tested his improvised firing position. Maybe partisans inside the bomb shelter already took the coding machines out and the partisans were heading back to the Marshes.

The bomb shelter hatch opened abruptly, and a man stuck his head out, followed by a flashlight that speared through the darkness. Sergeant Duncan froze behind his desks. The flashlight lingered on the desks, then went on. The guy pulled his head back and said something.

Russian. Sergeant Duncan was almost sure of that, but not sure enough to shoot. He watched the guy slip through the hatch and head for the door, flashlight playing across the room in quick, nervous arcs. The guy said in Russian, "Someone closed the door."

So, partisans did get into the bomb shelter.

"Where are our trucks?" That was in Russian too, from inside the bomb shelter.

The partisan peeked outside. "One truck, but it's damaged. Nobody around."

Where did the other partisans go? Maybe caught up in the wild fighting around Fort Seminole, though Sergeant Duncan hadn't heard any nearby fighting.

"Let's get the code machines up here." The partisan by the door turned and headed for the hatch. His flashlight played over Amber's overturned desks. He swore, then swung a pistol around. Amber shot him first. Sergeant Duncan launched himself toward the hatch. He grabbed the handle before it closed and jerked it further open. The partisan on the other side swung a pistol at him but kept one hand on the inside handle. Sergeant Duncan yanked the door further open, pulling the partisan off-balance. The pistol slammed into the doorframe, then fired, the sound deafening so close to Sergeant Duncan's ear. He slammed the hatch against the partisan's arm and shoulder. Amber grabbed the partisan's arm and levered his elbow against the door frame until he screamed and dropped the pistol. Sergeant Duncan yanked the hatch open again and punched the partisan in the nose, then slammed his head against the door frame.

More partisans surged toward the hatch. Sergeant Duncan threw the one he was holding toward them and started to close the hatch. Amber tossed something past him. "Grenade!" He slammed the hatch closed and felt the blast push against it. *Where did she get a grenade?* He pulled his sidearm, yanked open the hatch and fired into the chaos. Only one light bulb at the other end of the shelter survived the blast and it flickered wildly, the bare bulb dancing at the end of its cord. The partisans were down or stunned, but he shot them anyway, not letting them recover.

Amber turned a flashlight on. It highlighted a guy in civilian clothes and thick glasses. The guy raised his hands. "American!"

Amber kept the light on him. "Who are you?"

"I work with the code machines. They broke in and killed everyone else but kept me alive to help them."

Sergeant Duncan eyed the man. His English was perfect, but something about him seemed subtly off. *And my finger is throbbing again.*

Amber closed the hatch and checked the partisans for signs of life. Sergeant Duncan glanced at her. "You don't have to do that."

"Because I'm too delicate to be around bleeding corpses? You know better." She abruptly turned away and threw up, then swore. "That never happened."

"What didn't happen?"

Sergeant Duncan didn't blame her. The room smelled of gunpowder and death. "You shouldn't be near this crap."

"You mean I should sit and watch my dad move borders and armies around like chess pieces? I need to see this, not just read about it or imagine it."

She turned and retched again.

"Can I put my hands down?" The coding machine guy, if that was what he was, started to lower his hands.

"Not yet," Amber said. "We'll want to search you."

"I'm unarmed. I don't even know how to shoot a gun."

"That's the wrong thing to say." Amber swung her pistol around to point at him. "My dad doesn't waste manpower. The code machine people are all crack shots."

"Were they?" The man's expression grew subtly harder. "It didn't help them." He moved his hand down. "I guess I can get rid of these glasses. He flipped them into the air then drew a pistol, the move so fast that Sergeant Duncan didn't have time to fire before the weapon blazed.

Sergeant Duncan felt something tear through his upper thigh. He half jumped half fell and dropped his flashlight. Another shot blazed past him, hitting the remaining light bulb. The flashlight rolled, its light revealing only empty floor.

The shelter went silent except for Sergeant Duncan's breathing, which sounded loud in his ears, though it was mostly lost in the ringing from the shots and the grenade. He strained to see. Something loomed over him, barely visible. The partisan? Amber?

207

He wasn't sure enough to fire. Whoever it was merged into the darkness. Amber gasped, then someone swore in Russian. "Bitch!" A gun fired, monstrously loud and bright in the closed space. Sergeant Duncan blinked, his night vision gone. Someone stepped on his shoulder and went off-balance. Whoever it was merged back into the darkness. He heard someone opening the hatch. He fired toward it, hoping he wasn't shooting at Amber. The hatch slammed shut.

Was the phony coding machine guy gone? Sergeant Duncan retrieved the flashlight, which was still on, and held it at arm's length while he played it around the room. "He's gone."

"Not all of him," Amber said. "He tried to grab me. I bite."

Blood droplets led across the shelter to the hatch, almost lost among pools of blood from dead partisans. *And from me.* Sergeant Duncan turned the flashlight to his thigh, then turned it away. "It hurts more when I look at it." He turned to Amber. "Are you okay?"

She nodded. "So far, but the night is young."

"And if I had nine lives I'm into the bonus ones," Sergeant Duncan said. That suddenly seemed absurdly funny, and he laughed, the sound curiously far away. The flashlight sagged in his hands, and he couldn't pull it back up. He felt Amber grab his arm, then slumped to the floor, consciousness fading.

#

Captain Murphy got to the US unit without getting shot by either side, an accomplishment that felt better before he got a look at his new unit. There were around twenty men, part of an artillery company which had to abandon its guns when partisan tanks broke through and threatened to cut them off. About half had rifles. The rest had only sidearms. One guy carried a bazooka, but only had one rocket left. None of them had much ammunition.

"Partisan tanks went past us a few minutes ago," a sergeant said. He looked too young for his stripes and scared. He was also the highest-ranking man here except for Captain Murphy and sounded relieved to have someone else giving orders.

"We need to get back to our own lines," Captain Murphy said. That assumed there were still coherent US defensive lines out there, which seemed unlikely. Command was undoubtedly trying to stitch something together though and even these few troops might help.

How far into the night were they? He wasn't sure. Nothing in the eastern sky hinted of dawn. Would dawn help, or was Fort Seminole too far gone? Dawn might help the partisans hunt down US survivors. He pushed that gloomy thought aside. *If Fort Seminole falls, we'll make sure Stalin pays.*

There were tanks ahead. He glanced at the bazooka man with his one remaining rocket. Not much to fight a tank division. The Soviet jamming was still in place, still making radio communication impossible. There were phones in the now-deserted building, but partisan infiltrators had thoroughly destroyed the lines and switches. Did US troops at the rest of the front know partisans broke through here? Probably not in any coherent way, though wild morale-busting rumors were undoubtedly flying.

From what little he could see of the battle, the partisans were not much better off in controlling their men. They probably had a set plan at the start and lost control once their forces broke through. Without radios, tanks and trucks moved too fast for older types of communication to keep up. Two batches of fast-moving men with commanders reacting slower than Napoleon could have. Would the Soviets stop jamming now that they had their breakthrough?

The partisans at least had motorbike messengers. Captain Murphy and his men captured two, though they couldn't decode the messages.

The US remnants were moving slower than the partisan tanks and trucks ahead of them, but faster than partisan infantry marching up to consolidate their gains. The group picked up more US stragglers, swelling to over a hundred men, though with no heavy weapons. They could have grabbed abandoned US vehicles, but that would have bound them to the streets, a bad idea with enemy tanks prowling. The little group at least disrupted partisan resupply and communications, shooting up trucks and infantry heading to support the tanks, though they couldn't hold territory without heavy weapons. *We've only survived because of darkness and the jamming.*

They reached the airfields, which were mostly in partisan hands, and had to detour around them. They ran into a US front line of sorts, holding a corner of an airfield. But the bulk of a partisan tank division was between them and other US forces.

At least the partisans hadn't launched any more air raids. They probably couldn't now without hitting their own forces, given lack of communications and the way the forces were mixed.

Captain Murphy looked for some way out of the fiasco. US airpower would come into its own soon, hopefully at dawn. They would have no idea how dire the situation was, though they knew radio communications with the fort were out. *This is ridiculous. We are the world's only surviving great power and we're losing to a militia.* Ridiculous or not, what could the US do? Surrender? Not to the treatment the Soviet Union gave prisoners of war. *Take as many of them with us as we can?* He circled back to that, but Stalin wouldn't be impressed with a gallant defeat.

Amber said something about armored divisions in the works. If they didn't come soon, they wouldn't matter.

The partisans seemed to know they were on the verge of winning and spent men and material like water tonight. They threw men and tanks at the remaining US toehold on the airfields, took heavy casualties, but kept coming. Captain Murphy and his men kept hitting their logistics and communications with pinprick raids in the darkness, having brief firefights with partisan stragglers.

Where was Envoy McCormick? Would he bring in the Poles or Romanians now if he could? He couldn't now with the partisan jamming everything. Maybe someone else would give the order once US planes flew over and reported the situation. *And if the Poles come in, that's World War III.* Was that what Amber overheard? Her father giving orders that let the Poles come to the rescue? The situation wasn't bad enough to call the Poles in until it was too late to give that order, though.

Those thoughts flitted through his head, distracting him. He pushed them away. He was still technically in command of the scratch formation that formed around him, but several sergeants with combat experience made the tactical decisions and there was little they could do on a larger scale. They lurked among ruined buildings and tried to conserve their ammunition, grabbing what they could from captured partisan supply trucks.

They shouldn't be able to operate like this, even for a few hours, but the partisan commanders seemed to have lost control, at least away from the front lines. The partisans he encountered seemed more interested in looting than fighting.

The hit and run raids couldn't last forever. Could they last until dawn? Captain Murphy stared at the horizon, still dark, and wished for daybreak.

Chapter Thirty-Three: The Final Battle

Sergeant Duncan had one of those dreams when he suddenly discovered he was in public with no pants on. That wasn't a nightmare he had much anymore. War nightmares usually pushed mild embarrassment aside.

He gradually woke and realized he really didn't have pants on and that his leg hurt like somebody had branded him.

"I mostly stopped the bleeding," Amber said. "It's hard not to do more damage in this light." She had his leg cradled in her lap, taping gauze over it. "It keeps soaking through. Sorry. I'm not a nurse."

They were still in the bomb shelter, lit only by the flashlight. "How long has it been?"

"Maybe an hour," Amber said. "And so far, nobody has bothered us."

How long will that last? Probably not long with partisans loose in the fort. "Those trucks--they weren't just infiltrators. The partisans broke through to the heart of Fort Seminole."

Amber nodded. "And getting the code machines was a major goal for them, yet they seem to have gone away."

"Did they get what they came for?"

Amber shook her head. "I don't think anything is gone."

Sergeant Duncan looked around. Even in the semi-darkness, the bomb shelter looked as though a bomb had gone off in it, which made sense because a grenade *had* gone off there, plus a firefight or two. The code machine operators were dead, bodies stacked in a corner. The partisans still lay where they fell, the floor slippery with their blood.

The smell was worse now. He felt his nausea rise. "We need to get out of here."

"Not my top priority," Amber said. "You can't walk without breaking the wound open and somebody has to stay here to destroy the machines if the partisans come back."

"The operators didn't get it done?"

"No. The partisan who passed himself off as an operator must have talked his way in and killed them."

That made sense. "The guy was good at talking American," Sergeant Duncan said. "He sounded Iowa-bred. There was something off about him though."

"Your finger throbbing again?"

"It's been throbbing all night. It needs to tell me more than 'you're about to die, you idiot.'" He shifted his leg and groaned. "Did you have to take my pants off?"

"If you wanted to put them back on eventually."

"Does your dad really have armored divisions on the way?"

"Maybe. Don't count on them getting here in time."

He shook his head. "I don't know of any that could get here anywhere close to fast enough, at least not ours."

"Not ours," she said. "And not Poles. It may not come to anything. Don't get your hopes up."

"Why not get my hopes up?" He grimaced. "I could use some hope."

"Okay. Hope a couple armored divisions are close enough to get here by dawn."

"Are there?"

"Don't get your hopes up."

#

The siege of Fort Seminole ended in an anti-climax. At dawn, a Ruthenian armored division rolled into the ruins of Fort Seminole. It hit the partisan breakthrough from behind and routed them, throwing Czech-built Panthers and Hetzers against the partisan T-34s. Captain Murphy caught his first glimpse of the Ruthenian tanks and thought for a second that he was back in

World War II, in the middle of a German offensive. He caught a glimpse of the Ruthenian insignias on the tanks and relaxed a little. *Where did the Ruthenians get an armored division?*

Czechoslovakia probably. He remembered the Ruthenians Envoy McCormick claimed the Czechs were training. Czechoslovakia was a major center for German arms production late in the war.

He was too exhausted to feel much about the sudden turn of fortunes, his head buzzing and his steps coming with an effort. He was too busy trying to get his ad hoc group of stragglers out from between armored combatants to see much of what happened, but apparently more Ruthenian divisions hit the partisans who hadn't broken through, sending them fleeing along the highway. B-25s strafed the fleeing partisans, destroying vehicles and sending them back toward the Marshes on foot, without their heavy equipment, a broken army. Partisan stragglers and infiltrators held out in Fort Seminole, making the fort dangerous, but transports began arriving in the early afternoon, bringing in replacement troops and flying out the wounded. The rapid reaction force was too battered to chase the partisans, leaving that to the Ruthenians and the Air Force.

Captain Murphy didn't see much of that. He finally got back to US lines and fell asleep as soon as he was relieved.

Late in the afternoon, Colonel Rock called a staff meeting. Envoy McCormick was there. Most of the officers, including Colonel Rock, had wounds and too many familiar faces were missing. Colonel Rock said, "We dodged the bullet, but it came at a high price." He read off the names of dead officers, then paused. "And that doesn't even cover enlisted men. All of you probably have the same question I asked Envoy McCormick. Why the hell didn't we bring in the Ruthenians earlier?"

Envoy McCormick nodded. "I pushed the Czechs to keep the Ruthenians from crossing the border earlier because I was afraid that the Poles would send in exile militias and the two would spend most of their time fighting each other. The Ruthenians would probably win, then the Poles would send in their regular

214

army, and we would be on a short slide to World War III. I was worried about what the partisans had up their sleeves though and since the Poles were delaying our reinforcements, I put the Ruthenians in Czechoslovakia on a dead man switch. If I didn't say 'no' they would come in. When the partisans jammed us, I couldn't say no, so they came in." He suddenly looked exhausted. "Now, if we're very lucky, I can bribe or arm-twist the Poles into not sending in their militia, if the Ruthenians go back to Czechoslovakia. If they're smart they will. That way they keep the army without the restrictions they'd have if they stay here. Everyone knows the Ruthenians have an army just across the border. Now they know it's a potent little army. And if we're very lucky we'll have juggled another crisis that could have become World War III, turned it into a skirmish that people in the states will forget about by next week."

#

Dietrich Lang felt an overwhelming sense of an opportunity missed, but the more rational part of his mind didn't see the end of the Marsh War that way. He kept his interests mostly intact during the fighting, got action reports that told him a lot about the armies he would eventually have to face when Germany rearmed. Federov was no longer governor of the Marshes. Surrounding governors took the parts they were supposed to have controlled but couldn't until now. The Americans, through the UN, appointed a governor for what was left and sent troops to half-heartedly search for Federov loyalists. Federov himself was a fugitive, something that Lang found convenient. His organization helped the surviving partisans in small ways, while subtly, deniably, driving wedges between them and the Soviet government.

Lang saw one important gain from the war. Relations between the Poles and Americans were now frigid. The Poles occupied much of eastern Germany, not just the parts that had been disputed between the wars and they seemed intent on making much of that territory Polish, with harsh policies that forced remaining Germans to flee. They were the weakest, but also the most hated of the powers occupying Germany, so poorer relations between them and the US was a great thing.

Next time when we conquer the Poles they'll think the last time was a picnic. Lang smiled at the prospect.

He still had loose ends to tie up. Hannah Reitsch was the biggest one. Governor Meandrov would still want to show off his prize aviatrix and Lang couldn't stall him forever. Amber McCormick was an even bigger loose end. *I had her.* He wished that he could go back in time and simply put a bullet in the back of her head when he first ran into her. He knew he was getting obsessed with the woman. He remembered a surge of relief when he heard that his snipers had failed to kill the girl and wondered what was wrong with him.

Careful. She isn't a major threat now, but if I move too obviously against her she'll become one. Her dad was one of the most powerful men in the world and a sharp, cold political operator. It was obvious to Lang that McCormick lured the partisans into a bloody slugfest at a place of his choosing, let them bleed themselves white, then destroyed them, taking out the threat of a long-term struggle in the Marshes at the cost of a few thousand American lives. Clever and cold. *A man after my own heart, but I'm smarter. I'll bring him down and take his daughter.*

That was a long way off, though. For now, Lang had to be patient, something he found distasteful, close to cowardice, but had to cultivate. Amber McCormick should be dead or completely under his control, one of his playthings. Instead, she was out there, a symbol of lost opportunity and a threat. Someday, though, that would end.

The Ukrainians were another factor he could use. The Abwehr used Ukrainian nationalists early in World War II, only to kill or imprison most of them later, then, when the war grew desperate, turn to them again in a cynical alliance that both sides knew would end in betrayal. As long as the Ukraine wasn't officially a country, Ukrainians had to fear that the relative freedom they had might go away. They felt betrayed after the first World War when the peace settlement left them divided between Poland and the

Soviet Union and were afraid of a repeat. Lang's organization played on those fears, played on the disputes between Ukrainians and Poles. *Drive wedges between your enemies so they can't unite against you when they need each other.*

The Americans would eventually leave Europe and its ancient blood feuds. It was just a matter of how many lives and how much treasure they spent before they realized the continent couldn't be saved and went home to bask in their imagined security. *Then Germany will rise again.* Who would stop them? The French? If they could stop Germany from rising, they would have done it after victory in World War I left them with the biggest army in Europe and Germany disarmed. Britain? The British empire was over, a shambling corpse that didn't know it was dead yet, sustained by US aid as long as the Americans found the British useful.

The future belonged to Germany or the Soviet Union, despite their current weakness. Both countries would rise again, destroy the remnants of the west, then finally decide who would run the world. *And with me in charge, Germany will win.* Dietrich Lang believed that beyond any doubt. He just had to be patient.

#

Too many loose ends. Captain Murphy thought about those loose ends more than he wanted to. They haunted him, pushed into his thoughts, kept him from enjoying the hard-won victory at Fort Seminole. It *was* a hard-won victory, with far too many casualties. *And what did we win?* Stalin used up one of his pawns. He had plenty more. At least the war seemed to have made Stalin cautious. The Soviets said a lot of angry words but seemed to be gradually demobilizing. They needed the mobilized troops for the coming harvest.

Fort Seminole was a mess after the partisans bombed and occupied most of it, but once the runways were clear, the base quickly shaped up. New Memphis was bulldozed flat, with nothing to come back to, but merchants came back anyway and started rebuilding on the ruins. Fort Seminole had more troops now, nearly three times as many as had been based there before the war. It was still a ridiculously inadequate number, but an improvement. The base also got two dozen Sherman medium tanks to go with its light tanks, which was at least something.

Captain Murphy walked the fort's main street three days after the battle. Sergeant Duncan drove toward him in his battered jeep, with Amber McCormick beside him.

"I'm driving Miss McCormick to her flight," Sergeant Duncan said. "Apparently she's had enough of getting shot at." He sighed. "I've had enough for a lifetime." He pointed to his heavily bandaged thigh. "Bad enough to hurt like hell, but not bad enough to get me out of the army." He grinned. "Not that I really want out. I would go home, drink too much and get fat and useless. Here, I'm too scared to let myself get out of shape. And then there is Ruslana."

Amber leaned forward. "We will figure out who kidnapped Hannah and grabbed me. That won't stay a mystery." She paused. "I know you have your own mystery, and I hope you solve it."

They drove away, leaving Captain Murphy with his loose ends, the biggest and most personal one probably beyond solving.

Final Thoughts

Obviously this is going to need a sequel. I'll give it one soon.

In the meantime, look for more alternate history novels and story/essay collections under the Space Bats & Butterflies label and more stories in the Snapshot Universe.

Frequently asked questions:

What about nuclear weapons? Did the US have them? Yes, but due to the way the alternate World War II ended, the US has not used them in battle or publicly announced that they exist. Stalin is aware of the US atomic program, but not how far along it is. He has his own atomic weapons program, but it is still years away from done. The Soviet Union didn't have the resources to pour into it that they did historically and their access to the US program was cut off earlier in this scenario than it was historically.

Who is Dietrich Lang really? I left enough clues for people to speculate, but hopefully not to know definitively, at least not yet.

Did the US really have people as knowledgeable and devious as Envoy McCormick in charge? Probably not, though the early post-World War II leadership was, compared to say the Vietnam war era or Afghan war era leaderships, enormously better--smarter, less corrupt, maybe less arrogant.

Why the Alamo comparisons? The Alamo has taken on different and more divisive meanings in the last several decades, but in the late 1940s it was a symbol for most Americans. A few hundred Americans made a heroic stand against overwhelming odds and died gallantly. Of course there was more to the story and another side to it, but the references in this novel reflect what Americans of the era were taught and for the most part, believed.

Where can I find more background about the world this novel is set it? There is a very detailed, nearly novel-length scenario divided between the first two books of the Space Bats & Butterflies "Best Of" collections.

What else have I written that you might enjoy? If you like the alternate history in this novel, you might enjoy my Best of Spacebats & Butterflies collections, where a little over half of each collection is pure alternate history speculation. A third book in that collection should be out by the time you read this. If you enjoy more character-driven stories, you might enjoy Char or some of my Snapshot universe novels, especially The Necklace of Time. It's technically book two in a series but stands alone well and is in some ways the best introduction to the Snapshot universe.

If you like World War II alternate history, you might enjoy *Snapshot42: Stalingrad Run* and the two books of the New Galveston series.

Most of these stories are available in paperback and e-book formats. *Wrath of Athena*, a Snapshot universe novella, is also available in audiobook. For details, stop by my website at www.DaleCozort.com or look me up on Amazon.

You might also consider receiving my newsletter. It's free and infrequent. I send out updates on new books, appearances and discounts on current books every few months, depending on how busy my writing schedule is, along with insights into how books came about, what I'm currently working on, etc.

If you would like to get the newsletter, just send a message titled: "Please Send Me Your Newsletter" to:

DaleCoz2@gmail.com

Finally, if you enjoyed this novel and want to see more in the fictional universe, please review it on Goodreads or especially Amazon. Reviews make a huge difference. If you prefer to just leave a rating, that helps too.

Made in the USA
Thornton, CO
11/08/23 13:30:58

12c23c6f-80ef-4a69-89ca-f7c897ecc18fR01